"What's with You?"

he demanded. "This is the second time you've acted like a hysterical virgin when I came close to touching you."

Sydney felt foolish. Here she was, a thirty-year-old divorcée with children, shrinking from casual contact with a man who had made no intimate overtures. But perhaps it was for the best. She would seize the opening to make her position perfectly clear.

"Please don't take this personally, Daniel, but I prefer to keep our relationship entirely professional. I'm probably not your type any more than you're mine."

"You're damned right you're not my type! I've had enough of hard-shelled career women like you to last me a lifetime!"

CAROLE HALSTON

is an avid tennis player and a dedicated sailor. The author of two Silhouette Romances, this is her first Special Edition.

Dear Reader,

Silhouette Special Editions are an exciting new line of contemporary romances from Silhouette Books. Special Editions are written specifically for our readers who want a story with heightened romantic tension.

Special Editions have all the elements you've enjoyed in Silhouette Romances and *more*. These stories concentrate on romance in a longer, more realistic and sophisticated way, and they feature greater sensual detail.

I hope you enjoy this book and all the wonderful romances from Silhouette. We welcome any suggestions or comments and invite you to write to us at the address below.

Karen Solem
Editor-in-Chief
Silhouette Books
P.O. Box 769
New York, N. Y. 10019

CAROLE HALSTON
Keys to Daniel's House

Silhouette Special Edition

Published by Silhouette Books New York

America's Publisher of Contemporary Romance

Other Silhouette Books by Carole Halston

Stand-in Bride
Love Legacy

SILHOUETTE BOOKS, a Simon & Schuster Division of
GULF & WESTERN CORPORATION
1230 Avenue of the Americas, New York, N.Y. 10020

Copyright © 1982 by Carole Halston

Distributed by Pocket Books

ISBN: 0-671-53508-0

First Silhouette Books printing March, 1982

10 9 8 7 6 5 4 3 2 1

SILHOUETTE, SILHOUETTE SPECIAL EDITION
and colophon are trademarks of Simon & Schuster.

America's Publisher of Contemporary Romance

Printed in the U.S.A.

Keys to Daniel's House

Chapter One

*G*ood morning, Joan. Looks like a full house today," Sydney remarked pleasantly to the woman positioned behind the desk just inside the entrance of Pontchartrain Realty. Friday morning desk duty wasn't ever an easy assignment when all the agents gathered for the weekly sales meeting, but today the noise level seemed especially high to Sydney. She wondered how Joan Lemans managed to hear the voice of a caller when she answered the telephone.

No doubt one of the agents had just listed an especially valuable piece of property or made a sensational sale, judging from the undercurrent of excitement. She had only to join one of the chattering, laughing groups concentrated around the desks in the large open room in order to learn the latest hot item in the local real estate scene. Instead, she strode through the room, smiling and nodding to those who looked up and caught her eye, and went into Tim Atkins's office. Tim specialized in commercial properties and was the only agent with the St. Tammany Parish branch of Pontchartrain Realty to have a private office. The rest of them just had desks.

Sydney's was occupied at the moment by several part-time agents, but even if it had not been, the din would have prevented her from making effective use of it. Fifteen minutes remained until time for the meeting to begin, fifteen minutes that Sydney chose not to squander in idle conversation. She hadn't worked herself up to top agent in residential sales in two years' time by sitting around and visiting with the other agents, as so many were inclined to do when they dropped by the office. From time to time she found herself the object of resentment and occasionally was accused jokingly of being antisocial, but she wasn't in real estate to pick up a little extra spending money or just to "get out of the house," as were many of the other female agents whose husbands were successful executives or professional men in one high-paying job or another. Sydney was determined to prove to everyone, including her ex-husband, that she could support herself and her two children as well as any man could do, even though she didn't have a college degree.

Now, after just two years, she was earning enough money to tell Larry what he could do with his alimony payment. She wanted nothing from him. The child-support money for Stacy and Kevin went into trust accounts. When they came of age, they could do with it whatever they wished. In the meantime, with the help of Cora, she provided for all her children's needs, filling the roles of both mother and father.

Sitting at Tim's desk, Sydney made several telephone calls, addressed a birthday card to a former client, and checked her appointment book before going back to the seminar room at the rear of the building where the agents assembled each Friday morning. Will Donaldson, the manager of the St. Tammany branch of Pontchartrain Realty, always started the meeting promptly at nine and did a creditable job of curbing those who appeared willing to spend the entire day sitting around and chatting with one another.

His opening announcement today immediately clarified for her the reason for the excitement among her fellow agents. Via the grapevine he had heard that the current owner of the old Bates place had recently hired an appraiser in the area to give an estimate of the value of the house and property.

"As most of you already know, the house is a big old Louisiana cottage, the typical thing with high ceilings and fireplaces in all the bedrooms, a little rundown, so I've heard, and lacking some of the modern conveniences such as air-conditioning. But even without the house, the land is worth a bundle. Ten acres on Lake Pontchartrain west of the Causeway with a long stretch of beach. Heavily wooded with huge old live oak trees and magnolias. Personally, I'd price it conservatively at eight hundred thousand. Just think of the investment potential for a developer."

At this point Will was drowned out by comments from those who were personally familiar with the property. Sydney sat back in her chair and expelled a little sigh of impatience. Fortunately someone called out the question occupying her own thoughts, saving her the trouble of asking it.

"Is the present owner going to put the property on the market, Will?"

Will Donaldson stroked his bald pate in a gesture familiar to them all. "Old man Bates left the place to his nephew, same name as himself, Daniel Bates. The nephew is a geologist with one of the major oil companies. Seems he's being pressured to take an overseas assignment and hates to go off and leave the place vacant. He hasn't decided definitely, as least not so far as I know, to put the place on the market, but in case he does, I want Pontchartrain Realty to get the listing. That's the reason I want you all to be aware that he's a very likely client."

He paused as the hum of whispers and lowered tones welled up into a hubbub of excited voices. It was rare that any piece of lakefront property came on the market, and every agent in the room had in his client book the name of at least one person who had expressed interest in just such a place and could afford it. The lucky person who got the listing would be almost guaranteed a commission because, without a doubt, the property would sell, even at that price. And more often than not, the listing agent of a property was also the selling agent, since his or her name appeared in the newspaper advertisements.

Sydney did a rapid calculation in her head. If she could list *and* sell the Bates place, she wouldn't need to make another cent the rest of the year, and this was only the first of April! Her sales for the first quarter of the year already totaled half a million, more than some of the agents sold the entire year.

So absorbed was she in this intriguing speculation concerning the huge commission she could earn listing and selling the Bates property that she was only vaguely aware of several jaundiced glances in her direction. With difficulty she dragged her thoughts back to the meeting and forced herself to listen to several announcements Will was making in regard to workshops and seminars coming up in the next few weeks. She made a notation concerning one workshop which dealt with the concept of owner financing, which was becoming increasingly common since interest rates were so high.

"Sydney, you want to tell us about your two new listings in Country Club Estates?"

"Sure, Will."

She got up and handed out copies of the multilist forms used by nearly all the brokers in the parish and then described each of the houses briefly, taking care to emphasize their strongest selling points. The majority of the agents were far less painstaking in filling out all the blank spaces in the form, but Sydney measured every room in a house she listed and wrote down additional comments that would set the house apart from others similar to it.

Several other agents also had new listings to describe. When they had finished, everyone, including Will, went outside and piled into cars to go as a group to inspect each of the new properties. Sydney drove her car, a smart new Volvo sedan with which, along with her expensive slacks suit and leather briefcase, gave her the image of success she cultivated to such good effect. It was undeniably true, as Larry had always insisted, that success bred success.

Even in the early days of their marriage, when his salary was barely adequate to cover all expenses, he had worn expensive clothes and driven a Mercedes, albeit only a secondhand one in good condition, while she had shopped for herself and Stacy in thrift stores and coped with the vagaries of an aged Volkswagen Beetle. She hadn't minded at the time, believing that she was doing her part in building a future for her family. From the vantage point of the present, though, she bitterly regretted all the scrimping and careful budgeting of her limited household money when at the same time Larry had been enjoying two-martini lunches in the best New Orleans restaurants with colleagues and clients, all in the interest of "business," of course.

Chalk it up to experience. Goodness knows there were enough women who had made the same mistake she had, giving up her own college education and career for marriage to a young man with excellent prospects for providing for a family. What she and all those other misguided women hadn't anticipated was having a now-successful husband come home one day and, out of the blue, announce that he wasn't satisfied with *her* as his wife any longer. He had found someone else better suited for the position. In Sydney's own case, that had happened after nine years of marriage when her children were age eight and six.

She still boiled every time she let herself think about it. The anger had helped in a way, though, giving her the determination to get where she was today. Independent. Assured of her ability to take care of herself and her children. Perhaps she *had* become hard, as her mother lamented more and more often these days, but she'd be damned if she'd ever leave herself open again to the kind of hurt Larry had inflicted. Never again would she trust herself totally to the care of a man.

"How do you find the Bates place?"

Valerie Perkins's question brought Sydney back to the present, and she listened carefully to Joan Lemans's answer, having herself only a general knowledge of the location of the house and property Will had discussed so enthusiastically at the meeting a few minutes earlier.

"I really don't know why you even bother to ask,

though," Joan added. Some slight undertone prickled the hairs along Sydney's neck, warning her of something unpleasant to come. "We all know who will get that listing. After all, this Daniel Bates *is* a member of the male species." The little forced laugh didn't effectively palliate the sarcasm in the remark.

For just a moment Sydney felt the blazing fury befitting the red glints in her russet brown hair. This wasn't the first time Joan had made a catty remark like that, implying that Sydney's remarkable success in real estate depended entirely on her appearance, which was, without question, striking. She made no effort to minimize her height, wearing heels that put her within mere inches of six feet. Her skin was flawless, creamy and smooth-textured, her eyes intensely blue and fringed with long sable lashes. By anyone's standards, she was a noticeably attractive young woman.

But the truth was just the opposite of what Joan insinuated. The new Sydney, with her direct, almost brusque manner, was likely to intimidate many men, who preferred women to be soft and docile. For the most part, she was able to conceal the bitterness she felt about men in general these days, but now and then some chance comment would escape. Try as she might to soft-pedal the feminist instincts she had developed since the divorce, there was a certain brittle quality in her manner toward male colleagues and clients. Strangely enough, though, the men with whom she dealt seemed to respect her for those traits usually considered masculine: ambition, directness, aggressiveness.

The unfairness of Joan Lemans's innuendo made it rankle all the more, but Sydney bit back the retort that came to her lips, knowing it would only bring vindictive pleasure to the other woman. Throughout the remainder of the tour, one part of her mind grappled with some method of retaliating and putting to rest once and for all such snide implications, which had come to her ears with greater frequency the past few months. Her common sense told her some of the female agents in the office were small-minded people given to pettiness, but still, her pleasure in the day was spoiled.

That afternoon, when she parked her car under the carport of the house she rented and entered the kitchen, resentment was still seething at the back of her mind.

"Hi, yourself," she called absently in response to greetings from her two children, who were watching television with Cora in the living room section of the large room that took up much of the downstairs. The house had been designed in accordance with the popular Great Room concept, combining kitchen, dining and living rooms all into one.

Before joining them, she picked up the stack of mail on the end of the counter by the door and thumbed through it. Larry's child support check, utility bills, advertisements, a real estate magazine—nothing of a personal nature like cards or letters or invitations. But then, she could hardly expect that sort of thing since she never wrote any herself anymore. She just didn't have the time to keep up with friends who had moved away. All her time and energy went into her work. That was why Joan's insinuation that morning had been so unjust.

"Homework all done?" she inquired, walking the length of the room and sinking down on the couch where she could see Stacy and Kevin sprawled on their stomachs in front of the television. It was hardly necessary to ask. Cora Duval, bless her, ran the household like a benevolent general.

Sydney smiled fondly at the rawboned woman in her mid-fifties who sat in an armchair sewing a button on one of Kevin's school shirts. How fortunate the present living arrangement was for Sydney and her children, and hopefully for Cora, too, whose husband had died of a heart attack two years ago, leaving her practically penniless. His heavy drinking had kept him from being a good provider and made him brutal in his treatment of her, but she had never left him. Another example of unsung, unrewarded female loyalty, Sydney reflected dourly.

Cora's two daughters, married and with families of their own, could spare no extra money toward their mother's support, nor did either of them have room for her to live permanently with them without "imposing," as Cora put it. Thus she had found herself in the position of having to look for a job to support herself while having no particular training or skills except those of a housewife and mother. She wouldn't be eligible for a widow's social security benefits until she was sixty-two.

According to Cora, Sydney's newspaper ad for a mature, single woman to live in her home and do housework and child care was the answer to a prayer. Cora was certainly that for Sydney, who could concentrate on her job now and know the children were in excellent hands. In moments of honesty, Sydney admitted to herself that Cora was to her what most wives were to men: someone who could be relied upon to take care of things at home, to do the cleaning and cooking and discipline the children. But having been a wife herself, Sydney tried always to be appreciative and to make it clear to Cora that she was important to all of them as a person.

"I called Good Will today, like you said," Cora

announced now, snipping her thread and jabbing the needle into a pincushion shaped like an apple, a present from Stacy. "They said they'd send somebody here tomorrow to pick up the boxes of clothes."

"Great. Did you go through them and pick out anything your daughters or grandchildren might have a use for?" Sydney had just sorted through her clothes closet as well as Stacy's and Kevin's and eliminated all the garments that were outgrown or, as in her own case, out-dated or out of favor.

"Sarah and Caroline are both a lot heavier than you, but I kept out some of the kids' things for Micky and little Jane." Cora folded the small boy's shirt, the buttons all firmly sewn now. "Hard to believe *you* wore some of them clothes. They just don't look like you."

Sydney laughed. "I felt the same way when I was clearing them out of the closet. There's probably not a piece in the lot that wasn't bought off a clearance rack. Besides, you're right—my tastes have changed." Her tastes had grown considerably more expensive and she leaned now toward the tailored, with little frill and fuss.

"My ex-husband used to say clothes make the—" Sydney broke off midsentence. Without any warning inspiration had struck. She knew suddenly what she would do to rebut all those thinly veiled accusations that she depended upon her looks to make her a successful real estate agent. She'd get that Bates listing if it killed her in the process, but when she approached the owner, he'd think his homeliest maiden aunt looked beautiful in comparison to Sydney Cullen!

Chapter Two

"Cora, could I borrow your car this morning for a couple of hours? You're welcome to use mine if you need to go out."

The older woman was standing in front of the stove turning strips of bacon on the griddle and looked over her shoulder in surprise at this unprecedented request.

"Lord have mercy!" she gasped when she saw Sydney, who broke into a big grin of satisfaction at her reaction.

Kevin looked up from his favorite position on the floor in front of the television, where he was engrossed in Saturday morning cartoons. "Gosh, Mom, you look *ugly!*" he exclaimed.

Sydney couldn't have been more pleased by his response than if she had just been named a beauty-contest winner. She purposely hadn't told Cora or the children about what she planned to do, prefer-

ring to get their candid reactions to her masquerade,
for that was certainly what it was. She had looked
through the boxes of discarded clothes and selected a
khaki skirt, much longer than the current style, with
a short-sleeved belted jacket which did nothing for
her because the shoulders were too broad and it fit
so loosely it hid the contours of her breasts. The
outfit had been one of her most ill-advised purchases
during those years when she bought bargains in the
faith that somehow she would figure out a way to
make them becoming. The one other time she had
worn it, Larry had been scathing in his disapproval,
saying it fit her like a sack and was just as becoming.
She had been cruelly hurt by the blunt criticism, but
today, when she looked at herself in the mirror, she
had to admit he had been right.

Her sleek chestnut hair was pulled straight back
from her face and fastened with plain bobby pins.
She wore no makeup except for a heavy smear of
lipstick, inexpertly applied. Firmly in place on the
bridge of her nose were the plain dark-rimmed
glasses she normally used only at night when she had
removed her contact lenses. This morning she had
not put in the lenses, and her vision with the glasses
was less than perfect, a condition that doubtlessly
would cause her to peer and squint and further
enhance her disguise.

Perhaps she was overdoing things a bit, she admitted wryly to herself as she backed Cora's ten-year-
old Ford out of the driveway, but the Volvo just
wouldn't fit her purposes at all today. Just wait until
the gossips at the office saw her! Weekends were
prime working time in real estate so there should be
a sizable audience for her entrance.

Mary Linden was the agent on duty at the desk

just inside the door. "Can I help you?" she inquired cheerfully, glancing up as Sydney came through the plate-glass door and then staring incredulously. "Sydney?" she blurted uncertainly.

"Morning, Mary," Sydney greeted breezily and proceeded back to her own desk, ignoring curious looks from five or six agents seated at their own stations and involved in various tasks. Settling into the hard plastic contours of her chair, she made a big production of laying her briefcase flat on the desk top and picking up the telephone directory.

"Bates," she said loudly, thumbing through the pages. "Alistaire, Charles, Fred—no, Daniel. Hm-m-m. You suppose Daniel Bates doesn't have a telephone, or else has an unlisted number?"

The silence in the room, almost palpable, was interrupted by the buzz of the telephone and Mary's voice, "Good morning. Pontchartrain Realty."

"Oh, well, I guess I'll just have to pay Mr. Daniel Bates a personal visit." Sydney made this announcement to the room at large, got to her feet, and strode out, afraid she would burst if she didn't get outside and release the laughter swelling in her chest. The looks on their faces! If only she'd had a camera!

Born along on the wave of elation, she drove to the section of town where the Bates place was located and followed the directions Joan Lemans had given Valerie Perkins yesterday during the tour. It was like entering an era predating planned subdivisions. The streets were all haphazardly laid out, meandering around huge live oak trees with trunks eight or nine feet in diameter. The atmosphere was one of quiet and privacy; most of the houses were shielded by thick shrubbery and trees, some of the yards charming jungles of redbud, dogwood, and azalea, all in glorious bloom this time of year, along with trailing vines of purple wisteria and snowy bridal wreath shrubs.

The entrance to the Bates property was identifiable by a black mailbox mounted on a stout iron post with BATES lettered on the sides in silver paint. A massive wrought-iron gate was pulled back to one side of the driveway, allowing Sydney to drive between brick columns and proceed along the narrow, winding drive, the brittle white clam shells crunching under her tires. Without warning she emerged from the trees and heavy underbrush into a clearing and saw the house in front of her, a large old white frame building shaded by several enormous oak trees and the largest magnolia tree she had ever seen. Beyond the house a lawn sloped several hundred yards down to a white sand beach and then there was the blue-gray expanse of Lake Pontchartrain, with no end in sight.

The place was much as she had expected it to be from Will Donaldson's description, and yet it had a serenity and quiet charm that took her quite unawares so that, for several seconds after she had switched off the ignition, she just sat without moving, gazing around her with unexpected wistfulness. How could someone voluntarily give up a place like this? It had that air of tradition and stability that no new house, however expensive, could ever have. Something about this house and its setting soothed the spirit and made one want to absorb all that serenity and quietness into the soul.

A movement startled Sydney and brought her back to an awareness of the purpose of her call. A ladder was propped against the near side of the house and a man descended its rungs, a pail in one hand. He had been hidden from view by the branches of the magnolia tree. Like it, he, too, was of extraordinary size. Obviously a painter, judging by the pail and the paint brush he held, he wore old, faded denim trousers, and his torso was bare.

With deliberate movements he put down the bucket of paint and balanced the brush across the rim before approaching the parked car. Sydney climbed out, realizing as he came up close, stopping a few yards from her, that he was undoubtedly the largest man she had ever encountered in person. He towered over her, making him considerably above six feet in height; the span of his shoulders was incredibly broad, his chest deep and muscular and matted with dark hair.

If one admired that sort of rugged he-man build— as Sydney did *not*—he was undeniably a superb specimen. What a waste such a physique was on a house painter. The man should be making a fortune posing in macho magazine ads.

"I'm looking for Mr. Daniel Bates." Sydney smiled brightly at the house painter. One had to be indiscriminately friendly in real estate. Sooner or later almost everyone bought or sold a house. This man might be a potential client himself one of these days.

She noticed the unfriendly expression on his face with a twinge of irritation and then suddenly remembered what she looked like. It wasn't often that a man looked her over in that unflattering manner the way he was doing, a frown cutting little lines between his eyebrows, which were thick and craggy. They were the same dark brown as his hair, the unruly kind that had just enough curl to keep it from ever being neatly disciplined.

"I'm Daniel Bates. What can I do for you?"

His voice was deep and a little curt, as though he were forcing himself to be polite to this unprepossessing intruder driving a shabby old blue Ford Fairlane.

Sydney felt her mouth go a little slack with amazement. *This* man was Daniel Bates, her potential client? While she had not come with any preconceived image of him, she certainly had not expected this Herculean giant. Was he perhaps posing as Daniel Bates, acting as a shield for his employer? Undermining that hypothesis were his air of authority and the educated cadences of his voice.

"I'm Sydney Cullen, of Pontchartrain Realty," she announced, holding out a business card which he took in one large paint-spattered hand and studied briefly, as if to verify her identity. She found herself momentarily fascinated by the implicit strength in the long supple fingers. Her card seemed ridiculously insubstantial in their grasp.

"It looks like I've come at a very inconvenient time, Mr. Bates, but I have a client who is looking for a house and property like yours and can afford to pay the price if he likes it. If you should happen to be interested—now or in the near future—in selling, I hope you'll contact me."

Not exactly *true*, but she had no doubt she *would* have such a client in a short time if Daniel Bates decided to sell his property. She wondered what there was in what she had just said to make him look so displeased. She was only offering to perform a service for him should he decide to sell.

"I haven't made up my mind one way or the other—" he began, in a tone that told her she was about to be summarily dismissed.

"I can't blame you for not wanting to let go of a place like this," she interposed smoothly. "It must take a lot of constant care and upkeep, but no doubt it's worth it. I'll bet your wife and children love it, too." Now what had made her add that last conjecture? It was hardly designed to help her cause, which was to remind him of all the reasons he might not want to keep the property.

"My *ex*-wife hated it," he corrected curtly. "And we had no children." His dark eyes held an expression that matched the brooding regret in his tone as he added that last comment. He obviously had wanted children. Perhaps the failure to produce any was the cause for the breakup of his marriage. "Look, Miss er—"

"Cullen. Sydney Cullen." She pronounced her name slowly, as though she were speaking to a class of kindergarten children. Getting people to remember your name was one half of the battle.

"Right. Miss Cullen. If I decide definitely to sell the place, I promise you I'll get in touch with you. I'll try to hang on to your card." He looked down at the powerful expanse of naked chest as if realizing for the first time he was only partially clothed. After some hesitation, he shoved the business card into a hip pocket. Sydney knew the chances were good to certain it would go through the laundry along with the pants.

"You wouldn't regret working with me, Mr. Bates. I don't mean to boast, but my record speaks for itself. My manager, Will Donaldson, will tell you I'm the best agent he has in residential property. Would you mind if I checked back with you in a week or two?" She knew from the set of his mouth she was about to push him beyond the limits of his patience. "Thank you for your time, Mr. Bates. I look forward to hearing from you."

She climbed back into the car and proceeded to turn it around. As she left, she glanced in the rearview mirror and saw that he was already headed back to the ladder, no doubt to resume his painting. His back was as impressive as his chest, smooth and firmly muscled, tapering to a waistline proportionately narrow.

What a contrast he was to Larry Stanton, her ex-husband, and not just in physique either. How easily she could conjure up an image of Larry, tall—though not as tall as Daniel Bates, of course—slender and impeccably dressed in either an expensive business suit or white tennis togs. Larry was as fair as this man was dark, and he disdained any kind of physical labor that would involve getting dirty. No matter what he was doing, working or playing, he always looked like he could pose for a glossy magazine advertisement.

Sydney sighed, her thoughts bringing a familiar jab of pain to the area of her heart. Would she always have this feeling of loss when she thought of Larry? Why couldn't she get over caring about him when it was obvious she no longer meant much to him? While she would never admit as much to anyone else, one reason she drove herself so relentlessly in her work was to keep too busy to think about him . . . with Connie.

Stopping the car at the entrance of the Bates property, she dug in her purse and took out a pad and pencil to jot down the street address. Her gut instincts, like those of Will Donaldson, told her that Daniel Bates would eventually decide to sell. In the meantime, she meant to make sure he didn't forget her. At least once a week she would send him a note with a Pontchartrain Realty brochure designed to be a reminder to potential clients.

Feeling somewhat deflated after her earlier exhilaration, she drove home and shed her disguise before returning to the office. The afternoon passed quickly as she drove a new client, a corporate executive being transferred to New Orleans, all over the parish so that he could decide where he would prefer to start looking at houses. Not surprisingly, he was most impressed with the several country club subdivisions in the vicinity of Lake Pontchartrain. He could commute across the twenty-four-mile Causeway and arrive at his company office in New Orleans in forty minutes.

By the time she returned home late in the afternoon, Sydney had entirely forgotten about Daniel Bates and her impulsive masquerade of the morning. Cora and the children were awaiting her arrival excitedly. The weekend edition of the local newspaper, the *St. Tammany News Herald*, contained an article about her as Top Real Estate Agent of the Month.

"Look-a-here, Mom! You're right on the front page!" Kevin called out as soon as she opened the door from the carport into the kitchen. He held up the magazine section devoted entirely to real estate, and Sydney's own face smiled back at her. SYDNEY CULLEN—PONTCHARTRAIN REALTY'S SUPERAGENT read the headline.

"Guess your mother is famous," she said, smiling indulgently and ruffling the fine sandy hair so like his father's. For pragmatic reasons she was actually quite pleased with the coverage. It was invaluable advertising, a fact which Cora confirmed by telling her several people had called during the afternoon, leaving messages for Sydney to call back on real estate matters. No telling how many new clients she would pick up because of the article.

"That's probably another one of them now," Cora said as the telephone rang.

"I'll get it," Sydney said, rising swiftly to her feet and moving to the wall telephone in the kitchen. "Hello. Sydney Cullen speaking."

"Just what the hell are you trying to pull, Miss Cullen?" came a low, angry voice she was able to place almost immediately as belonging to Daniel Bates. The newspaper article! He must have seen it! The possibility that he would see her picture and read the article hadn't even occurred to her. But now she remembered seeing the blue plastic tube for the *News Herald* affixed to the same post that supported the mailbox at the entrance to his property. He sounded furious.

"Mr. Bates, I can explain—"

"Explain what, Miss Cullen? That you're trying to make some kind of fool of me? I'm sure the St. Tammany Board of Realtors will be interested in your little masquerade. They may find your ethics as questionable as I do."

"Mr. Bates—please—"

"I think I'll drop by your office tomorrow and let your manager know what I think of his top agent's shenanigans."

Sydney winced at the sharp sound of the receiver being slammed down to sever the connection. What a mess this was. It wasn't just the embarrassment of having everybody in the office know how her plan had miscarried. What really scared her was Daniel Bates's threat to press charges against her with the board of realtors. Even if she were found innocent, as she surely would be, the blot against her name would remain. People had a way of remembering things like that. If she had any ambitions of being elected to offices in the state realty hierarchy, she couldn't afford to have her image besmirched.

What was she going to do?

Sydney pondered this disturbing question while she helped Cora put dinner on the table, finding it difficult to concentrate on what she was doing. Several times while she was tossing the salad and separating it into individual bowls she became motionless for an indeterminate time, only to be roused to the present by Cora or one of the children.

During the meal she only half listened to the conversation and then discovered she should have been more attentive when a question Stacy was posing finally sank in.

"Well, Mom. Can I?"

"Can you what?" She knew vaguely that her ten-year-old daughter had been prattling on about a letter she had received in response to a drawing she had sent in to an art contest. There was something about a correspondence course.

"You haven't been listening!" Stacy accused, the dark blue eyes identical to Sydney's shooting sparks of indignation. "Can I enroll in the correspondence course to learn to draw? I bet daddy will pay for it."

"Oh, I see. It's just as I suspected. Your so-called art contest is just a come-on to get people to enroll in a correspondence course. Honey, I know you have a real knack for drawing, but *everybody* who sends in an entry gets the same letter you did. It's a racket." Sydney felt a rush of sympathy when she saw how crestfallen Stacy was at her mother's matter-of-fact words. Darn it all! Stacy was really serious about this interest in art.

"Sweetheart, maybe we can find someone in the area who gives art lessons. That way you could learn the basics. And you *don't* have to ask your father to pay for it."

Stacy brightened at that news. "You won't forget to find out, will you, Mom?" she urged several times, causing Sydney a twinge of guilt. Achieving success in the real estate world took its toll of her time and resources. She didn't spend as much time with the children now as she once had, before the divorce. No wonder they were so persistent in pleading their interests whenever they could capture her attention.

"I won't forget, honey," Sydney promised, and then turned to regard her son warily. "Okay, buster, what's on your mind?" Two years younger than his sister, Kevin had been wriggling with impatience, waiting for the conversation between Sydney and Stacy to end.

"Mom, *all* the other boys in my class are going out for Junior Football. They'll be practicing during the summer. Please, can I? I'll be real careful—I promise I will!" Golden hazel eyes much like his father's were eloquent with pleading.

Sydney took a deep breath. Why did they both have to tackle her at the same time, especially when she had other things, important things, on her mind? But then, she had to keep reminding herself, what might seem trivial to her could be of monumental importance to a child.

"Kevin, we've been through this time and time again. You *know* your father refuses to have you play football." Honesty compelled her to add, "And

I agree with him. Most bone specialists say it isn't good for young bones like yours to be subjected to the stress of football."

"But, mom, *everybody* but me is going out for it. Their parents must think it's all right for *their* bones," he reasoned desperately, huge tears glistening in his golden eyes.

Sydney wrestled with the temptation to say those words familiar in nearly every household with children: *You'll have to talk to your father.* No, she would not take the coward's way out. Nobody had ever said it would be easy for her to rear her two children alone.

"I'm very sorry, Kevin, but I care about you and your bones," she said firmly, and then escaped from the room, reminding Stacy it was her turn to help Cora clean up after dinner.

Strange that, even after a year and a half, the length of time Cora had been living with them, Sydney still felt vaguely guilty about sitting down to a meal at her own table that she hadn't prepared or getting up afterward without cleaning up. Most of the time, when she was home, she pitched in and helped Cora with whatever household task she was doing, but tonight Sydney had a more pressing matter to attend to.

She had to see Daniel Bates and reason with him, if necessary *beg* him not to bring charges against her with the board of realtors. Once he understood the reason for her imposture, the essential innocence behind it, surely he would no longer be angry.

"Cora, I'll be back in a little while," she promised, leaving the house a few minutes after touching up her makeup and combing her hair.

On the way to the Bates property, she rehearsed

in her mind the explanation she would give him. Only when she had reached the residential section near the lake did she realize how impulsively she was acting—going at this time of night to see a man she had met briefly only once. It was dark and quiet driving along the deserted streets, almost spooky. She could imagine how inky black the driveway leading to the old house would be. The dense shrubbery and sprawling old live oak trees on both sides of her seemed somehow menacing, hiding heaven knew what kind of danger to a lone young woman out at night on a mission inspired by desperation.

Sydney shivered, rolling up the window and locking both doors as she proceeded along the narrow street leading to the Bates property. Disappointment was matched only by relief when she turned into the driveway and saw that her way was barred by the heavy wrought-iron gate which had been swung to one side earlier in the day. There was no doubt that it was locked; she could see the stout length of chain connected by a massive padlock.

For a fleeting moment she considered several impulsive plans to reach Daniel Bates. Dare she leave her car parked here and try to make her way through the woods to the house, managing somehow to get over or under or through the fence? Might she drive some distance farther down where she could walk to the beach and approach his house that way?

Suddenly she came to her senses. What could she be *thinking* of even to consider such harebrained schemes? Chances were good to certain that, even if she *did* manage to call on Daniel Bates in such a manner, he would see her actions in a most uncomplimentary light. His conception of her as an unscrupulous real estate agent who would go to any lengths for a sale would only be strengthened.

Without further mental debate, Sydney backed out of the driveway and drove back home, a somber and troubled young woman.

Up early the next morning after a night of fitful sleep, she couldn't remember her dreams clearly, but there remained a strong impression of some kind of trial with searing accusations against her and desperate attempts on her part to defend herself. In the light of day, she could explain the dream as the result of her anxiety over Daniel Bates's anger at her, but a strong feeling of dread persisted as she dressed in a dark blue linen suit with a sedately striped silk blouse with long ties that could be knotted or tied into a bow at the throat. The outfit was new and smartly tailored, making her look every inch the smooth professional.

Cora was already up, sitting at the kitchen table with a cup of coffee at hand and the Sunday *New Orleans Times-Picayune* spread open in front of her. She looked up and noted Sydney's appearance with narrowed eyes.

"You haven't forgotten?" she said doubtfully.

Sydney expelled a deep sigh. "No, Cora, I haven't forgotten that today's Dad's birthday. But something's come up—something really urgent—and I have to go down to the office this morning. I'll do everything I can to make it to Mom's for lunch."

She went over to the counter and took a cup down from those hanging on brass hooks underneath the wall cabinet. After pouring herself a cup of coffee, she came back to the table and perched on the edge of a chair at the end opposite Cora, her whole demeanor bespeaking nervous haste.

"Would you mind dropping the kids off at Mom's this morning? They can go to church with her and Dad."

Cora's look said what she refrained from putting into words. Pauline Cullen wasn't going to be happy over Sydney's allowing business to take precedence on this day, which was not only the Sabbath but also her father's birthday. Cora and Sydney both knew Sydney would be hearing from her mother at the office before the morning was over.

Sydney had tried to convince her mother for the past two years that weekends were busy work days for real estate agents, since people with normal work schedules had time on Saturday and Sunday to get out and look at property, but as far as Pauline was concerned, Sunday was a day of worship and rest, a time to be spent with the family. Sometimes Sydney envied her brother, Fred Junior; he lived in the northern part of the state and could return home only several times a year on visits. The rest of the time he was free from his mother's loving scrutiny.

Whenever this thought happened to occur, Sydney always squashed it instantly, regretting her ingratitude and childishness. Nor for anything would she want to deprive Stacy and Kevin of the opportunity to know and love their grandparents. Immediately after Sydney's separation from Larry her mother had been strongly supportive, taking care of the children while Sydney went to real estate school and got herself established in the field. It was Sydney, not Pauline herself, who had worried about the drain on the older woman's energies and the interruption of her customary involvement in community and church activities.

"I really *have* to go to the office this morning,

Cora." Sydney's voice held a note of anxiety twisting her insides. Tersely, driven by a sense of urgency that bade her hurry up and get to the office, she told Cora about the episode with Daniel Bates.

Cora didn't interrupt during the brief narrative, but nodded her head thoughtfully when it had ended. Her shrewd eyes skimmed over the sleek russet hair, the arresting blue eyes, which seemed darker this morning because of the color of the suit, and the faint dark smudges beneath them, the slender shoulders held so erect under the superbly fitting material. For a moment Sydney imagined she saw an expression of ruefulness, almost regret, pass through the older woman's eyes.

"Don't worry about Pauline. I'll take care of her," Cora promised, and Sydney relaxed perceptibly at the assurance.

Cora and her mother got along well in spite of a certain understandable tinge of reserve on the part of Pauline who made it clear to everyone that *she* was Stacy and Kevin's grandmother. In her quiet wisdom Cora always kept herself out of the picture when Pauline entertained Sydney and the children at her house. Cora usually managed to have other plans which kept her from accepting Pauline's perfunctory invitations. Today, for example, she was driving to New Orleans to visit her two daughters and their families.

"You just run along to the office now and don't worry about a thing," Cora ordered briskly, returning her attention to the newspaper in front of her. "I'll see that the kids are dressed up to Pauline's standards. I hemmed Stacy's new dress yesterday."

For just a second Sydney wavered on the verge of going around the table and giving the calmly implacable woman a hug around her rawboned shoulders. But lacking the nerve to initiate an intimacy that might not be welcomed, she said instead, "Cora, I don't know what I would do without you."

It was ridiculously early to go to the office, but she went anyway, unlocking the front door with her own key, turning on the overhead neon lights and opening all the venetian blinds. When Valerie Perkins arrived for early-morning desk duty she didn't appear surprised to see Sydney seated at her desk and going through the real estate section of the New Orleans paper, several pages of which were devoted entirely to property in St. Tammany Parish.

Sydney made it her business to keep up not only with the listings of Pontchartrain Realty but with those of the other agencies as well. Her commission for selling their properties was not as large as selling those of her own agency, but the important thing was to fulfill the customer's needs. A satisfied client usually came back to the same agent when he was ready to sell or to invest in additional property.

Today Sydney's concentration was much poorer than usual. When she received telephone calls in reference to her advertised listings in the newspaper her training enabled her to convey just enough information to pique the caller's curiosity, but she didn't come across with her usual enthusiasm. Her attention strayed constantly to the plate-glass door, seeking the appearance of a tall giant of a man with dark unruly hair and a frowning countenance, for in her imagination the man she had met yesterday was of mythic proportions, making his probable censure all the more terrible. Was he really as huge as she remembered him? If so, she doubted he would be able to walk through the door without stooping.

"I'm sorry, Mr. Lane, I can't show you the house this morning . . . Not this afternoon either, I'm afraid . . . My father's birthday party . . . I appreciate your being so understanding . . . Yes, certainly, any afternoon this week would be fine. Or any evening, for that matter—"

Sydney heard the abstracted note in her voice and silently cursed the circumstances which rendered her so helpless to do her job effectively. Then, abruptly, she stopped listening to the male voice on the telephone. It was getting close to twelve o'clock by now and she had almost given up on the appearance of Daniel Bates, reasoning hopefully that he had much better things to do with his Sunday on such a beautiful day than to come down to Pontchartrain Realty and cause her trouble.

But there, coming through the door, was the same giant she had seen yesterday in paint-spattered jeans and no shirt. Somehow he seemed even larger in casual beltless slacks and an open-throated knit sport shirt. He stopped just inside the door, looking around the large open room, the "bull pen," as the agents mockingly labeled it.

"Mr. Lane, I'll have to call you back—" Sydney broke into the man's explanation, which she hadn't even been hearing, and hung up, thinking bitterly to herself, *Well, Mr. Daniel Bates, I hope you're satisfied. You just cost me one possible sale.*

Rising swiftly, she walked toward the man who stood with his powerfully muscled arms akimbo, his hands balanced on hips that looked preposterously slim in contrast to the massive span of his shoulders. He watched her approach him with swift strides, his eyes sweeping her slender length from satin mahogany head to high-heeled pumps.

"Mr. Bates," she said in a voice that held an undertone of pleading as she came to a stop right in front of him, amazed that she had to bend her head so far back to look up into his face. It was not, as she had imagined, horribly constricted with anger, but rather, calmly watchful.

"Please, Mr. Bates, don't say anything," she begged in a voice that was scarcely audible, grasping him by the forearm and giving a little tug as if to lead him over to her desk. The hair on the firm skin tickled her palm, and the flesh felt more like solid iron than mere human muscle and sinew. She might have been trying to budge a span of the Causeway, judging by the effect she was having.

"Miss Cullen, you do look *different* today," he drawled, his dark eyes narrowed and flicking over her.

She felt relief wash over her in a welcome but weakening tide. He was still irritated, there was no doubt of that, but he wasn't the raging nemesis there to destroy her real estate career as she had feared. With some luck, and considerable verbal skill, she could talk him out of his sense of injury and perhaps even cajole him into not holding a grudge against the whole agency because of her own impulsive actions. While she had unquestionably lost all possibility of getting his listing if he decided to sell, perhaps some other agent with Pontchartrain Realty could get it.

"If you'll just come back here to my desk, Mr. Bates, we can talk." Her voice was pitched low but openly beseeched his cooperation, as did the blue eyes opened wide between their sweep of dark lashes.

After a brief hesitation, during which he seemed to be resisting the power of her appeal, he allowed her to guide him to the desk placed against the wall at the rear left-hand side of the room. Fortunately, the several other agents in the room were occupied with clients, and the level of noise gave her the privacy she sought.

"Please. Sit down, Mr. Bates," she urged, indicating a chair close beside her desk. "Oh, damn!" she muttered as a button on her telephone lighted up, accompanied by a beeping signal. "Excuse me one moment," she begged breathlessly, picking up the receiver and keeping her eyes fixed on the man who continued to stand beside her, as though she feared he might try to escape while she was engaged in conversation.

He thrust his hands casually into the pockets of his tan slacks and she noticed irrelevantly how the cream-colored fabric of his knit shirt, loose-woven and knobby in texture, suggested the hardness and immense power of his chest and shoulders. He must have played football or trained as a weightlifter to develop his body like that, she reflected with instinctive disdain.

"Hello . . . Mom, I really don't have time now to talk . . . no, of course, I didn't forget, but. . . Mom, I have *not* forgotten it's Dad's birthday . . ." Sydney averted her head and spoke in a low, desperate tone. What an incredibly bad time for her mother to telephone and make a big production of Sydney's not being on time for her father's birthday lunch. Sydney felt like a child being scolded for wrongdoing, and something in the tall man's quiet presence made her sense he perceived her discomfort and was amused by it.

"Mom, I have a client with me right at this very moment. I'll be there as soon as I can . . . I promise . . . Good-bye, Mom." This last was said gently but firmly and she placed the receiver in its cradle without waiting to determine if the conversation was over.

For a moment she closed her eyes, running manicured fingers through her sleek mahogany hair, which settled silkily into place without appearing in the least mussed. Then, steeling her resolve, she dropped into the chair behind the desk, hoping he would now take the chair she had indicated. If she could face him on eye level she would feel less at a psychological disadvantage.

But he remained standing, and she was forced to push her chair back several feet so that she wouldn't get a cramp in her neck looking up at him.

"Mr. Bates, if you could give me just fifteen minutes of your time I could explain the reason for my imposture yesterday. It had *nothing* to do with you, I promise you."

Sydney glanced nervously around the room to reassure herself that no one in the vicinity was taking particular notice of her and Daniel Bates and then down at her watch. "Today is my father's birthday and I'm expected to be present for a family dinner or I'd offer to take you to lunch somewhere." The strain induced by her circumstances showed in the tautness of her features and the intense blueness of her eyes as they searched his calm, expressionless countenance for an assent to her request for a hearing.

"I'll drive you to your dinner appointment."

It was a most unexpected offer, delivered not as a suggestion but as a statement. Ordinarily she would have informed him that she had her own car and was capable of driving herself, but now was hardly the time, nor was the office the place to argue with Daniel Bates. Her father could give her a lift back to the office later in the afternoon.

Snapping her briefcase closed and taking her handbag from a drawer in the desk, she indicated her acceptance of his offer and followed him outside the office to his car, a brown Buick several years old. Automatically, she found herself comparing it to Larry's silver Mercedes sports model. Daniel Bates obviously didn't share her ex-husband's concern for projecting the right kind of image, or maybe geologists didn't have to worry about creating the impression of material success.

By coincidence, the Buick was parked right next to Sydney's own smart gold Volvo and looked conservative and drab in contrast. Daniel Bates paused in the act of opening the passenger door and glanced around at the other cars parked in front of the office building.

"I don't see your car," he commented dryly.

Acting on reflex, Sydney glanced over at the Volvo and then avoided his eyes, feeling warmth suffuse her face and neck under his cynical survey. He held the door open for her.

"You certainly went to a lot of trouble, Miss Cullen, even to borrowing a car to fit your disguise. Your name really *is* Miss Cullen, I take it?"

She stepped into the car with as much dignity as possible and waited for him to come around and slide in under the steering wheel before replying to the jibe. "My name *is* Sydney Cullen, Mr. Bates." She didn't bother to explain that it had been Stanton for nine years, and that after the divorce she had resumed the use of her maiden name, going to the trouble of changing all her identification, including her social security card and driver's license. Her mother had objected, pointing out that her name would be different from her children's, but Sydney had been determined that she wouldn't keep Larry's name if he didn't want her as his wife.

The interior of the Buick was roomy, but the man in the driver's seat seemed to fill in with his great size. Sydney was intensely conscious of him, the length and muscular power of his arms and legs, the breadth of his shoulders, as he fitted the key into the ignition and started the engine. Intuitively, she rejected the masculine dominance he emanated. No doubt his mentality was as macho as his appearance. Even in high school, when the other girls had drooled over the starting line-up of the football team, she had preferred boys with less brawn and more social finesse and intelligence.

"Where to?"

He had backed the car from its position between her Volvo and Valerie Perkins's Lincoln Continental and was looking over inquiringly at her for directions.

"My folks live in the old part of Mandeville, on Carroll Street," she began and elaborated no further when he sent the car forward immediately, ostensibly requiring no additional instructions at this point. Sydney waited until he had accelerated out onto the highway before commencing the explanation she had promised him.

"I heard at our sales meeting Friday morning that you—that is, the new owner—of the old Bates property on the lake might be putting it up for sale in the near future. Knowing how expensive land on the lake is and how many people would give their right arm to own it, I decided I would get the listing if indeed you—the new owner—decided to sell. Of course, every agent in the office was hoping to do the same thing."

She allowed a little pause at this juncture, but he seemed totally absorbed in his driving and made no use of it to insert a question or comment. Darting a quick look at his profile, Sydney found it quite impassive and continued.

"Then something happened that really upset me. One of the agents in the office implied that if anyone got the listing, *I* would because . . ." Sydney floundered in the effort to verbalize the accusation that she exploited her female looks in dealing with clients of the opposite sex. "Well, because I'm a woman and younger and more attractive than some of the other agents. Most of the agents in our office who deal in residential property are women," she added quickly to cover the awkwardness she felt as he shot her an assessing glance, as if weighing the truth of her alleged feminine allure.

"At first I was so mad I couldn't see straight— because it's not at all true, you see. The only reason I've done so well in such a short time is that I work twice as hard as anyone else on this side of the lake. And even though I knew I shouldn't let the incident bother me, it did."

He still didn't say anything. By now Larry would have thoroughly cross-examined her, eliciting answers that supported whatever preconceived opinion he held of her actions. It was a good thing Daniel Bates hadn't chosen to go into law, she reflected with a touch of asperity.

"All day I kept wishing there was *some* way I could prove that the way I look has nothing to do with my success in real estate. Then came the inspiration to make myself ugly and go to see the owner of the Bates property. You know the rest."

She glanced at him inquiringly, expecting some response and hoping that it would be understanding of her motives and actions.

"What did you do before you went into real estate?"

Sydney failed to discern any relevance in the question unless he suspected she might be a frustrated actress. "I was a housewife," she replied evenly, carefully keeping her tone free of the rancor that could easily creep in when she thought of the nine wasted years of her marriage to Larry. Well, not really wasted, since she had Stacy and Kevin out of the deal. And there had been happy times, too.

"That's not a job in great demand these days," Daniel Bates said shortly, jolting her to attention.

The implied criticism hit a sensitive spot, and she spoke hotly, without thinking. "Like a lot of other women, I didn't quit the job, Mr. Bates. My services were no longer required." The words were out before she could stop them, dripping scorn for those of his sex short on fidelity, which in her opinion constituted a majority of men. Immediately, she realized how foolish she was to take the chance of offending him needlessly. When would she ever learn to control that temper of hers, which invariably erupted through her tongue?

Trying to repair whatever damage might have been done, she suggested in a calmer, more reasonable tone, "Look, what do you say we just forget I came to your house yesterday? I can't blame you for getting riled up at me the way you did, but there wasn't really any harm done, was there?"

Silence hung between them as he executed a

right-hand turn onto Carroll Street. In Sydney's opinion he had to be one of the least talka-
tive men she had ever encountered, and trying to
carry on a conversation with him was frustrating
indeed.

In minutes they would be arriving at her parents'
house, and after that she wouldn't ever have any
contact with the laconic man again. In the meantime, she might as well make a plea for large-
mindedness in the hope that he would not hold a
grudge against Pontchartrain Realty just because of
her.

"If you should decide to sell your place, Pontchartrain Realty will do a better job for you than any
other agency on this side of the lake," she said
casually. A probing glance from the dark eyes re-
leased another scalding tide of indignation which she
struggled fiercely to repress. "I am *not* even hinting
that you should list with me. There are other good
agents in the office—stop up ahead. The white frame
house with the green shutters."

Seldom during the past year, when she had come
to enjoy a pleasurable new sense of control in her
relations with people, had Sydney felt so ineffectual.
This man beside her was totally inscrutable, like a
granite boulder, showing not a dent under the
persistent onslaught of her words. She was totally
unable to read him, to gauge his reaction to what she
had said.

As he obeyed her directions and pulled into the
driveway of her parents' home, something occurred
to trigger the instincts of the mother inside her,
making her temporarily oblivious to any other concern except the well-being of her child. Kevin had
bounded into sight around the corner of the house,
still dressed in his Sunday clothes, a big red setter in

close pursuit. Spying the strange automobile turning into the driveway, the boy stopped suddenly and was hurled to the concrete of the driveway by the impact of the dog's body.

Sydney jerked open the door of the car and in seconds was on her knees beside her son, her heart pounding with fear. "Kevin, baby, are you hurt?" she demanded breathlessly, gathering his small body up against her very carefully. He submitted for just a moment and then pushed away from her with boyish independence.

"Aw, I'm okay, Mom. It was my fault. I shouldna stopped so quick like that. Old Red couldn't change gears."

His limpid golden eyes widened with interest as he looked up at the man who had come to stand behind his mother. "Boy, you're big!" he proclaimed, clearly impressed. "I wish I'd grow up big like you."

"Kevin, this is Mr. Daniel Bates. Mr. Bates, my son, Kevin, whose greatest ambition in life is to be a football player." Sydney's tone was gently disparaging as she made this explanation by way of an apology for Kevin's childish candor. Against her son's will, she smoothed his ruffled hair and tucked his shirt neatly into his pants before straightening.

Suddenly an embarrassing thought struck her. "Not that there's anything wrong with being a football player," she said hastily, glancing obliquely at Daniel Bates only to find him smiling with evident amusement at her chagrin over having made yet another blunder. The smile transformed his rugged features, making him almost handsome.

"All-American," he murmured, confirming her earlier conjecture that he had probably played football.

"Does that mean I can play Junior Football, mom?" Kevin spoke up eagerly in response to his mother's unprecedented approval of playing football. "I don't want to play dumb old tennis—"

"We'll discuss this later, Kevin," Sydney interrupted in a tone that told her son he had better drop the subject immediately.

"KEV–IN! GRANDMA SAYS TO COME GET WASHED UP FOR DIN–NER—Oh, hi, Mom; I didn't know you were here already." Stacy had come skipping around the corner of the house bellowing her message ahead of her and skidded now to a halt as she spied her mother. One glance told Sydney the reason for her daughter's wariness. The front of her pastel blue dress had several vivid splashes of color identifiable to Sydney as daubs of paint.

"Stacy Stanton! Your new dress! What have you done to it?" Sydney demanded as though she didn't already know the answer.

"I *had* to finish Grandpa's picture for his birthday," Stacy offered shamefacedly, coming forward a few halting steps. "Grandma says she thinks it will come out."

Sydney suddenly became aware that Daniel Bates was regarding the two children and herself with unabashed interest. "Both of you go and wash up for dinner. Tell Grandma I'll be right there," she ordered in her best Authoritative Mother tone. She watched her two offspring dash off toward the rear of the house and disappear from sight before bringing her attention back to the tall man next to her. He looked perfectly relaxed and unhurried, standing with his weight evenly balanced on both feet and his hands thrust casually into his pockets.

"Sorry you had to be subjected to this domestic

scene, Mr. Bates," she said crisply, turning to go back to the car and retrieve her briefcase and handbag, which she had left behind in her anxiety over Kevin's tumble.

"Syd, honey, the food's on the table! We're all waiting for you."

Sydney groaned audibly, turning around slowly to see her mother standing on the front porch, her Sunday dress protected by a white ruffled apron with dainty appliqué designs. It looked as though Daniel Bates would be confronted with the whole family before she could manage to get rid of him. Yet he displayed no eagerness to escape, giving Sydney little choice other than to introduce him to her mother.

"Mom, this is Daniel Bates. He owns a house and ten acres on the lake. My mother, Pauline Cullen."

Sydney had deliberately injected the identifying information to dispel the gleam of interest in her mother's eyes as she gazed from her daughter to the man beside her. Sydney wouldn't put it past her mother to invite this total stranger to join the family for dinner if she thought he was a potential suitor for Sydney. If Pauline believed Daniel Bates was a very important client she might be too intimidated to make such an offer.

"Happy to make your acquaintance, Mr. Bates. You won't be sorry my daughter is your real estate agent. She's the top selling agent in this whole area." Pauline folded her smooth, plump arms across her middle, smiling proudly at Sydney, whose cheeks were suffused with the telltale warmth of a blush, an indicator of embarrassment she had never learned to control.

"Really, Mom, Mr. Bates doesn't care to hear—"

"I gathered as much about your daughter from the article in the *News Herald* yesterday, Mrs. Cullen. It's a pleasure to meet you, but I don't want to delay your dinner any longer. If you'll excuse me—" Daniel Bates inclined his head in a courtly gesture and turned to leave, again showing no evidence of haste.

Sydney felt a rush of helplessness, knowing what would happen next as well as she knew her own name and age. Her mother and Daniel Bates were like two actors speaking well-rehearsed parts, both of them knowing the outcome.

"Wouldn't you like to stay and have dinner with us, Mr. Bates? You're more than welcome. And there's plenty of food, too," Pauline urged.

"Oh, thank you for offering, Mrs. Cullen, but I wouldn't think of barging in." The demur was spoken with just the right shade of wistfulness.

"You wouldn't be barging in. It's just Mr. Cullen and myself, Sydney and the two grandchildren. We'd love to have you, wouldn't we, Syd?" Pauline looked convincingly at him, as if nothing would please her more than to have him accept her impromptu invitation. She eyed her daughter a trifle disapprovingly, finding her slow in confirming the welcome.

Sydney had the uncomfortable sensation that Daniel Bates had perceived her own irritation and was enjoying her helplessness. "Mom, I'm sure Mr. Bates has other plans for lunch," she protested.

"Actually I don't," he contradicted, brown eyes glinting with humor as they met hers. "The prospect of a real home-cooked meal is always appealing to a single man."

Spoken by a man of such obvious eligibility, those

were the words guaranteed to ignite hope in the heart of a mother whose daughter has two wonderful children and no husband. Sydney knew she had lost the battle even before her mother chirped, "That settles it, then. Come along, both of you, before everything gets cold."

Chapter Three

$\mathcal{W}$hat could Sydney do? Nothing except submit as gracefully as she could manage to the inevitable.

She found Daniel Bates's behavior truly baffling— how many men would voluntarily spend a Sunday afternoon with strangers engaged in a birthday celebration? But on the positive side, she reflected with a certain measure of calculation that he was unlikely to accept her parents' hospitality and then later cause trouble for their daughter over an innocent charade, about which Pauline and Fred knew nothing.

Refusing his offer to carry her briefcase, she preceded him into the house through the front door. They entered the living room, which bore the evidence of Pauline Cullen's mastery of various kinds of needlework, from the crocheted arm covers on the sofa and deeply cushioned chairs to the framed tapestries on the wall. Sydney could tell Daniel

Bates was noting his surroundings with far more than
casual interest, lagging behind her so that she
stopped in the archway between the living and
dining rooms and glanced over her shoulder at him
with open impatience. He was inspecting an embroi-
dered forest scene with a mother deer and fawn and
looked around to meet Sydney's gaze. For a moment
she thought he was about to make a comment, but
then he apparently changed his mind, following her
into the dining room.

The table was resplendent with the good china and
silver and laden with bowls and platters of food
prepared according to Fred Cullen's preferences,
since he was the one having the birthday. There was
a beautiful baked ham decorated with cherries and
studded with fragrant cloves, creamed yams with
marshmallow topping, corn on the cob, green peas
with pearl onions, plus various relishes and pickles
Pauline had put up herself. Everything was delicious, and Pauline beamed with pleasure at the
hearty portions consumed by her husband and spur-
of-the-moment guest, who insisted everyone call
him Daniel.

The birthday cake, contrary to the usual, was a
superb German chocolate cake which, at the children's insistence, bore candles inscribing Fred Cullen's age in arabic numerals. He blew out the candles
and then relit them twice so that both Stacy and
Kevin could take turns blowing them out, insisting
that each of them make a special wish for him.

Daniel seemed not in the least bored or impatient
with the interlude dominated by the children and, on
top of the large meal he had just consumed, accepted a generous slice of cake topped with a scoop
of ice cream.

Next came the time the children had been awaiting

with great anticipation, their grandfather's opening of his presents. After all, what else were birthdays for?

Kevin had taken his own money and purchased several exotic fishing lures, apparently guided by the supposition that the gaudier the color and the larger the feather, the greater the appeal to an unsuspecting fish.

"Say, I should be able to catch some big ones with these!" Fred declared, inspecting each one with such close interest that Kevin wriggled with pleasure. Only a faint twinkle in Fred's eyes as they locked fleetingly with Daniel's made Sydney wonder if the lures were even suitable for fishing in the surrounding area.

Stacy watched with an expression blending eagerness with apprehension as her grandfather opened her present, a portrait she had done of Red, the Cullens' setter. "Careful, Grandpa, it's still a little wet," she cautioned, glancing down at the front of her dress and then quickly over at her mother.

"Say, that's a really a good likeness," Fred praised. "Take a look at that, Daniel." He handed the painting to the man sitting on his immediate right.

Daniel regarded it thoughtfully for several seconds and then turned his head and spoke directly to Sydney, who sat next to him, thanks to her mother's less than subtle manipulation. "Your daughter is obviously talented."

Glancing across the table at Stacy, Sydney was forced to concede that the glow on the girl's face was worth the price of the dress she might have ruined. With the discernment of the very young, Stacy recognized the genuineness of Daniel's compliment, lacking as it did the effusiveness of obligatory praise.

"Mom promised I can take art lessons this summer," she volunteered. "If she can find a teacher."

"There should be no problem finding a competent teacher," he said, looking from Stacy's thin young face, illuminated with hope at this welcome assurance, to Sydney's, which suggested he mind his own business and let her worry about art lessons for her daughter. Ignoring the message in the latter, he continued, "You have an active artists' association in this parish. Probably all you have to do is contact them and get the names and telephone numbers of those members who give private instructions to juniors."

The suggestion was so entirely reasonable and so obvious now he had stated it that Sydney wondered why she hadn't thought of it herself. "That's a good idea," she admitted grudgingly and then smiled across at Stacy. "I'll call the association tomorrow," she promised.

During this conversation Kevin had managed to sit as still as could be expected of an eight-year-old boy. Sydney recognized the telltale signs of restlessness and excused him and Stacy from the table. Then she rose and began to help her mother carry the remaining dishes out to the kitchen, assuming that Daniel would accompany her father to the living room or—a more likely possibility—seize the opportunity to take his leave. In fact, he did neither.

She was running warm water into one half of the double sink in preparation for washing the dishes that wouldn't fit into the dishwasher, which was already filled, when he entered the kitchen carrying a stack of dessert plates and came over to place them on the counter by the sink.

Sydney grinned wickedly up at him. "You were batting a thousand up until now, my friend, but you just committed the unpardonable sin for a southern male." She clucked in mock disapproval. "Helping clear the table is bad enough any time. But on Sunday? Horrors!"

She was only half joking, having grown up in a home where duties were clearly divided between women's work and men's work. Her father, so far as she knew, had never cooked a single meal for himself or loaded soiled clothes into the washing machine, nor would her mother dream of mowing the lawn or carrying the big aluminum garbage cans out to the edge of the driveway on garbage pickup days.

The only difference in Sydney's own married life had been her assumption of some of the duties her father performed at home. While Larry never openly refused to mow the lawn, he never seemed to get around to it, preferring to spend weekends playing tennis or going out sailing with some of his friends at the local yacht club. On garbage collection days he simply forgot to take out the big plastic cans unless she nagged, and eventually he solved the problem to his satisfaction by buying a trolley so that she could wheel them to the edge of the lawn without straining herself carrying them.

Certainly it would never have occurred to Larry, in his own home or anyone else's, to rise from the dining room table and carry a dish out to the kitchen. Nor, as Sydney would have to admit if she were honest, had she ever expected him to do so.

"Better pay attention to what you're doing."

A big hand came into her line of vision and turned off the tap. The sink was three-quarters full of sudsy water and she had been staring down at it, lost in her own thoughts, while he went out into the dining room and returned with a stack of cups cradled

carefully in his hands, which though large were
sensitively shaped and not at all awkward, as she had
noticed yesterday. They were capable hands, sure of
themselves and used to doing things. No doubt they
were also skilled in molding the curves of a woman's
body. . . .

Disturbed by this totally unexpected foray of her
mind into forbidden territory, Sydney turned
abruptly away from the sink to remove her suit
jacket, which she draped over the back of a kitchen
chair, and then began methodically to unbutton the
cuffs of her silk blouse and fold back the sleeves
above her elbows. The last thing she welcomed at
this particular juncture in her life was physical
attraction to a man, any man, but certainly not to
Daniel Bates, who was not her type under any
circumstances. He was entirely too overpoweringly
male, with all that brawn and muscle. She preferred
intelligence and sensitivity.

When she turned around it was to note with
astonishment that Daniel now stood in front of the
sink calmly and efficiently washing dishes, rinsing
them, and placing them in the drain beside the other
half of the sink. For the first time it occurred to her
that her mother was conspicuously absent from the
kitchen.

"What happened to my mother?" she demanded,
as though suspecting some skulduggery.

"Out on the back porch with your father enjoying
a well-deserved rest after preparing that superb
meal."

He glanced over his shoulder, his eyes traveling
slowly down her figure, the curves of her breasts and
hips more noticeable now after the removal of her
suit jacket. The surge of response his gaze aroused in
her body both shocked and annoyed her. To combat

it, she moved briskly over to the counter, picked up
a dish towel and began to dry the dishes in the drain
with hands that were far from steady.

What was wrong with her today? she fumed.
Turning weak-kneed because a man looked at her.
More than one of her friends had warned her with
varying degrees of subtlety after the separation. *You
won't be able to live without a man, Sydney. Face the
facts and don't be shocked at yourself. Women have
biological needs, just like men.*

Their intentions were good, she knew, so she
hadn't bothered to argue with them. They were
only recommending discretion in order to avoid
the kind of gossip that would bring harm to those
she loved, in particular her children and parents.
How often she had heard remarks about divorced
women who "went wild" and "slept with anything
in pants."

What her friends hadn't realized, and she hadn't
bothered to explain, was that her sexuality had
been anesthetized—perhaps even killed—by the
shattering emotional trauma of Larry's rejection.
Sex represented surrender and vulnerability, and she
desired neither. It was with a certain fierce sense of
triumph during the past few months that she had
tested her imperviousness to the male of the species,
going out several times with men and even suffering
them to kiss her good night. She had felt nothing,
not the slightest stirring of passion, and had
concluded with satisfaction that she was immune to
men.

But was she? Daniel Bates had just raised some
alarming doubts about her passivity. Even now,
standing as far away from him as she dared without
appearing ridiculously obvious, she was acutely
aware of him even though he didn't try to engage her

in conversation and seemed totally unaffected himself by her presence. It was with relief that she noted he had finished washing the last of the dishes.

"Why don't you go out and join Mom and Dad?" she suggested, concentrating all her attention on the bowl she was drying. "I'll wipe the counters and put on a fresh pot of coffee."

He was half turned at the sink, watching her. She resisted the magnetic force of his gaze, keeping her profile to him as she placed the bowl on the counter. Before she could take up another wet dish from the drain, he reached out his hands toward her. Involuntarily, she shrank away, realizing too late that all he intended was to dry his hands on her dish towel. Hoping her reflexive reaction had gone unnoticed, she thrust the towel toward him, bracing herself for what she might see when she looked up into his face.

His expression was a blend of awareness, curiosity and detachment she perceived with more dissatisfaction than relief. He backed off a few steps so that he could lean against the counter running along the wall. His scrutiny contained no element of intimacy. She might as well have been a rock sample he was examining with geological interest.

"I've never seen a woman more out of place in a kitchen."

The remark was so unexpected Sydney didn't know whether she should interpret it as an insult or a compliment, but thought somehow it wasn't the latter. Curbing the impulse to make a sarcastic retort about the emancipation of women from domestic bondage, she picked up the wet sponge and commenced a less than thorough swiping motion across the counter top, calculated to inforce his impression of her ineptitude.

"You, on the other hand, look thoroughly comfortable up to your elbows in dishwater," she observed coolly. Then, after tossing the sponge carelessly into the sink, she smoothed down the sleeves of her blouse and applied herself to buttoning the cuffs. As though it were an afterthought instead of a deliberate provocation, she added, "You'd make some working woman a good house-husband."

"Someone like yourself, for example?"

Her cuffs neatly buttoned, she crossed her arms under her breasts and tilted her head to one side as if giving serious consideration to his terse rejoinder.

"No, someone who isn't as *lucky* as I am. I have a perfectly good housekeeper."

Her softly spoken barb evidently hit her target. For a long, breathless moment Sydney wondered if she had been foolhardy in challenging Daniel Bates. He straightened and tensed as if about to spring at an adversary, something primitive and dangerous flaming up in his dark eyes and inducing in her a strange sense of paralysis in the face of his male power and dominance. She was keenly aware of danger and yet too helpless to flee, prey to a swelling exhilaration inexplicable in one about to be conquered by a stronger foe. Later she would berate herself with disgust for acting like some stereotypical cave woman, defiant and yet thrilled to the core at the prospect of being dragged off to her brutish captor's lair.

"You two going to take all day to wash a few dishes?" Pauline inquired from the doorway.

The tension ebbed almost visibly from Daniel's powerful body, and suddenly he was no longer a primitive man brandishing a club over the head of a foolishly rebellious member of the weaker sex. He was just an exceptionally large man who had been temporarily angered by a woman's needling.

Sydney might almost have imagined the strange contest of wills that had throbbed between them in some dimension removed from ordinary time and place, every nerve and muscle and fiber in her body straining in resistance to him and yet thrilling to the inevitability of the eventual surrender. There was at first an unaccountable sensation of letdown at the interruption rather than the relief she should have felt. She almost resented her mother for intruding.

"We were just finishing," she said, going over to pick up her jacket from the back of the kitchen chair, a sense of normalcy returning. Was something wrong with her, causing her to indulge in all manner of strange fantasies today? Some hormonal imbalance or vitamin deficiency? More than likely she was just suffering a reaction from the strain she'd been under ever since last evening when Daniel Bates had telephoned with his threats to brand her as an unscrupulous real estate agent.

Her best course was to blank him entirely from her mind, pretend she had never made that ill-fated visit to his house. A few minutes more and she would make some excuse to return to the office. After that, with any luck, she would see no more of Daniel Bates.

If Pauline detected anything but friendliness between her daughter and her guest she gave no indication. "Daniel, you go on out to the back porch and keep Fred company while Syd and I make some more coffee," she ordered cheerfully, her eyes inspecting the kitchen in a way that told Sydney it didn't measure up to her own standards of perfection.

Daniel obeyed without sparing Sydney so much as another glance. When she accompanied her mother out onto the screened back porch a few minutes later, he was deep in conversation with her father about the older man's job with the state highway department.

Then the talk shifted to Daniel's job. He explained that more and more of late he found himself confined in an office when what he really enjoyed was being outdoors working in the oil fields. "That's one reason I'm considering accepting a position overseas for a few years."

This was news to Pauline, whose voice held discernible disappointment as she asked, "Is that why you're thinking of selling your house and land?"

"More or less."

Sydney watched his features settle into a brooding expression tinged with sadness and something akin to anger. He had looked the same way yesterday morning when she broached the subject of his selling the valuable piece of property he had inherited from his uncle. Apparently he had just now conducted a debate within himself as to whether he should further explain his reasons for selling or not selling and had decided to elaborate.

"I have no need for the money the property would bring. On my salary I can buy whatever I want and need." Sydney had a mental vision of the brown Buick parked outside in the driveway and guessed his tastes must be modest in other respects as well, but she didn't speak her thoughts as he continued. "I love the old house and the land. I spent most of my summers there with my Uncle Daniel when I was a kid. He was pretty much the epitome of the independent old bachelor and something of an eccentric. He bought the place long before the Causeway was built connecting Mandeville to New Orleans, back in the days when all these fancy country club subdivisions were nothing but forests and nobody dreamed this end of the parish would turn into a corporate bedroom community."

Sydney stirred restlessly, not liking the turn of this whole conversation. Her livelihood not only depended but flourished on these changes his tone disparaged. The affluent residents of the subdivisions to which he referred were transferred by companies to the New Orleans area for usually no longer than five years and frequently only two or three. As a result, the turnover in ownership of houses was almost constant, making residential real estate a thriving business.

"If you don't need the money and you have such a strong attachment to the place, why sell?" she asked, speaking for the first time since coming out from the kitchen. Her voice was sharper than she had intended and drew surprised looks from both her parents in addition to the narrowed gaze of the man she addressed.

"That's a good question. I'm not sure the answer is one someone like yourself—a member of the real estate profession—is capable of understanding." His antagonism was less blatant than her own had been, possibly discernible only to herself. Transferring his attention back to her parents, he continued in the same reflective manner as before, ignoring the brief interchange.

"It seems not just selfish for me to hold on to the property, but . . . *unjust* to it." He hesitated, as if searching for the right words. "This sounds really far out, but in some weird way I've begun to feel the chain of ownership needs to be broken. The last Daniel Bates lived in that big old house all by himself, but he did share it with me in the summers.

Now I own it and—and like him—I'm single. No kids and no prospects of having any."

The explanation obviously cost him some effort, noticeable more in the lack of expression in his quiet voice than from the regret one might expect. Pauline's lip quivered with sympathy, but before she could speak, he was continuing.

"I'd gladly—well, not gladly, but willingly—give the place up to some family with kids, preferably four or five. It's a paradise for a kid, at least it was for me. The beach with all its treasures, swimming and fishing in the lake, climbing trees with branches so big you can stretch out and take a nap on them, the woods with all kinds of wildlife and imaginary dangers and adventure . . ."

Daniel seemed oblivious to their presence for a long moment, lost in his own recollections. Then his face hardened. "What I *don't* want is to let some developer get his hands on the land and chop it up into lots."

Which was the most likely future for the property. Sydney's unspoken thought hung in the air like some evil specter. Suddenly both of her parents were looking at her as though expecting some assurance that what Daniel feared could be prevented from happening. Feeling herself uncomfortably allied in all their minds with the hypothetical villains who lurked around the corners of the future, waiting to get greedy hands on Daniel's beautiful acres and despoil them into orderly lots, she jumped to her feet.

"I still have some things to do at the office before I can call it a day. Could one of you give me a ride?" She looked from Daniel to her father, signifying that it didn't matter which one volunteered.

"Just leave the kids. Fred will take them home

later." Pauline settled the matter, taking it for granted that Daniel would drive Sydney back to the office.

Sydney gave tacit assent to the arrangement. "Cora should be back at the house by now." She glanced at her watch. "But you'd better call to make sure before you take the kids over. I can always come back and pick them up here."

The lengthy leave-taking tried Sydney's patience more than it ordinarily would have. Her parents sometimes carried the southern hospitality concept a little too far, and how many times did Daniel Bates have to thank her mother for the meal and impress upon her and Fred how much he had enjoyed the entire afternoon? Finally she found herself in the car and moving.

They hadn't gone far when she noticed he was not taking the most direct route to the Pontchartrain Realty office. A few minutes later she began to wonder if he had forgotten the way.

"Where are you going?"

He didn't answer directly. "You have listing contracts in your briefcase?"

"Why, yes." He *couldn't* mean—? Some reticence on her part forbade her from openly asking the question dominating her thoughts, and they rode in silence a few minutes longer until it became evident he was taking her to his house.

"You're not seriously thinking of letting *me* list your property?" she blurted incredulously when he swung the car into the open entrance of his driveway.

"Why not? If I'm going to sell it, I might as well go with the best agent in the parish."

Sydney was dumbfounded, and not in the least elated at the prospect of the biggest commission she had yet to earn. "But you haven't even decided you definitely want to sell."

"I've decided. Today helped me to decide."

Whatever the meaning behind that cryptic statement, he evidently had no intention of explaining it to her, and her sense of dismay grew as the car entered the clearing and came to a stop near the small back porch.

"Daniel—" She turned toward him before he could get out of the car. "I think you're acting impulsively. Why don't you take some more time and think about it?"

He regarded her intently, as if registering her words and examining them with great caution. No doubt he thought she was up to some underhanded real estate trick, she reflected in exasperation.

"Look," she reasoned, "nobody can give you any promises about what will be done with this property once it's sold. Aside from zoning restrictions, people in this country can do what they choose with their own property. You know that." Why did she feel so angry? Was it because her deepest instincts were in conflict with her common sense and self-interest? Or was it because he looked as though he was still wary of her motives in trying to dissuade him from selling?

"Think of this possibility before you definitely make up your mind to sell. Somebody could buy this place and tear down the house, board by board, and sell it to a builder—old cypress goes for a premium price. Could you stand that?"

She turned her head and looked at the old white frame building in question. What she had just suggested seemed a desecration to her, and she was looking at the house for only the second time. She could imagine how he felt.

"No, I couldn't stand it. But I won't even know. Once I sell this place I don't intend to come back and see what happens to it. Not ever." He spoke with clipped savagery. "I've been mooning around like some kind of idealistic moron the last year, refusing to face up to reality. Well, I'm facing it now. Are you interested in handling the listing for me—or not?"

His eyes bored into hers, probing them for the answer. She gazed back, mesmerized, trying desperately to summon the words she knew instinctively she should say. *No, I do not want to list for you.* She was a real estate agent dealing in the transfer of properties, intricacies of mortgages and loans, legal contracts—not a psychologist or a counselor. There was entirely too much emotion involved here, and she should refuse to have any further dealings with Daniel Bates. He wasn't what he appeared to be: an oversized ex-football player who by rights should be forthright and simplistic, not this complex man with philosophic depths that enticed and frightened her.

"Yes."

The word originated from some source she couldn't indentify or control, and she regretted it as soon as it passed her lips.

"Good," he said matter-of-factly and leaned across her to open her door.

Sydney flinched automatically, flattening herself against the back of the seat to avoid contact with the masculine shoulder and upper arm extended in front of her breasts. Her recoil was entirely involuntary, and she didn't even realize she was holding her breath to keep the warm musky scent of him out of her nostrils.

Sensing her reaction, he froze in place, turning his head to see her face. Surprise shaded into irritation as he noted the rigidity of her shoulders and the pale tautness of her features. Slowly, she expelled her breath, realizing that her dizziness was resulting from the shortage of oxygen in her lungs.

He straightened without opening the door. "What's with you? This is the second time today you've acted like a hysterical virgin when I came close to touching you." He sounded more puzzled than angry.

Sydney felt extremely foolish seeing her actions through his eyes. Here she was, a thirty-year-old divorcee with two children, shrinking from casual contact with a man who had made no intimate overtures toward her. No wonder he was provoked. But perhaps what had just happened was all for the best. She would seize the opening to make her position in regard to him perfectly clear. Then they would be able to work together with no misconceptions on either side.

"Please don't take this personally, Daniel, but I prefer to keep our relationship entirely professional." He was looking at her with open incredulity, apparently unable to believe he was hearing what he was. Maybe he *was* macho where women were concerned, after all. With that in mind, she made an effort to soothe his injured ego. "Probably I'm not your type any more than you're mine . . ." That had not come out quite the way she intended, but she lost all opportunity to amend it.

"You're damned right you're not my type! I've had enough of hard-shelled career women like you to last me a lifetime!"

The words exploded from him, reminding Sydney uncomfortably of the barely leashed savagery she'd witnessed in him earlier that afternoon in her mother's kitchen. She must be crazy to prod a man like him to anger. He could strangle the breath out of her with one hand. Her fear must have shown in her eyes, and it did nothing to quench the blaze of his fury.

"For your information, I have never found it necessary to rape a woman to sate my uncontrollable male lust, and you don't even tempt me. I prefer a woman who looks and acts like a woman, not a man."

That stung. Sydney forgot she was afraid of him.

"A petite blonde is probably more to your taste, I suppose. The kind who bats her eyelashes and coos over your muscles." She gave him a demonstration with eyelashes fully suited for the purpose and softened her tone to a sugary drawl on the last words.

"Actually, I'm partial to the voluptuous type," he said coolly, flicking a derogatory glance over her own slender figure, which had never been accused of being voluptuous.

Sydney drew in her breath with an audible hiss and turned her head to stare out the window. Never in her life had she been so *insulted* by a man, not even Larry during their fiercest quarrels. This man had galling nerve!

Suddenly it occurred to her that she had been literally *brawling* with an almost total stranger, and all over nothing. A few seconds ago she would have liked to bash him over the head, and she suspected he would have liked to do the same to her.

Hesitantly, she turned her head and met his eyes, seeing there an awareness that matched her own and, like hers, threatened any second to give way to amusement. Her lips twitched irrepressibly and then they were grinning sheepishly at each other.

"I guess we've established rather thoroughly that

we don't appeal to each other," she quipped. He *did* have a nice smile. It changed his whole face and crinkled the outside corners of his eyes.

"This time you can open your own door," he said wryly, getting out of the car.

The next two hours were all business. Sydney went from room to room in the house, measuring, making notations, thinking aloud as she anticipated objections and thought of improvements she would suggest when showing the house.

"What a shame someone *painted* this lovely beaded wainscoting," she lamented in one of the bedrooms. "I don't suppose it could be stripped and varnished?"

"Not easily," he agreed. "You could strip the flat surfaces and paint the crevices a dark color, maybe black, and then varnish over the whole thing. But it would be a lot of trouble."

"That's a clever idea," she approved, visualizing the effect he described.

"Not bad for a guy who went to college on a football scholarship, hm?"

The needling was good-natured now, and she was quick to retaliate. "Imagine what you might have been able to think up if you hadn't got all those knocks on the head."

"It wasn't my head that took the brunt of it."

The rueful note caught her attention, and she looked questioningly at him for an explanation.

"The knees, especially the right one. Jogging and tennis are out for me."

"A fate worse than death," she said sarcastically. "They're both so fashionable these days."

His eyebrows lifted a fraction. "You don't like tennis players and joggers either?"

She flashed him a smile that conceded a point for

his side of the scoreboard. "Joggers are so sanctimonious. And I guess my husband turned me off tennis. He's a fanatic about it and determined that Kevin is going to be the next child pro. It's so ironic—Kevin is thinking more in terms of being the next . . ." She searched her mind for the name of a current football celebrity and drew a blank. "Star quarterback, I guess," she finally finished.

"Is Kevin a Saints fan?"

"Unflagging. Whether they happen to win a game the whole season or not." Even she knew the New Orleans Saints' chronic failure to reward their zealous fans with a winning season. She'd have to have been deaf and blind not to know, considering the emphasis local newsmen gave the subject.

"Does he go to any of the home games in the Superdome?"

Sydney shook her head. "Larry has a low opinion of all team sports, but especially football. He thinks the emphasis in school is all wrong. That kids should learn individual sports they can pursue all their lives."

She thought he might present an opposing view, defending his own role in team sports and pointing out benefits they offered, but he didn't. Instead, he shook he head slightly. "If I were going to be around this fall, I'd take him."

The lighthearted atmosphere evaporated and silence fell between them. Daniel seemed preoccupied with thoughts that were not particularly cheerful, judging from the somber cast of his expression. As she busied herself measuring the remaining upstairs rooms, Sydney pondered the conversation which apparently had triggered his change in mood. Did he resent the fact that he had no children while other men, Larry, for example, had been more fortunate and did not even seem to appreciate their children, seeing them only occasionally when the impulse to act the generous father struck. Considering the brief time she had known Daniel, it surprised her that she could be so utterly confident that he would have made an excellent father, with the right combination of firmness and indulgence.

"Well, that does it!" she declared when she had finished the last room.

"How about a drink?"

"Hm. I guess so. If I can use your phone, I'll check in with Cora and let her know where I am."

They sat out on the steps of the wide front veranda which faced the lake. In the fading light it gleamed like a vast opal, pearly lavender, pink, and palest aqua blending into the horizon so there was no division between sky and water. The effect was one of unearthly beauty and it cast a spell of serenity over the two people gazing out at it.

"What a luxury to have a view like this," Sydney observed dreamily.

"It's never exactly the same twice," he replied. "The infinite variety is part of the charm."

They sipped their drinks in companionable silence as dusk fell and then Daniel went back into the house and mixed refills. Sydney seldom drank except at parties, which had become extremely infrequent occasions now that she was divorced, and the alcohol had a relaxing effect upon her. Succumbing to a pleasant languor, she leaned back and rested her elbows on the planking of the veranda behind her. The small sigh she gave was one of utter content- ment. It was so seldom she relaxed anymore. There was always so much to occupy her mind, most of it related to work. People to telephone, appointments to keep, records to check at the zoning office of the courthouse, loan officers who had to be reminded to contract deadlines. When she wasn't actually *doing* real estate work, she was *thinking* about it.

A glance at the man seated beside her revealed that he was lost in his own reflections. What was he thinking about? He was certainly given to being quiet for long stretches.

"Penny?" she queried lightly.

He made a visible effort to return from the solitary plane of his introspection. She waited with a curious sense of expectation for his answer.

"Women like your mother are a dying breed these days."

He wasn't deliberately baiting her. She could tell from his quietly reflective tone that he was simply obliging her bid for conversation. But she was nonetheless irked by the comment, finding in it an implied criticism of ambitious women like herself.

"There's damned good reason for that," she said, sitting up straight. "You men want everything. The sweet little housewife with all the domestic talents to soften and beautify your nest and the bright career girl on the side as your mistress—to provide stimulation and excitement."

He had sat up, too. She could read the skepticism on his features in the semidarkness.

"I can't quite visualize *you* in the role of 'sweet little housewife.'"

"I have the family albums to prove it," she jeered cynically. "For nine years I kept the house spotless, did the laundry and shopping and cooking, took care of the kids—all with the foolish belief that Larry Stanton wanted an 'old-fashioned' wife." Her voice sharpened with bitterness on the last three words.

"Then, guess what? He discovered he didn't want that at all. He wanted a woman with a mind. A woman who could function intelligently in a man's world." She was quoting Larry almost verbatim on that last.

Daniel was giving her his full attention, but when she paused he uttered no comment or question, a restraint she was coming to recognize as typical of him. It revealed a patience most people lacked. He was content to let her tell her story her own way without prompting or guiding.

"It wouldn't have been so bad, I think, if he hadn't fallen for his law associate, Connie Bell, who was everything I had wanted to be nine years earlier and gave up to marry *him!*"

"You wanted to be a lawyer?" She had surprised him out of his silence.

"I was in prelaw when I met Larry. He was in his last year of law school at Tulane. 'One lawyer in the family is enough,' he said. The *bastard!*" Tears burned her eyes. She blinked furiously, grateful now for the screen of darkness and at the same time angry with herself for feeling so deeply even after two years.

Daniel let the silence eddy around them. When she didn't continue, he spoke. "You seem to have done very well for yourself."

"Yes, I have," she confirmed grimly. "For two years I've lived and breathed real estate, and it's beginning to pay off. I don't need a penny of Larry Stanton's money now. He still pays child support, but I don't really need that either. I put it in an account for the kids. For their education or whatever when they're grown."

He made a sound in his throat. "Life is so **d**amned crazy. Your husband decides he wants a career woman, turns his back on his wife and two great kids, when I—" He broke off abruptly, but she knew what he had been about to say. He would have given a great deal to have what Larry threw away.

Suddenly she was curious about the kind of woman he had married. "What was your wife like, Daniel?"

"Petite. Blonde." Sydney felt the irony of his gaze slicing through the darkness and remembered her sarcastic supposition about his preference in women. "Lovely and delicate, like a porcelain doll. The kind of feminine woman a man instinctively wants to protect and cherish, instincts that are quite unnecessary in Deborah's case. She manages very well to take care of herself. I don't think she really needs anybody on a permanent basis."

"Where does she live? What does she do?"

"She lives on the West Coast now, since her last promotion. She's the regional sales manager out there for Glamour Girl cosmetics. She started as a sales rep for the New Orleans area and worked herself up from there. It won't surprise me if she makes it all the way to the top of the corporation before she's through."

"She didn't want children?"

"No. But she never openly admitted it until our marriage was over. Before that, it was just never the right time. She knew from the beginning, too, that I wanted kids."

Sydney was drawn to the man beside her, deeply touched by the dark emotion of his tone, a combination of despair, resignation, and anger. How well she understood the sense of frustration and bafflement when one's marriage and whole course of life turn out to be a disappointment. The sense of undeserved wrong, of years wasted.

In the spirit of one human being desiring to comfort another, she moved closer to him on the step, laying a hand on his bare forearm as if to say: *I know how you feel. I, too, have suffered.* It seemed entirely natural for him to turn toward her and take her into his arms, equally as natural for her to slip her arms around his waist and rest her cheek against the warm hardness of his chest. She felt secure and protected in a way she hadn't known for a very long time.

His large hands were infinitely gentle as they smoothed her hair, slipped underneath it to massage her neck, and then slid down her back, stroking and soothing as though *she* were the one who needed consoling. Sydney wasn't quite sure when her sensations of pervasive warmth and closeness changed to something more intense, perhaps when his lips pushed under the heavy screen of silky hair and found her bare neck. The heat of his breath against her skin caused her to arch her back, bringing the thrust of her breasts against his chest. Her hands flattened against the solid tautness of his back, and she had a fleeting vision of the way it had looked the day before, smooth and hard-muscled and bare.

His mouth worked slowly up to her cheek, moving in unhurried little circles as if tasting the creamy texture of her skin, and then finally found her mouth, which quivered in readiness and made no pretense of evading his. After that there was an explosion of sensations for which she was totally unprepared. Daniel's mouth devoured hers with insatiable hunger, and she kissed him back in full measure, their passion feeding on the meeting and clinging of exploring tongues and the savage meshing of their lips.

Hands grown urgent and seeking molded the slimness of her waist, the curve of her hips, and then came up and pressed against her back, crushing her breasts against his chest. Breathless and gasping air into their lungs, they finally pulled their lips apart as Daniel fell back onto the planks of the veranda behind them, bringing her with him so that she lay on top of his chest, imprisoned in the powerful circle of his arms. She could feel the violent tremors coursing through his body and the thunder of his heartbeat penetrating her own chest cavity.

What she couldn't understand in her passion-drugged state was why he was just lying there holding her pinned against him so that she couldn't move an inch. Why didn't he kiss her again, move those marvelously strong and gentle hands of his all over her body, caressing and stroking every inch of her? Oh, how she wanted that! Hadn't she guessed they would know how to touch a woman's body?

"For heaven's sake, be still, Sydney. I'm having a hell of a time stopping as it is."

The ragged desperation of his tone more than the actual words first penetrated her consciousness. Her initial reaction was to protest that she didn't want him to stop. Her body was aflame with a crying need she hadn't known in two years and not even before that with this same urgency. She wanted him to make love to her, right now, right here on the veranda in the cool darkness with the lake out there not far away and the open expanse of sky overhead.

Before she could express all of this, a tiny needle of doubt thrust its way into her mind, pushing and penetrating until she could ignore it no longer. He evidently *did* want to stop. In her arousal she'd forgotten completely how brutally clear he had made his feelings about her earlier. She wasn't his type.

Stiffening in instinctive withdrawal, mental as well as physical, she tried to draw away from him. At first, her effort was entirely futile against the tensile steel of his arms, but then, without warning, they loosened their hold and she moved away from him to crouch on the edge of the step they had abandoned. Trembling with the upheaval of her emotions, she didn't know whether to maintain a cold, injured silence or to vent her indignation with words. The latter urge won. She would burst if she didn't tell him what she thought of his behavior.

"I've heard women accused of being teases," she burst out, "but never a man."

He moved with a quickness astonishing for someone his size, rising to his feet and going down the steps to stand at the bottom, an immense shadowy figure. "What the hell are you talking about?" His voice was ragged and strained.

"You had no right to start something you didn't intend to finish," she said stiffly. "If I'm not your type, you shouldn't have—have . . ." Her voice trailed off in embarrassment.

She could discern the slow movement of his head from side to side. "I don't believe this. Are you the same woman who announced in no uncertain terms a few hours ago that our relationship was to be strictly professional?"

She had completely forgotten that. There remained the fact, however, that he had made overtures and she was still quivering inside and feeling horribly frustrated. "Why did you kiss me, then?"

He sat down on the top step again, but as far away from her as its width permitted. "Good Lord, Sydney, I should think that was obvious. You *were* married for nine years. I wanted you. I still want you."

He bent over, resting his forearms on his knees and staring downward as though scrutinizing, in the

darkness, the plank on which his feet rested. Sydney
slanted a glance over at him and perceived the
weariness in the slope of his immense shoulders. In
spite of her sense of pique, she wished she could
reach over and stroke them, soothe away the fatigue
which was more than physical. Such a gesture from
her was out of the question now, though. She
wouldn't dare touch him again after what had just
happened. She had only meant to be sympathetic
when she laid her hand on his arm. Apparently he
had misread her sympathy as an invitation. But why
had he stopped without making love to her if he
were telling the truth when he said he wanted her? It
didn't make sense.

As if reading the question plaguing her mind, he
raised his head and looked toward her. "You have
no reason to feel insulted. The only reason I forced
myself to stop—and it wasn't easy, believe me—is
that I don't think either of us is emotionally ready
for a love affair. We both still have all sorts of
hang-ups from our marriages. We're not whole
people yet, Sydney. I'm afraid we'd just succeed in
opening up some new wounds in each other. Don't
you agree?"

Sydney did agree and she felt intolerably small and
petty for not having understood without having it
explained to her, simply, patiently, as though she
were an adolescent.

"I do agree, Daniel," she said contritely. "Tomorrow I'll thank you with all my heart, I'm sure. I guess
it must have been the drinks. I haven't felt anything
sexual for two years." His honesty deserved to be
reciprocated with her own. Now that her passion had
abated, she wasn't sure whether she had been at-
tracted to Daniel personally or if her biological
needs were just asserting themselves after a long

period of abstinence and he just happened to be the closest man when it happened.

Something hesitant in his manner made her suspect he wanted to say something more but was fearful of doing so. "Go ahead," she urged. "Whatever it is, I can take it."

"I haven't felt so strongly about a woman in almost a year. Tonight took me by surprise, too."

They eyed each other across the darkness with the openness of people who've survived a life-testing ordeal together and have seen each other at less than their best. For all practical purposes, nothing had happened to change their status since they had glared at each other that afternoon in the car. Although they had spoken then with the intent to injure and insult, each had been speaking the truth. Daniel Bates wasn't Sydney's kind of man. Nor was she his type of woman. The passionate interlude of a few minutes ago did nothing to alter matters.

Chapter Four

*Y*ou know—something has been puzzling me," Daniel remarked on the drive to the office of Pontchartrain Realty.

"What's that?"

"How did you happen to get the name of Sydney? It seems so . . . oh, unsouthern, I suppose. And now that I've met your mother, I'd expect her to choose a name like Cynthia or Sarah, not Sydney."

Laughter bubbled up inside Sydney's throat. "Pregnant women are sometimes prey to strange impulses. My mother got the fixation that she would name me something *different*. She was sick and tired of Carolyn and Linda and Mary, and even Michelle and Dawn were getting terribly common. But hard as she thought and much as she looked, she couldn't find anything she liked that wasn't already used. The last couple of months of her pregnancy she took to scouring novels. According to Dad, she would bring home stacks of them from the library, not to read, but to scan for the names of female characters. She'd decided I was going to be a girl, you see. Then *one* day . . ." She paused theatrically.

"A character named Sydney?"

"Exactly. And the beautiful thing about the name was that she could use it for either a boy or a girl, just spell it with an *i* if her intuition proved to be wrong and she produced another son."

Sydney loved to tell this family anecdote. Perhaps because it proved that even her practical mother could be subject to whimsy. She continued in the same lighthearted tone. "I'll have to say the name was just what she was looking for, too, at least in this area. Not once in school did I encounter another Sydney, and the teachers never had trouble remembering my name."

Not long after she had satisfied his curiosity on the subject of her name, they arrived at the realty office, where the only car remaining was her Volvo. The sight of it set her mind running along its usual channels, all related to business.

"I'll get this listing contract typed tomorrow and bring it over for you to sign. What time would be convenient?"

"I'm usually home from work by six at the latest, unless I stay in the city for dinner. I'll make it my business not to tomorrow. You can drop by any time after six."

She thought of him alone in that quiet roomy old house. It was wonderfully peaceful and private there —but didn't he get lonely? She always had someone to go home to. Funny, she hadn't given that circumstance of her life much thought; there hadn't been any reason to before now. But it occurred to her that having the kids waiting for her when she got home—

lying in wait might be a more accurate description!—
was kind of nice. Nine times out of ten they were
preparing to present their latest scheme, but still
they were happy to see her, assuring her in dozens of
ways besides words that she was central to their
world.

"Would you like to come over to my house and
sign the contract? You could have dinner with us, if
you like. Cora's not as passionate about feeding
people as my mother, but she's a good cook." The
invitation was entirely impulsive, arising out of what
was more than likely misguided sympathy.

"I'd like that." He accepted with alacrity and
sounded as if he meant it. "I can't wait to meet the
formidable Cora. You can be sure I'll be on my best
behavior or she'll probably poison my food," he
added.

The image he had conjured up was puzzling to
Sydney. Surely she hadn't conveyed such in her
mention of her housekeeper. "Did my mother say
something to you about Cora? Sometimes I'm afraid
she may be a little jealous of her."

"No. I'm going strictly on my own impressions
from talking to Cora over the telephone."

"You talked to Cora! When?"

"This morning."

His eyes took in the incredulous expression on her
face, and he continued calmly, before she could
interrupt again. "When I got up this morning I read
the article about you again, looked at the picture,
and didn't feel any of the outrage I had felt last
night. More than anything else, I was curious to find
out why you had disguised yourself. You'd already
left for the office when I telephoned your house.
Cora answered—I didn't know who she was then, of
course—and managed to ascertain who I was. She

proceeded to chew me out for frightening you the way I evidently had, threatening to ruin your career, according to her. By the time she had finished you were a heroic figure struggling against daunting odds to support yourself and two babies—she made them sound like children out of a Dickens novel—and *I* was the blackest kind of villain."

"*Cora* said all this?" Sydney shook her head doubtfully, trying to reconcile the fierce advocate he conjured with the taciturn, unflappable woman she lived with.

He nodded. "Properly chastened, once I managed to get off the telephone, I tried to call you at the real estate office, but the line was busy."

"It's not easy to get through on weekends," she admitted. "People call in about the newspaper ads, at least half of them purely out of idle curiosity."

"After trying several times, I decided I would just wait until I went out for lunch and drop into the office on the chance of finding you there."

"So you *weren't* angry anymore when you came by the office . . . and you *already* knew why . . ." Sydney was seeing the whole scene between him and herself in light of this new knowledge and was rapidly working her way toward being indignant. "Why didn't you put my mind at ease right away instead of letting me go on and on the way I did?"

His shoulders moved in a shrug that held the same rueful apology as his faint smile. "I guess I started enjoying myself, and it's become a rare feeling the last couple of years. Now don't go climbing up on your high horse. I wasn't making fun of you." He read with unerring accuracy the tilt of her chin, the compression of her lips.

"There was nothing contrived about what happened this afternoon," he continued. "Nor about my driving you to your parents' house and then accepting your mother's invitation to dinner. It was Sunday. I'd worked hard the day before and felt I'd earned some leisure. I had nowhere to be. All of a sudden I found myself right in the middle of your family—Kevin, Stacy, your mother. It was all so normal and pleasant I couldn't resist staying." He shrugged again as if to say the explanation might not be convincing but it was true.

How could Sydney maintain a sense of outrage in the face of such disarming candor? It simply was not possible. And besides, the events of the afternoon now seemed to have occurred days ago, not mere hours. Never in her life had she gotten to know someone as fast as she'd gotten to know Daniel.

"Don't worry about Cora. She'll be a lamb when she finds out about the whopping commission I'll make on this listing."

Sydney reached for the door handle and, seeing that he intended to get out of the car, demurred, "Don't bother. I can open the door for myself."

His glance said that he, too, remembered the awkward moment that afternoon when he had reached across her and she had shrunk away from his touch. An intense awareness quivered between them, banishing the casual camaraderie of just moments ago. His eyes dropped to her mouth as if looking there for visible evidence that it had been crushed and bruised by his during that searing interlude when both of them had been swept along in the combined torrents of their revitalized passions.

Sydney pushed open the door and stepped out onto the pavement, bending down to pick up her briefcase from where it had sat on the floor beside her feet. Her breath was coming quickly, and her knees had a strange unsteadiness. But now she knew it wasn't a vitamin deficiency. It was a condition universal in humans and animals alike—plain old birds-and-bees sex. That had been a close call on Daniel's veranda tonight. She really had to thank him for having more control and retaining his perspective, even in the height of arousal, but proximity wasn't doing anything to develop either of those strengths in herself at the moment.

"Good night. And thanks for the ride."

"What time tomorrow night?"

"Six thirty. I hope that's not too early. The kids have to be in bed by a reasonable time, and they'll be excited at having company." She had no doubt that he would be in for a barrage of questions from Kevin about his football experiences, and that the compliment today on Stacy's painting was going to entitle him to a tour of her room with all her drawings and cherished treasures. Judging from his behavior at her mother's today, though, Sydney didn't think Daniel was going to mind.

"By the way, how do I get to your house?"

She told him, bade him good-bye, and walked over to the plate-glass door of the office. He still hadn't started the car when she fitted her key into the lock and twisted it in preparation for pulling the door open. She looked back over her shoulder at him.

"You don't have to wait. I just want to get something from my desk."

He glanced around the empty parking lot, as if emphasizing the isolation of the building beside busy Highway 190. Although the area was quickly becoming built up, there still were no other businesses close by.

"This doesn't look like a safe place for a woman to be alone this time of night."

"I do it all the time," Sydney burst out indignantly. Her words were braver than they had a right to be, though. She didn't feel safe in the office at night, but combatted the fear by locking herself in and then making a dash to her car when she was ready to leave. Something about the silence of the man behind the wheel of the Buick told her she might as well not argue. He had no intention of leaving until she did.

When she emerged a scant two or three minutes later, having found without any trouble the folder she wanted, he started the engine of his car while she relocked the glass door, but he didn't back out immediately. When Sydney had accelerated briskly out onto the highway she looked in her rearview mirror and saw him behind her. Before long she turned off and he kept going straight, back toward the lake.

Her reaction to his small act of male chivalry was mixed. In a way it irritated her because it challenged her independence and self-sufficiency. And yet it warmed her, made her remember how nice it was to have a man concerned about her safety. Larry had refused to allow her to drive anywhere alone at night. She had insisted he was being silly but had secretly reveled in being bossed for her own good. What woman who was really honest wouldn't admit to having felt the same way? That still didn't mean Sydney had any intentions of enslaving herself to a man ever again. No siree—once was enough.

A listing contract wasn't really binding until it had been signed by the property owner, but Sydney couldn't resist confiding her good news to Will

Donaldson, who gave out such a roar of excitement it brought five agents crowding curiously around the door to his office. At that point the news was out, and it caused a furor of excitement.

Valerie Perkins, who had been the agent on duty yesterday when Daniel came into the office, wanted to know if the "big hunk" Sidney had left with yesterday was Daniel Bates. Sydney had to admit that he was and couldn't miss the glances passing between Valerie and her crony, Joan Lemans. Sydney mentally shrugged indifference as she should have done a couple of days earlier when Joan made the catty prediction that Sydney would undoubtedly be the one to get the Bates listing. Let them whisper and waggle their eyebrows all they pleased. She had too much to do to worry about them.

Mondays were usually busy and this one was no exception. The first half of the day she had desk duty and received numerous inquiries on property advertised in the Sunday papers. After lunch she had an act of sale to attend in Covington, a nearby town. It was late afternoon before she could get around to typing up Daniel's listing form, and by the time she finished it was nearly six, later than she had intended to stay since she had wanted to get home in time to bathe and change clothes before he arrived.

Just as she rose from her desk, ready to leave, the telephone rang. It was Mr. Lane, the client whose call she had terminated so abruptly yesterday when Daniel appeared, and he wanted to know if she could show him that house he was interested in tonight. His wife was "giving him fits" to get her and the kids out of the city. He could be over by seven thirty, if that was all right with her.

Some sixth sense told Sydney she was talking to a man in the psychological frame of mind to buy. His

voice had that harried tone of the busy man who is
being pressured from several directions at once and
is going to do something soon, just to get relief. The
house he wanted to see, and which his wife had
already enthusiastically approved, was located in the
newest and most expensive of the country club
developments, and Mr. Lane could easily afford it.
She had already "qualified" him, a procedure which
required a delicate mixture of directness and tact,
since she had to elicit information such as the client's
income and present financial obligations in order to
determine if he could afford the property in which he
expressed interest. There was no point in selling a
person on something he couldn't buy no matter how
much he liked it.

If she refused to show Mr. Lane that house tonight
she wouldn't put it past him to hang up and call
another agent. Lots of clients worked with more
than one, making the job of selling real estate a kind
of psychological Russian roulette. You just hoped
you were the one present when the urge to buy
struck.

"I'll have to call the owner first, Mr. Lane, and
make sure it's all right for us to come by and see the
house. It's a little late notice, but I'll see what I can
arrange."

She heard herself speaking the words, a little note
of censure in her voice to impress upon the man at
the other end of the line that she was putting herself
out for him. The real estate agent in her had taken
over. Daniel would just have to understand that
what had happened was beyond her control. Surely
his work was important to him, too.

By the time she had called the owner of the house
and got permission to show it, all but promising that

her client would buy it, and then called Mr. Lane back, it was quarter past six. If she really hurried, she might still get home before Daniel arrived. It had been a long, grueling day. She would give almost anything for a long soak in the tub, but now she'd have to settle for a shower, and a quick one at that.

The brown Buick was already parked in the driveway, blocking the entrance to the carport. Sydney saw it with a mixture of frustration and resignation. Parking behind it, she consoled herself that it was probably just as well he was so prompt. This way she'd be sure to get the listing form signed before she left again, and now he wouldn't have to move his car when it came time for her to leave, which wouldn't be long from now, she realized, striding quickly to the front door.

Her briefcase weighed a ton, and she felt like a hag as she opened the door and went through the hall to the main room at the rear of the house. She could hear voices coming from it, the young excited tones of Kevin and Stacy and then a deep, spontaneous laugh that had to be Daniel's. She hadn't heard it before, and its carefree quality took her by surprise.

Daniel was lounging on the sofa, Kevin and Stacy sitting cross-legged a few feet away on the carpet and Cora busy in the kitchen. His appearance was a direct affront to Sydney, who saw at a glance that *he* had evidently had time to shower and change. His hair was still damp, and he looked fresh and utterly relaxed. Suddenly she resented feeling so grubby and rushed and uptight.

"Sorry I'm late," she announced tersely to the company at large and stood for a moment, caught up in indecision. She glanced over at the table, which was already set for supper, down at her watch which said she had less than an hour to shower, dress, eat, and get back to the office, and then at the briefcase which, besides dragging her arm from the socket, reminded her that she needed to get Daniel to sign the contract. To make matters worse, he was watching her as if he could read the conflicts pulling at her and was not especially sympathetic.

"Mom, did you call about the art teacher today?"

Stacy had risen up on her knees, her hands clasped together in an eager gesture which was a combination of excitement and supplication. When she saw the answer written clearly on her mother's face, she sank back down on the carpet. "I thought you said you would," she murmured disconsolately.

Sydney hadn't given the art teacher a thought. She'd been so damned busy all day. "Honey, I'm sorry," she said irritably, walking over and dropping tiredly into an armchair set at an angle to the sofa. "I had desk duty all morning, an act of sale this afternoon, and tonight I have to show a client a house. I haven't had a spare moment. Maybe things won't be so hectic tomorrow."

A silence followed her words. She wished fervently she hadn't sounded so crabby, but they didn't all have to stare at her like she was a time bomb about to explode. The warning constriction in her throat told her that if she didn't unwind a little, the next thing she knew she'd be in tears, and it would be humiliating to break down in front of Daniel Bates.

She bent over and opened the briefcase at her feet, taking out the neatly typed listing contract and offering it to him. "It's exactly like the one I went over with you and filled out in rough."

He nodded, taking it from her and studying it briefly. "There's one thing I need to talk to you about before I sign it."

Sydney's already overtaxed nervous system sounded an alarm. Had he changed his mind about selling after all? After she'd already told everybody about her big listing? That would be all she needed right now to send her over the edge.

"I want to place certain restrictions on showing the place."

She breathed a sigh of relief. "I shouldn't be too late getting back tonight. We can talk then if you wouldn't mind waiting for me. You *are* going to stay and have dinner with Stacy and Kevin and Cora, aren't you?"

Stacy and Kevin both spoke up enthusiastically at this point, making it impossible for him to refuse without disappointing them.

"Aren't you eating?" he asked.

She stood up. "Not now. I don't have time to eat and clean up, too, and right at this moment, the shower wins without a contest." She was proud of the light tone, but a glance at her watch tightened the coils in her midriff. She excused herself and fled to her room, glad to escape those eyes of his which seemed to see too much.

Having showered and changed into fresh clothes, a cool green slacks outfit, she felt somewhat rejuvenated when she stopped by the door to the big combination room to say good-bye. They were all seated at the dining table, eating and talking and giving every indication of enjoying themselves thoroughly without her. The responses to her "See you later" were absent-minded.

"Gosh! You were a *center!*" she heard Kevin

marvel as she closed the front door behind her. His tone was reverent, as though he was in the presence of some supernatural being.

It was silly of her to feel as excluded as she did. She should be relieved that Daniel showed no sign of being piqued that she had invited him over to dinner and then made another appointment. There wasn't time to mull over her contradictory feelings, however, for in a short time she had arrived at the office, where Mr. Lane already awaited her in a brand-new Lincoln Mark VI.

Even before she got out of her car she had slipped into the role of real estate agent, professional, pleasant, knowledgeable. It wasn't a pretense either. She was all of those things, and she loved her work—the challenge, the stimulation, even the hectic pace and the pressure, except at times like tonight, when she felt pulled in too many directions at once, unable to be what everyone wanted her to be.

Her instincts about Mr. Lane proved to have been unerring. He said little as he followed Sydney from room to room in the house, but when the tour was over, they had barely climbed back into her car when he pronounced, "I'll buy it."

Jubilation rose inside Sydney, eradicating the fatigue, the empty hunger, making the duress of the long day worthwhile. She always felt like this, as though every sale were the first. Automatically, she said the right words to reinforce him in his decision and lost no time driving him back to the office, where she took him inside and sat down to write up a purchase agreement.

Once, when she glanced at her watch, she remembered that Daniel was waiting for her, but nothing short of a dire emergency was cause to break the cardinal rule she had learned in real estate school: Get the client's signature while he is in the mood to buy. Don't give him a chance to catch buyer's remorse.

When the purchase agreement was typed and signed and Mr. Lane sent on his way, it still wasn't quite ten o'clock. If this sale went through, and she had hardly a doubt it would since Mr. Lane was offering almost the full asking price, she would earn more in commission than a well-paid secretary in the area would earn in two months. All because she had followed her instincts and taken the time tonight to show the house.

Deciding to wait until she got home to telephone the listing agent of the house and notify her of the contract, Sydney turned off the lights, except for those left on all night, and left the office. The sight of her lone car parked in front reminded her of last night, when Daniel had insisted upon waiting until she came out of the building before he left. Suddenly she was gladdened at the thought that he would be there at her house when she arrived. She looked forward to telling him about her sale.

He was sitting in the living room area with Cora, watching the ten o'clock news. Sydney greeted them with a triumphant smile and a brief account of her success, then excused herself to go to her bedroom and change into more comfortable attire. She didn't mention her real reason—to use her extension to call the listing agent of the house she had sold.

That task accomplished, she stripped down to bikini panties and donned a cotton caftan that came down to her ankles. It was the only one of her "bargains" she had kept. Larry hadn't liked it any more than he had liked most of the clothes she purchased during her marriage, but she loved to lounge around in it at night, finding a deep satisfaction in the bold abstract design whose dominant colors were black and shades of brown.

Cora was gone when Sydney returned to the living room. The television had been switched off, and Daniel was still sitting in one of the two deep armchairs. Sydney succumbed to the enticement of the sofa, piling all the throw pillows at one end and flopping down on her back full-length.

"This feels incredibly good." She expelled a deep sigh of satisfaction. "What a day!"

She asked him how he had fared with the children, and his answers confirmed her earlier predictions. Apparently he had enjoyed himself, if she could judge from the amused tone of voice and the smile playing around the corners of his mouth as he admitted that there *had* been some discussion of football between himself and Kevin. He also divulged that Stacy had given him a guided tour of her room and had offered to paint a picture of his house for him. That last reminded her of what he had mentioned earlier.

"By the way, what was there about showing the house you wanted to discuss with me?"

"I'd like to stipulate that nobody can see the house unless you're present. I don't like the idea of just any Tom, Dick and Harry of an agent strolling around the place."

Sydney was quiet for several seconds, her mind coping with the complications such a restriction would impose. The other agents in the area wouldn't be thrilled about it, that much she knew. But it wasn't unheard of either.

"I can write that into the contract. I'll bring it over for you to sign tomorrow night."

"I've already signed it."

Her eyes widened a little. "That was trusting of you."

He shrugged. "You wouldn't be my agent if I couldn't trust you."

Sydney knew then what troubled her about his restriction on showing the property. Daniel wasn't expecting her to screen potential buyers, was he? To make sure the kind of person he would approve of bought the property?

"Are you hungry?" he broke into her somber reflections.

"Not really. Just tired and terribly comfortable. Not very stimulating company, I'm afraid."

Her eyelids drooped a little. She was coming down from her high over selling the house tonight, but her neck and shoulders still felt like the muscles and tendons were tied into hard little knots. She rolled her head from side to side and shrugged her shoulders trying to loosen up.

"Turn over and I'll give you a rubdown," Daniel ordered, getting up and coming over to get down on his knees beside the couch.

She complied readily, sliding down a little farther so that her head wasn't propped up on the pillows. He began to massage her neck and shoulders and back with steady circular motions that made her gasp in delight.

"Where did you learn to do that?" she murmured into the cushion under her cheek. The answer was pretty obvious, though: in the locker rooms of football stadiums. He had been an athlete and apparently a very good one. He hadn't said he would give her a massage, but a "rubdown."

His hands were finding all the knots and snarls and pressing them into smooth skeins. His fingers and palms slid, kneading and pushing, down the planes of her back and found the bones below her waist. Sydney felt as though she were disintegrating into a puddle of melted bones and flesh. She moaned aloud in bliss. What wonderful hands he had. So strong and yet so gentle.

"You're too thin."

"I know," she murmured contentedly. "Tall and skinny. Not your type at all."

One of his hands strayed down to curve around a buttock, measuring its firmness, while the other one worked its way up the vertebrae of her spine. The wayward hand went lower, sliding over the back of a long, slender thigh and calf down to a narrow ankle and then dipping under the material of the caftan and working its way slowly upward.

Sydney lost track of the other hand altogether. Her flesh was beginning to congeal around the bones again, and the sensation was as pleasurable as the melting had been. Nerve cells prickled in advance of the hand that slid over bare skin until it reached her panties and paused there to savor the silken texture and the resilient shape underneath.

Suddenly she located the position of the other hand. It had made its way up to her shoulder and was turning her over on her back. The hand beneath the caftan slid around to the front of her, spreading so that it seemed to cover the tautness of her flat stomach and then sliding up to her breasts and tracing the tender curves with fingertips that didn't criticize or compare. Her nipples stood out eagerly and were pinched gently between thumb and forefinger.

Sydney lay with her head thrown back and her eyes closed, floating in a sea of exquisite sensations. "You have the most marvelous hands," she murmured and then half opened her eyes to look at him.

He was gazing intently at her mouth, as if drawing it to him by magnetic force.

She reached out her hands and clasped him around the head, drawing him to her, anticipating with every fiber and pore of her body the meeting of his lips with hers. It seemed to take a long time for him to reach her, but there was nothing tentative about the contact. Their lips burned with a raging fire that consumed them without abating any of their urgent hunger. Daniel's tongue thrust into her mouth and found hers, curling around it, searching and insatiable, seeking some merger of flesh with flesh.

The caftan was up around her hips and then higher. She was only vaguely aware of its ascent until he pulled away from her mouth and tugged the garment over her head. She felt freer once it was gone and rejoiced in its absence as he bent his head to her breasts, feasted on the firm curves and took the nipples by turn into his mouth, teasing them with his tongue and arousing shooting spasms of delight that made her grasp his head and press it harder against her.

In the sweeping intensity of her pleasure there was no room for thought of any kind, not even that she was lying near-naked and then completely naked on her living room sofa, or that privacy was not guaranteed. Cora or one of the children could walk in at any moment, an unlikely prospect, but certainly possible.

Nor did the thought enter her head, anesthetized as her faculties were by passion, that *her* pleasure, *her* needs, were foremost during the entire span of time she lay on the sofa and submitted to the delights of his ministrations. She had no concept of the ordinary units of time, seconds and minutes and hours. Time was sensation and spiraling pleasure, the warm roughness of a questing tongue, the sliding caress of a mouth, and hands that knew everything about her body and its awakened, urgent needs.

Low gasps of sound came from her throat when the bliss became more than she could bear. She murmured his name, tried to push him away and then immediately grasped his head and shoulders and drew him against her as she was seized by a shattering paroxysm that began and seemed never to stop. She was riding the zephyr at Pontchartrain Beach, and everything was out of control. Higher and higher she went until she had reached the peak of the nervewracking course. The track was rough and bumpy, clattering bone against bone. Never before had she stayed so long at the top without moving forward. Any second now she should be swooping down, her stomach jumping out to take a slower route.

As reality slowly returned Sydney realized that the tweedy fabric against her bare back wasn't the hard metal of the roller coaster at the big amusement park called Pontchartrain Beach. It was the upholstery of her own sofa in her own house, and she was lying on it spent and a little dazed. Daniel's head lay heavy on her stomach. Idly she fondled the hard cheekbone, smoothed the ruffled hair the same way she did Kevin's. Glancing down, she saw that he was completely clothed while she was naked, and the realization of what had just occurred sank in.

"What about *you*, Daniel?" she murmured.

He raised his head and sat up, leaning back against the sofa. "Me? I'm okay." He sounded calm and in control, but his dark eyes held a turbulence she found flustering. Her hair was touseled about her face, which must contain vestiges of her recent abandonment. She felt unbearably vulnerable under that gaze and sat up, looking around for her caftan. Belatedly, she considered all the possibilities of discovery by Cora or one of the children.

"Here." Daniel reached over, picked up the voluminous garment from the floor and handed it to her. She pulled it over her head and stood up, letting the long folds cover her like a protective tent.

"Would you like something to drink? Some coffee?" she offered.

"That sounds good." He got to his feet, towering above her even more now that she lacked the extra inches her heels usually provided. She padded ahead of him into the kitchen, feeling the linoleum cool under her bare feet.

"I'll bet you're hungry," he remarked, leaning against a counter and watching her as she ran water into the kettle and set it on a burner on the range top.

"I'm starving," she admitted, realizing the reason for the contractions in her stomach. "Would you like a snack?"

"Maybe just a tiny sliver of that apple pie we had for dessert tonight."

Sydney got the white enameled coffee pot ready, spooning dark roast coffee grounds into the central compartment. She had grown up drinking coffee brewed in the French Market fashion and preferred the rich flavor of dripped coffee to the "boiled" taste of percolated coffee. And as far as she was concerned, instant coffee wasn't coffee at all. There wasn't even a jar in the house.

Next she got the leftovers from dinner out of the refrigerator, meatloaf and potatoes au gratin plus the remainder of the apple pie. "Sure you wouldn't like some, too?" she queried as she put a portion of meatloaf and potatoes on a paper plate and stuck it into the microwave oven.

"I'm sure."

He was pouring boiling water into the top of the coffeepot, and the fragrant aroma of brewing coffee soon filled the kitchen.

They sat on stools at the counter which divided the kitchen from the dining area. Daniel's piece of pie was somewhat larger than a "sliver," Sydney couldn't help noticing. She herself ate hungrily, enjoying the food.

"Do you often show people property at night?"

He asked this question after they had taken their second cups of coffee over to the sitting area, she sinking down at one end of the sofa with her feet curled under her and he taking one of the armchairs.

"More often than I'd like," she admitted. "Some of my clients are terribly busy people—but then people with money usually are, aren't they?—and I have to adjust my schedule to fit theirs or they'll find an agent who will."

He didn't reply directly to that. "I hope you don't mind, but I mentioned to Kevin and Stacy that I'd like to invite them over this weekend, either Saturday or Sunday—it doesn't matter which. We can all have a picnic down on the beach, swim, fish, or whatever they want to do."

His words had the beguiling effect of a glossy brochure describing the enticements of a Caribbean island resort. Sydney groaned. "That sounds heavenly, but weekends are my busiest times. I pretty much have to leave myself free for whatever comes up."

"You don't mean you work every weekend?"

"Just about."

He didn't have to say what was on his mind. She

could guess the reason for that little frown cutting twin lines between his heavy eyebrows. "I don't need *you* on my back, too, Daniel. My mother is enough. I give the kids all the attention I can manage. Do they look to you like they're neglected? It's not my fault I have to be their father as well as their mother."

He didn't back off. "But they have a father. He may not afford them much of his time, but he *is* paying money toward their support, and he *was* paying toward yours until you refused to accept it. Isn't that what you told me?"

"You don't think the kids and I could live the way we do on Larry's alimony and child support payments?" Sydney scoffed. "How many women can *really* live 'in the style to which they're accustomed' after a divorce? Damned few!"

He shifted impatiently in his chair. "I don't doubt that, or the fact that it's necessary for you to supplement your income. But is it necessary for you to drive yourself the way you're doing?"

Sydney stiffened so that she sat bolt upright on the sofa, and her voice had a strident edge when she spoke. "What you're really saying is that I'm on an ego trip, isn't it, Daniel?" For two cents, she'd tell him to mind his own business even if he was an important client.

He studied the empty coffee mug cradled in his hands, hands that looked as if they could crumble it into bits of ceramic rubble if they wanted to. "There's nothing wrong with working for your own personal satisfaction. Ideally, every job should offer that. But when it starts to take precedence over everything else, something's wrong."

"I don't suppose that would ever happen to you!" Sydney flung at him, irritated to the core. He had an answer for everything, did he? Well, then, why was his life in such a shambles?

"It threatens every man with a career that holds the promise of advancement. Every woman, too, I suppose." A brooding note in his voice on that last reminded Sydney of what he had told her about Déborah, his wife. Apparently she had been one of those who considered her career more important than anything else, including her husband and marriage.

Sydney was still irked at the conversation, but understanding the reason Daniel disapproved of—maybe *distrusted* was a more accurate word—her devotion to her work kept her from resenting him personally. How could she hold a grudge when he spoke so reasonably, obviously without any intent to hurt? He just didn't understand what it felt like to be a woman on her own at twenty-eight, as she had been two years ago, with no particularly marketable skills. Every listing and sale she made increased her measure of confidence, but she didn't dare slack off. Not yet.

"I'll do the best I can to get some time off this weekend, but I'm not making any promises." Insofar as she was concerned, the discussion was over.

"In that case, I won't count on you. Do you have any objections to my having the kids over without you?"

"Of course not. Why should I?"

She thought he might have had the tact to *pretend* it made a difference to him whether she could manage to join him and her children. She was beginning to wonder if she had been included in the invitation to begin with only out of politeness. Now that she thought of it, he hadn't shown any disappointment that she wouldn't be present at dinner tonight either. She wasn't so petty, though, that she would deprive the children of a day of fun just because she felt a little disgruntled at her own tepid welcome. And she did trust Daniel to look out for their safety.

"Great. Why don't we settle on Saturday, then. I wouldn't be surprised if your parents count on having the kids over on Sunday."

He was right, of course. They did. But how had he known that? Again Sydney found her attitude toward him confused. On the one hand, she admired his awareness of other people's feelings. But at the same time, she resented his being so sensitive. Every time she looked at him, she saw the abnormal size of him: the height, the large bone structure, the muscles and brawn. Her brain repeated its initial message—*not your type of man, Sydney*. And then he said things, *did* things, no man who looked like that should say and do. It was confusing and altogether disturbing.

He left soon afterward. Sydney trailed him to the door, wondering if he would kiss her good night, if he would assume a right to do so after the intimacy between them earlier. She didn't know whether she wanted him to kiss her or not—she rather thought *not*. But when he showed no inclination to touch her she was disappointed and a little put out.

He was out of the door when he stopped and turned around. "I guess I had the carport blocked. Give me your car key and I'll pull your car under it after I get mine out of the way."

For some perverse reason, she didn't want him to do that. "No. It won't hurt it to stay out one night. Speaking of keys, though, I'll need one to your house."

He glanced out at the street, where she had

parked her car so as not to block his in the driveway, but he didn't argue with her refusal. Reaching into his trouser pocket, he extracted two keys on a ring and held them out toward her.

"I'd forgotten about these. The brass-colored one is for the padlock on the gate and the other one's for the house. I'll pick up Stacy and Kevin about nine Saturday. All they need are bathing suits and some grubby clothes they don't have to worry about getting dirty."

Without any further ado or farewell he turned and strode to his car. Sydney would have liked to stand there in the open door and watch him while he got into the car, backed it out onto the street, and drove off, but she didn't permit herself to do it. Instead, she closed the door quickly and went back into the kitchen to put the few dirty dishes in the sink and threw the paper plates and napkins into the garbage pail. That done, she went to bed and immediately to sleep.

Chapter Five

$\mathcal{T}$he next morning it seemed entirely unreal, something she had dreamed, lying naked on her sofa the night before, oblivious to everything except the pleasure enveloping her at the stroke of Daniel's hand, the drugging warmth of his mouth, the maddening exploration of his tongue.

At breakfast Kevin and Stacy chattered excitedly about Daniel's invitation for that weekend.

"I'm going to paint Daniel a picture of his house," Stacy announced importantly. "That way, when it's sold, it'll still be like it's his."

Kevin was more interested in the pleasures of the moment. "Daniel says we can swim in the lake and fish off his pier." He wriggled in his chair at the prospect.

"Daniel has his own beach, you know," Stacy added. "We're going to have a picnic on the sand. I wish it wasn't only Tuesday." She sighed at the thought of the interminable days still to live through.

Sydney got up from the table and went to the kitchen to pour herself another cup of coffee. "You'd think," she remarked dryly to Cora, "these two had been locked in the attic to hear them talk."

"They had a good time last night," Cora said, smiling fondly at her two charges. "Trouble was, they both wanted all his attention. He managed to handle them without any trouble, though."

From the older woman's tone, Sydney rather suspected Daniel had effectively "handled" *her,* too.

"Mom, how did Daniel get so big?" Kevin wanted to know when she returned to the table.

"I guess he just inherited big genes from his parents, honey."

He considered that information while he chewed on a bite of toast heavily smeared with blackberry jelly. "You think I might inherit some big genes like that, too, Mom?"

Sydney laughed delightedly. "I guess we'll just have to wait and see, won't we?" One of the pleasures she found in her children was the constant freshness of their observations. Last night Daniel had implied she should spend more time with them. Although she had reacted irritably at the time, she knew she *was* missing a lot now that she was so busy with her real estate career. She'd just have to take more time out for them later in the summer when the spring buying frenzy had calmed down. This time of year people got the bug to get out and ride around and look at property.

During the next few days she was too busy to give more than an occasional thought to Daniel. The first ads on his property wouldn't appear until Sunday. After that, she would undoubtedly be driving over to his house frequently, since he had stipulated she must be present when his property was shown. In the meantime, she concentrated on other transactions in various stages of completion. Most people seemed to think real estate agents merely showed houses and then collected fat commissions, but there was far more to it than that.

In January she had sold a house that was almost a hundred years old. The act of sale still hadn't taken place because of a title problem dating back fifty years. The owner had already moved to Phoenix and was anxious for his money; the new buyer had wanted to move in months ago to get his children settled in the Mandeville school system. In the meantime, both owner and buyer called her almost daily as though *she* should be able to cure the title problem. She, in turn, called the law firm handling the work.

She was also turning over heaven and earth trying to get financing for a young couple who wanted to buy a little house on one acre on the outskirts of Covington. The couple's income was not large enough to qualify them for a conventional loan. She was trying to interest the owner of the house in some form of alternative financing, preferably owner financing, where he would hold a mortgage on the property himself, thereby earning interest as well as receiving the principal in installments. The commission involved wasn't large, but she liked the young couple and sympathized with their desire for a home of their own with a yard big enough for their two toddlers to play in.

Friday morning passed with the usual sales meeting and tour of the new listings, including the Bates place, and then that afternoon she made house calls in a small subdivision she was "farming" with great success. None of the other agents in the office deigned to put out the effort required for this kind of venture, where an agent makes it his or her business to become a familiar face in a certain area, calling periodically with a brochure or newsletter or even a little gift.

Sydney had been shy at first about ringing doorbells at the houses of strangers or walking up to people working out in their yards, but she soon discovered everyone was intrigued with the subject of real estate values, especially where their own homes were concerned. In most cases, a home was the largest investment the couple would ever make.

Several families in the subdivision had decided to sell their homes since she had begun "farming" it, and two of them had listed with her. That success reinforced her efforts, not to mention the fact that she was warmly welcomed by a number of women who seemed to look forward to her brief visits. It wasn't always easy to make her departure.

Friday evening she drove to New Orleans to a seminar called "Alternative Methods of Home Finance." It turned out to be extremely informative, but anything but simple, so the discussion went on until almost midnight. Afterward, most of those present decided to go over to Morning Call across from Lakeside Shopping Center and have *café au lait* and *beignets*.

A few years ago the historic old coffeeshop had moved from the French Quarter, or *vieux carré,* out to the suburb of Metairie, bringing along the entire original interior right down to the light fixtures, which were merely unadorned light bulbs, and counters and stools. The same elderly waiters served the thick black coffee heavily laced with boiled milk and the crispy deep-fried pastries.

It was one o'clock by the time Sydney set out across the twenty-four-mile bridge connecting greater New Orleans to the north shore of Lake Pontchartrain. The house was quiet when she let herself in. On impulse, she decided not to set her alarm clock as she usually did. It was a luxury she hadn't allowed herself with any frequency during the past two years.

The following morning she was awakened from a sound sleep by voices and then the closing of a door. She rolled over on her side and peered nearsightedly at the clock on her bedside table. Nine o'clock! Had she really slept that late?

It wasn't until she had pulled on a robe over her nightgown and gone out to the kitchen for a cup of coffee that she remembered. Daniel was taking the kids out to his place for a picnic today. The sounds of their leave-taking must have awakened her.

Suddenly she was struck with an impulse entirely foreign to her normally well-ordered routine—why didn't she take off from work today, not go into the office at all? She could put on some old shorts and a shirt over her swimsuit and drive out to join Daniel and the kids. It promised to be another gorgeous spring day. The weather had been almost up to eighty the past week. The trees were all in glorious green foliage again and flowers were in riotous bloom: azalea, wisteria, bridal wreath.

But her conscience held out for duty. Even though she didn't have any appointments there were sure to be clients calling in to inquire about her listings. The news about Daniel's property had already spread by word of mouth. Nine chances out of ten, she would have to show it once or twice before the day was over. No, spring was too busy a period for her to take a whole Saturday off.

Feeling like a martyr, Sydney dressed and drove to

the office. But try as she might, she couldn't muster any enthusiasm for the familiar routine of work. She flipped idly through her book of clients and saw there were several she should call just to keep herself fresh in their memories: "Have you thought any more about the Johnson farm? It would be a great place to keep horses." And so on.

Instead she gazed out the window, thinking how nice it would be out there by the lake in the bright sunshine instead of in this noisy office with all these people puffing away at cigarettes and clouding the air with acrid smoke. Finally, when she had been in the office for a little over an hour, she knew her conscience had lost the battle with some errant part of her that wanted the day off. Certainly she *deserved* one off, for a change.

With that bit of self-justification, she packed up her briefcase, marched out of the office without leaving any message as to where she would be all afternoon, and drove home. It took no more than fifteen minutes to change, even allowing for the time she spent regarding herself critically in the mirror.

No sign of a tan, since she hadn't had time for sunbathing last summer. Two-piece green bathing suit, modest as bikinis go—she hadn't gotten around to buying herself one of those sleek one-piece suits so in vogue. Figure not really bad: legs long but shapely, waist narrow, hips slim, stomach flat, bosom not in the voluptuous category but at least rounded and firm. On the whole, matters could be a lot worse, she decided, donning a pair of white denim shorts and a long-sleeved pale yellow shirt, which she knotted at the waist.

Her skin would not be able to tolerate hours of direct sunlight the first day out. With that thought in mind, she set a floppy-brimmed straw hat on her head, slipped her feet into a pair of sandals, and set off, so buoyant and carefree that she felt closer to Stacy's age than her own.

When she climbed out of her car at Daniel's house and scanned the beach directly in front of it, there was no sign of him and the two children. But after walking down to the edge of the sand she saw them off to the right. A weathered pier with railings on each side extended some considerable distance out into the Lake. Daniel sat near the end of it, and Stacy and Kevin were splashing and swimming about in the water not far from him.

To prevent her sandals from filling up with the silky white sand, Sydney slipped them off and held them in one hand while she walked along the beach in the direction of the pier. When she came close to it she noticed a picnic hamper and cooler sitting some distance from the sand on the grass beneath an oak tree.

Taking off her shorts, she left them, with her sandals, on the grass near the lunch containers before proceeding out along the pier. Kevin was the first to acknowledge her presence. "Hey, there's Mom!" and then Stacy chimed in with her own greeting. Daniel didn't say anything as he turned and looked over his shoulder. The only emotion he betrayed was surprise.

"You're all a terrible influence," she accused playfully, stopping a few yards away from him and leaning over the railing to smile down at the children splashing happily in the water.

Kevin wore flippers and a face mask which he had pushed up on his forehead at her arrival. "Watch me dive, Mom!" he shouted and proceeded to plunge headfirst into the water, forgetting the face mask was out of place and coming up sputtering to adjust it for a repeat performance.

"Are you coming in swimming with us, Mom?" Stacy urged, paddling around, her hair, ordinarily a shade lighter than Sydney's, when it wasn't wet, sleek against her head.

"I think I will."

Sydney shivered in anticipation as she took off her shirt, dropped it to the pier and placed her hat on top of it. Daniel was leaning back on his elbows now, his body half turned so that he could watch her. His gaze made her self-conscious so that she hurried behind him to the end of the pier, where a wooden ladder descended into the water. She backed down it and then dangled her foot in the water to test the temperature.

"It's ice-cold!" she protested, having known it would be this early in the year. By summer it would be almost too sultry to be refreshing.

"Oh, come on in," Stacy begged. "It feels good when you get used to it."

Sydney turned around and dived head first, gasping with the shock, and then swimming a little distance out. The lake shelved so gradually that even this far out she could stand up and the water was not over her head.

Turning over on her back, she swam back toward the children, able to hear them, when she got close, urging Daniel to come back into the water, too. Sliding over on her stomach, she looked up at the pier where he had been sitting, unprepared for the sight that met her eyes. Aside from the fact that his torso was bare, she hadn't really noticed what he was wearing. But now he stood on the pier, bending slightly forward so that he could rest his hands on the railing. Sydney stared.

In plain black swimming briefs made of nylon, like those competitive swimmers wear, he was magnificent. Like a larger-than-life statue of a Greek athlete, his body was beautifully proportioned with muscles that were hard and clearly defined and yet smooth. For Sydney to ignore his maleness was out of the question.

She forced herself to look away, disconcerted by the surging responses her body made to the view of Daniel standing there so lightly clothed, virile and manly and apparently not conscious of being either. She had managed, up until now, to put out of her mind the one-sided lovemaking between them the previous Monday evening, but now it emerged to dominate her thoughts.

To hide her discomfort, she pinched her nose between thumb and forefinger and sat down on the sandy bottom of the lake, digging around and uncovering several hard little clams. When she surfaced with her treasures in her hand, Daniel had entered the water and was moving toward her.

"Hey, Kevin, look what Mom found!" Stacy shouted, and immediately lamented the fact *she* couldn't go down to the bottom herself and find some clams since *she* didn't have flippers and a face mask like Kevin.

"You don't need them. Just hold your nose and let yourself sink down to the bottom," Sydney explained, and then watched as a doubtful Stacy attempted to follow her instructions. She was strongly conscious that Daniel had come up close and was watching her as well as Stacy.

"Do you swim much in the lake?" she asked,

looking around at him and meeting dark eyes which held a quizzical expression as they slid over her plastered-down hair and spiky eyelashes.

"More this time of year than later in the summer. It's a nuisance to have to wade so far out, though."

The proximity of his wide shoulders and chest, the latter with its thick growth of curly dark hair, made foremost in her mind the question that popped out next. "How do you stay in such good condition? If you can't run, that is."

He smiled. "I do believe you have slipped up and paid me a back-handed compliment. At least, I'll take it as one. There's a racquet ball and exercise club right in the same building as my company's offices. It has an indoor pool and sauna plus all kinds of exercise facilities. I swim and work out there an average of three times a week, sometimes more. It helps keep the flab at bay. How do *you* keep in shape?"

Either she was already used to the coolness of the water or else the look in his eyes was heating her blood. They seemed to be saying that, in their estimation, she *was* in very good shape.

"I don't really do anything. I tried jogging and detested it. It's so boring. Larry made a half-hearted attempt to teach me tennis, but I had three left hands and no right one at all. Besides, it wasn't easy to get the time to play with two small kids at home. I enjoy swimming and bike riding, but I don't do much of either, especially now that I'm working."

"I'm glad you could join us after all."

That remark, combined with the admiring expression in his eyes, made her toasty warm even though she had been just standing still in the water, not moving enough to keep her blood pumping vigorously through her veins. To hide the fact that she was flustered, she quipped, "You may not be so glad when you realize your real estate agent isn't available to show your house."

Stacy and Kevin had been engaged in a contest to see who could dig up the most clams, but they had tolerated being ignored by the adults long enough and now clamored for attention. Some minutes later, Daniel wanted to know, "Isn't anybody except me hungry?" It turned out that they all were.

Lunch did not consist of premade sandwiches, as Sydney had expected. She hadn't noticed the hibachi already filled with charcoal and waiting to be lit. Daniel had hamburger patties made up to cook and delighted the children by insisting they had to help tend their own.

Sydney sat on a beach towel spread on the grass a few yards away from the scene of cooking. "Medium," she answered when Daniel inquired how she liked her hamburger cooked.

It tasted delicious, as did the potato chips and cole slaw, the latter, he had to admit, bought from a delicatessen counter. They drank canned soft drinks chilled to icy coldness in the cooler and then feasted on rich devil's-food cookies for dessert. By the time the meal was over Sydney had begun to have suspicions about Daniel's incredible ability to predict her children's favorite foods.

"They must have given you some hints the other night," she suggested.

"One or two," he admitted with a broad grin. "I think your daughter may have the makings of a good manager."

After lunch Stacy wanted to begin her painting of Daniel's house, and Kevin begged to see the tree house in the woods Daniel had built when he was a teenager spending his summers with his uncle. Sydney walked down to the area of beach directly in front of the house and spread her towel on the sand to sunbathe. Stacy sat nearby with sketchbook and pencil, chattering happily as she worked on one of the art lessons her mother had arranged for the summer.

It became more and more difficult for Sydney to concentrate on the conversation as she became increasingly drowsy. Lying in the sun always relaxed her this way and made her sleepy.

"Better put these on."

The words jolted her awake just before the weight of her shirt and hat dropped onto her midriff. Shielding her eyes with her hands, she gazed up at Daniel. He towered over her, his legs braced apart and his hands resting on his hips. Lying on the sand, warm and relaxed and half asleep, she was particularly responsive to the blatant maleness of his stance and instinctively wanted to hold a hand up to him. Whether she wanted him to come down beside her or to grasp the hand and pull her up to him wasn't clear in her mind, but, fortunately, Kevin came up at that moment and said something to his sister about her drawing. Sydney came to her senses.

Sitting up, she pulled on the shirt and set the hat on her head, wondering how long she had been lying there asleep in the sun. He was probably right in judging she had had enough direct sunlight on the more tender areas of skin.

Daniel had gone over to kneel in the sand just behind Stacy so that he could see how far she had progressed. Sydney took advantage of the opportunity to study him. From the brownness of his skin, he obviously had already spent some time in the sun this spring, but then, someone with his dark coloring tanned easily. His back was broad at the shoulders, smoothly contoured and tapering to his waist and hips. His thighs were powerfully muscled, as were his calves. In repose, his body was taut and suggestive of alertness, with the symmetry and grace of classical sculptures of mythical Greek gods. Names like Poseidon and Atlas came vaguely to mind.

Then, to her embarrassment, he glanced around and caught her staring absorbedly at him. Her face burned with the inevitable blush she had never been able to control. What was wrong with her, mooning about like a high school cheerleader trying to get a date with the star quarterback? It was unnerving to act like this. She had to stop this errant sensuality which threatened to take control whenever she happened to be in Daniel's company.

Not that she didn't like him and admire him for his good qualities. There was no disputing his intelligence, and he was, in fact, more likable and considerate than the majority of the men she had known. But the fact remained that he didn't want any involvement with her—he'd made that clear. And she liked her life exactly as it was, man-free. The problem lately was that her head and her body weren't always in agreement, and the head seemed to win fewer and fewer points. Sydney just had to get herself in hand.

For the remainder of the afternoon she controlled her reactions firmly. Not once did she allow herself to stare at Daniel's superb physique, which meant looking his way as little as possible. To accomplish that objective, she participated in games with the children with more enthusiasm than might ordinarily have been her wont. The four of them competed in building sand sculptures until the need for physical activity led them into raucous games of catch played with a beach ball in the shallow water at the edge of the sand, always the boys against the girls, and the boys won easily.

When the sun had descended far into the west Daniel got out casting rods and lures, and they all went back out onto the pier to try their luck at fishing. Nobody seemed to mind that they caught nothing. Sydney even suspected Daniel hadn't expected them to.

Kevin was intrigued with zinging the lure out over the surface of the water and then reeling it in fast so that it wriggled furiously. Sydney made little pretext of trying to entice some unwary fish to take her lure. Sitting on the edge of the pier facing the west, she let her red-feathered plastic bug float idly while she watched the pageantry of the sunset, the horizon a constantly changing abstract painting with purple and crimson overpowering the more delicate hues of pink and lavender and gold. Why did looking at a spectacular sunset like this always make her long to capture it somehow? Trap it on film or canvas? Much of its beauty was its ephemeral quality, the knowledge that it was like this now and would never be so again, not exactly the same.

Daniel sat down beside her and smiled into her bemused face. His bare muscular thigh was just inches away from her own, which was either reflecting the vivid color from the setting sun or showing evidence of sunburn. She tended to believe the latter because her face and shoulders and back were also uncomfortably hot. He confirmed her fears.

"Your nose is giving some competition to the sunset, I'm afraid. I was a little late in warning you to cover up," he said ruefully.

She laid the fishing rod on the pier beside her and leaned back on her hands. "So it's your fault. I'll be needing somebody to blame when I can't stand to put on clothes tomorrow."

His eyes narrowed between his eyelashes as though he were giving literal consideration to her comment, which had not been deliberately provocative. "Imagine what your female colleagues at the agency will say about your sales record then."

Sydney giggled appreciatively, and he seemed to listen with special attention to the rippling sound. "It's hard to believe *this* you, with the red nose and flyaway hair, is really my real estate agent. I get glimpses of Stacy every now and then."

At that moment Stacy was lying flat on her stomach and looking over the edge of the pier into the water. Sydney cast a tender look in her direction, seeing the youth and vulnerability and eager hopefulness. Life was an adventure at that age, full of unlimited possibilities. Unfortunately, one had to grow up sooner or later. Sydney said as much to Daniel.

Not long after that conversation, they all picked up the fishing equipment and trooped back to the house. The day's outing was over. Stacy and Kevin were too tired to demur.

Sydney wondered if Daniel would make some suggestion that the two of them get together later in the evening, pondered what she would say if he did, and then was strangely disgruntled when he didn't. She added her thanks to Kevin's and Stacy's, silently seconding their candid hopefulness that they could do this again sometime soon, and then drove off with the image of him in her rearview mirror.

Toward the last he had become the brooding, quiet person she had come to expect whenever shadows from the past shaded the present. Once she had been on the verge of inviting him to come over to her house later that night for a drink, but then pride intervened. If he wanted her company he could make some overtures to that effect.

She *had* overdone it her first day out in the sun, that much was dismally evident when she stepped out of the shower, gingerly blotted herself dry and looked at her reflection in the mirrored wall over the built-in vanity. She was a fire-engine-red woman dressed in a white bathing suit.

She was in her bedroom a few minutes later, feeling somewhat cooled by the shower and the medicated lotion she had smoothed onto her skin, when the telephone rang.

"Sydney, I've been trying to get you all day!" Valerie Perkins said in an accusing voice, not bothering with preliminary greetings. "I've got a client who's in town on business and is dying to see the Bates property."

"I can take you over tomorrow," Sydney began.

"That'd be great except he's catching a plane out of Moisant at one A.M.," Valerie cut in impatiently. "Look, Sydney, I've been working with this man for almost a year now, trying to find him something on the lake. He called this afternoon just to say he's in town, do I have anything he might be interested in, and *you're* nowhere to be found. Where were you, for Pete's sake?"

Sydney was tempted to tell her it was none of her business, but that wouldn't have improved the woman's already aggrieved attitude toward her. And, in truth, she could understand Valerie's frustration under the trying circumstances.

"Sorry you couldn't get in touch with me, Valerie. I took the day off with the kids. Give me a few minutes and I'll call Daniel Bates and ask if he would mind if we brought your client over tonight. Of course, he won't be able to see much of the grounds."

There was no answer when Sydney dialed Daniel's number. She let the telephone ring at least twenty times just in case he might be outside but in hearing distance. Hesitating for only a moment as to what she should do, she wondered if he had gone out for the evening and if he would mind if she brought Valerie and her client over without any advance notice. He hadn't put any time restrictions on showing the house, only the condition that she herself be present when it was shown.

After calling Valerie back and arranging to meet her and her client at the office in thirty minutes, Sydney donned a soft cotton knit pullover and a wraparound skirt, omitting bra and panty hose because of her tender skin. After all, this client was not hers personally and she need not worry about impressing him.

The makeup she used on her face toned down its color somewhat, but it was obvious she had spent the day in the sunshine. After buckling on wedge-heeled sandals, she was ready.

Valerie was waiting for her at the office and waved her to lead the way. Sydney understood and did not resent the other agent's failure to invite her to ride along in the same car with the client. Including a third person, particularly the listing agent, would alter the openness between agent and client. Besides, Valerie probably wanted her client to have as little opportunity as possible to talk to Sydney for fear he might be more impressed with her than with Valerie.

The gate was still open, as it had been earlier when Sydney drove herself and the children home.

Daniel's brown Buick was not in sight, but the big double doors of the detached garage were closed and the car might be in there, Sydney reasoned, as she brought her car to a stop and got out.

After she had been introduced to John Wainwright, a burly man with florid features and small restless eyes, she led him and Valerie to the steps at the rear of the house. Standing on the small covered porch, she knocked several times and called out Daniel's name until she was satisfied he was not in the house.

Although she accompanied Valerie and John Wainwright from room to room, she stayed in the background and offered nothing without first being asked, knowing such behavior was what Valerie wanted and expected. Indeed, Sydney was a little surprised at her own lack of interest in the conversation between the other two. She found herself watching the potential buyer of Daniel's house closely as though on the alert for clues to his personality and character. What kind of person was he? Why was he so interested in property on the lake? A summer house? Permanent residence? Speculative investment?

Following him and Valerie down the stairs when the tour of the upstairs, including Daniel's own bedroom, was completed, Sydney wondered why she felt so little enthusiasm at this showing, considering the commission that was at stake. Why did she almost resent the presence of Valerie and this stranger in Daniel's house? She must just be tired after being outside all day, exposed to wind and sun and exercising more than usual, chasing that silly beach ball around and swimming.

"And out here is the front veranda overlooking the lake," Valerie was saying, leading the way through the front door. "You can't see at night, of course . . ."

Sydney didn't follow behind them. The idea was repugnant for reasons she couldn't fathom. Instead, she walked back to the kitchen and sat down at the table, which was round, supported by a massive central pedestal and painted the same soft gray color as the tall wooden cabinets with their clear glass panels showing the contents. She was sitting there glumly, her chin resting on her fists, when she heard the sound of a car outside. Daniel had returned!

Heart pounding with dread, she thought of him driving up to his house and seeing her car and the strange one he wouldn't recognize. He would put one and one together immediately and come up with the correct answer, but what would his reaction be? Why did she feel like such an intruder being here like this in his house when she had every right? He had listed the house with her. That meant he had entrusted her with the job of selling it, no matter how reluctantly he had decided to part with it.

All the conflicting feelings that churned inside her—apology, apprehension, defensiveness—must have shown on her face when she looked up at him as he entered the kitchen from the big central hallway running through the middle of the house. He looked vital and masculine in western-style denim jeans that emphasized the length and power of his legs. His dark blue knit shirt was open at the neck. He carried a bucket of fried chicken in one hand and a white paper bag from the same franchise in the other. Cole slaw or potato salad, she guessed.

After studying her slump-shouldered posture at the table and the uncertain expression on her face for long seconds, he came over to the table and set down the bucket and the bag.

"You're just in time for supper," he said lightly.

Sydney's reaction surprised her with its poignant emotion. Tears burned her eyelids and clogged her throat so that she had to blink hard and clear her throat. Why hadn't he asked what the hell she was doing dragging strangers into his house at this hour of the night or something comparable? Then she would have been able to bristle and defend herself.

"I'm sorry. I tried to call and didn't get an answer. Valerie had been trying to get in touch with me all day. Her client is here just for today. She's been trying to find lakefront property for him for a whole year now." Sydney hadn't meant to sound so apologetic.

Valerie and John Wainwright were coming back into the hallway now, their voices floating clearly through the opened door. Daniel showed the first sign of annoyance as he glanced over his shoulder in the direction of the sounds.

"I don't want to talk to them," he said tersely.

Sydney acted without hesitation, getting up from her chair and striding quickly out into the hall, closing the kitchen door behind her. Valerie noticed the action and exchanged a questioning glance with her. Obviously she read the message because she didn't demur when Sydney hurried them out of the house. Mr. Wainwright would have lingered a while longer, but he was clearly outnumbered as the two agents ushered him out to Valerie's car.

"They're gone."

Sydney found Daniel leaning against a counter, his arms folded across his chest, his expression impossible for her to read.

"I'm sorry," she said again. "I did try to call." He didn't answer and, not knowing what else to do, she turned to go.

"Have you eaten?"

She stopped in surprise and looked around at him. "No. I just went home and showered, then Valerie called."

"Stay and eat with me—if you don't mind a catered meal," he invited lightly and turned to the wall cabinets behind him to take dishes from the shelves. A platter, a bowl, two plates.

"Are you sure?" she inquired hesitantly. If he had wanted company tonight, why hadn't he asked her . . . ?

"It's the least you can do since you didn't see fit to invite me for one of Cora's home-cooked meals," he cut into her doubtful thoughts as he opened the bucket and put pieces of fried chicken on the platter.

"I started to—but I didn't know if—I thought you'd say something to *me* . . ." Sydney stammered in her confusion and then came over to the table and opened the white paper sack. Taking out the carton inside, she discovered it was potato salad and scooped it out into the bowl with the spoon he handed her.

"What would you like to drink? I have milk, beer, a few cans of soft drinks left over from lunch and some superior jug wine."

She considered the choices with exaggerated seriousness. "Wine, I think."

He got out two stemmed goblets and set them on the table, then took the bottle of wine from the refrigerator. "Anything missing?" He looked at the table and then at her.

"Not that I can see."

He had set out forks and knives and paper napkins, salt and pepper shakers. The aroma of the fried chicken had her mouth watering. It seemed a long time now since lunch.

"Hm-m-m-m. Good," she murmured a few minutes later, taking a respite from chewing. "I didn't realize how *hungry* I was."

"A day out in the sun and wind will do it to you every time." He glanced at her face and the portion of her neck and shoulders the pullover left in view. "Are you very uncomfortable with that burn?"

"A little," she admitted. "I put some medicated lotion on it right after I took a shower, but the cooling effect's worn off."

"I have something that will do the trick," he assured her, but did not explain any further.

When they had finished eating and cleared the table, stacking the dishes in the sink and leaving them at his insistence, they took their glasses of wine out to the front veranda and sat in wood-slatted lounge chairs, choosing, as if by unspoken agreement, not to sit on the steps as they had that other night, almost a week ago.

Sydney asked him about his background and learned he had grown up in New Orleans, in the older uptown section, and had attended a Catholic boys' school.

"You know how New Orleans people are," he mused. "They've never really believed in public education, and my parents were no exception. They'd have done without the necessities, if necessary, to see that I got to attend what they considered a first-class high school."

"You played football in high school?"

"Yes. We went to the state play-off my last two years in high school. I got offers of football scholarships from eight or ten good universities. I chose LSU because it was close to home, and my folks weren't getting any younger. They didn't have me until they were past the age when most people start having a family. I don't doubt I was an accident. Also, LSU has a good program in geology, which is what I intended to major in."

The wine hadn't done anything to combat the deep relaxation Sydney was experiencing after a day outdoors and then, more recently, a satisfying meal. She lay back in her chair and thought of a much younger Daniel.

"Guess you must have gotten a lot of attention from the girls. Being a big football jock, I mean."

"A little more than I knew how to handle. In college, I mean. High school was all boys. You see, my parents were old-fashioned. My father always pulled out my mother's chair at the supper table at night. I was trained to stand up if a lady entered the room." He chuckled. "It came as quite a shock to find out how different girls were from what I'd been led to believe. And, of course, I loved it. At least, at first."

"Why only *at first?*" Sydney's voice was patently dubious. "Old hat after a while, huh?" Her tone held a trace of her old condescension for the stereotyped football jock with his retinue of female hangers-on. His answer wasn't at all what she had anticipated.

"Not at all. I just didn't have the time to reciprocate. Being an athlete on scholarship isn't easy. It takes every spare moment not required for studying."

Sydney was skeptical. "I thought athletes breezed through their courses with the help of the coaches."

"That's what a lot of people think. It might be true in some places—though, frankly, I doubt it—but I can promise you it isn't true at LSU. I had very little time for partying."

"When did you meet Deborah?"

"Not until I was in graduate school. She was in her senior year of undergraduate work at LSU. We started going together and got engaged that year. But we didn't get married until we both got the degrees we were working on, her first and my second."

A silence followed during which they both gazed out at the darkness. The lake was out there, but they couldn't see it. Sydney slapped absently at a mosquito buzzing around her head.

"I wish I'd known you then, Daniel."

It was the wrong thing to say. She realized that too late; it was already out. Did he, too, feel the way she did—that here was a person she would like to have met a long time ago before she made her choice in lifemates and was so devastatingly disappointed? Now everything had been spoiled: the hope, the anticipation for the future. It was too late.

"How's your sunburn?" His voice was terse, vaguely angry.

"It hurts."

He got to his feet. "Don't call me a witch doctor, but I've got a magic cure."

She followed him into the house. He led her into the kitchen, where he took a clay pot containing a cactuslike plant from the window sill behind the sink. He set it on the countertop.

"This is an aloe plant. It has healing properties for burns." He broke off a long narrow leaf and cracked it open down the full length. "The jellylike substance inside soothes and heals." He gently smoothed the inside of the leaf against her neck, steadying her when she would have moved warily away, and she felt the cooling relief immediately.

"Hm-m-m. That feels good."

Carefully, he applied the natural unguent to her

nose and cheeks and then instructed, "Turn around and lift your shirt."

She obeyed, holding the shirt over her head and flinching involuntarily at the coolness of the jelly substance he spread over her reddened skin.

"You want to do the rest, or you want me to do it?"

With only the slightest hesitation, she pulled the blouse off and turned around. He was careful not to brush her skin with the spiky exterior of the leaves as he attended to her throat and neck and midriff.

"Take off the skirt."

She complied, standing in nothing but her bikini panties while he broke off leaf after leaf and applied the jelly to her lower abdomen and thighs and then to the back of her.

When he had finished, she felt considerably cooler than she had before. While he gathered up the remains of the leaves he had used and put them in the garbage pail in the pantry she slipped her shirt back on over her head and wrapped her skirt around her waist.

"Thanks, Doctor Bates," she said lightly. "I feel better already."

"With any luck, you shouldn't peel now," he promised.

Sydney had the vague intuition he was ready for her to leave. He didn't offer any opposition when she said it was time for her to get home, adding, "Tomorrow's Sunday and the first day your property will be advertised in the papers. I expect to get some action."

He walked with her outside to her car, opened the door and held it wide for her to get in. She looked up at him in the darkness, strangely unwilling to slide under the wheel and drive off, just like that.

"The kids had a wonderful time today, Daniel. So did I. The lunch was great. Hamburgers are Kevin and Stacy's favorite meal in the world. You went to a lot of trouble . . ." She was chattering on like a nervous fool.

"It was no trouble. No trouble at all." He bent down and kissed her on the lips, not lightly, but not hard either. "Good night."

Only then did she know what she had been waiting for, standing there, putting off the moment when she would get into the car and drive away. She'd wanted Daniel to kiss her, touch her, make some sign that the two of them had passed beyond the stage of just polite acquaintances. Much to her disappointment and slight chagrin, the kiss seemed to be bestowed more in the spirit of cooperation than spontaneity. It was as though he recognized and conceded to *her* need, not his own.

Without further delay she climbed into the car and fitted her key into the ignition.

Chapter Six

*H*er prediction proved all too true. The ads on Daniel's house and acreage brought an avalanche of inquiries from agents and prospective buyers alike. It seemed to Sydney that she did little else on Sunday besides give out information on the Bates place and show it.

Daniel was evidently away for the day, for there was no sign of him during the three occasions when she accompanied agents and their clients while they viewed his house and property. She wondered where he had gone, with whom he was spending the day. And each time she followed an agent and client from room to room in the house she found herself studying the prospective buyer critically, as she had Mr. Wainwright the previous evening.

It was ridiculous for her to feel the way she did, that she was searching for the "right" kind of person to buy Daniel's house. So far, everyone lacked the mysterious qualifications, whatever they were.

Each time she entered the old-fashioned, roomy kitchen, she eyed the aloe plant on the window sill and remembered last night when Daniel had applied the jellylike contents of the leaves to her inflamed skin with hands whose infinite gentleness belied their great strength and size. This morning she had been amazed and relieved to note that her sunburn was not nearly so severe as she had feared. She doubted that she would peel.

Where *was* Daniel today? Who was he with?

These questions sank to the back of her mind during the next few days as she found herself engrossed in the business of real estate. Then, on Wednesday, the mail brought an invitation that called into question her confidence in her "new" self since the divorce. Every year at this time Gladys and Emory Parker, the latter a senior partner in Larry's law firm, had a big spring gala at their modern showplace of a home located in a very exclusive area near the lake on the New Orleans side. Since the divorce, Sydney had not been invited, but apparently Gladys had decided to include her this time. The printed invitation contained a handwritten message.

Sydney, darling, we've missed you. Larry assures me everything is entirely civil between the two of you and that he doesn't object in the least to my inviting you. I do hope you'll come. We'd love to see you again. Gladys.

Sydney's first reaction was that she would not consider going. Larry was certain to be present—with Connie, of course. But then she reconsidered. Wasn't this the opportunity she had secretly been waiting for? A meeting with Larry that would demonstrate dramatically the change in herself from "little woman" to independent career woman? Until now she had managed to avoid him on the infrequent occasions when he came over and picked up Stacy and Kevin. She had been motivated by self-defense—she hadn't been *ready* to face Larry. But now she was. Perhaps, deep down, she had been waiting, plotting, until enough time had elapsed and the transformation in herself had become complete.

The only problem was that she did not want to go to the party alone. That would never do. But who could she take along as an escort? The answer was immediately obvious: Daniel. But would he be willing?

The rest of the week the thought of the party lurked in the back of her mind when it wasn't foremost. The invitation had said *rsvp*. She would have to let Gladys know one way or the other, and soon. The party was a week from Saturday night.

In the meantime, she heard nothing from Daniel, so there was no opportunity to ask him casually if he would be interested in attending a cocktail party with her in New Orleans. Saturday morning she arose with the determination to telephone him. After all, she had every reason to call and report the interest in his property, the number of times it had been shown, and so on. It was standard procedure to keep a client informed of such matters.

To her disappointment, there was no answer when she dialed his number. After several attempts she went on to the office and became busy with a half-dozen details related to ongoing transactions plus the usual calls of inquiry about properties. At eleven thirty an agent from Pontchartrain Realty's strongest competitor called and asked to show the

Bates property. Sydney arranged to meet him there in half an hour and, once again, dialed Daniel's number to warn him of the showing. Once again, there was no answer.

Therefore, it came as a surprise when she pulled up into his driveway half an hour later and saw his brown Buick parked in the garage, the double doors standing wide open. When she stepped out of her car she heard the sound of a lawn mower coming from the front of the house and surmised both his whereabouts and the reason he hadn't answered the phone.

The other agent, a man named Jerry Simpson who sold real estate in addition to his regular job, had shown Daniel's place once before under Sydney's silent surveillance, and she didn't see any necessity to tag along with him now from room to room. Instead, she took him and his clients into the house and then walked out onto the front veranda, where she stood watching Daniel as he pushed a lawn mower with vigorous strides across the section of lawn down nearest the beach.

The fragrance of cut grass was fresh and sweet on the air. He must have been working all morning because he was almost finished, and the cleared grounds on either side of the house and extending down to the lake far exceeded those of an ordinary house in a subdivision.

He wore old faded denim pants, possibly the same ones he had worn the first day she had seen him, painting the outside of the house. His shoulders and chest were bare and he glistened with sweat. When he turned and began pushing the mower in the direction of the house he looked up and saw her on the veranda. She waved and he lifted a hand in acknowledgment of her presence.

Watching him as he strode along, pushing the mower effortlessly back and forth across the small remaining swath of uncut grass, she remembered that first glimpse of him as he backed down the ladder with a paint brush and pail in hand, looking much as he did now. She had mistaken him for a laborer because he had looked so utterly competent and assured in his task, not like a white-collar executive trying to do small jobs around the house and not feeling at all in his element. Today, as on that other day, Daniel looked firmly in command of the task at hand and—here was the *real* difference between him and the majority of weekend handymen—as though he took pleasure in the hard, physical work he was doing, finding it not in the least demeaning or irksome.

A vivid picture flashed into her mind. Larry just arriving home from a tennis game and herself out in the yard mowing the grass. He stood looking at her with an expression she read easily: He felt he *should* offer to take the lawn mower and finish cutting the lawn, but the prospect was deeply distasteful. He much preferred to go inside and take a shower and change into clean clothes.

Sydney left the mower running and walked over to him where he stood on the concrete driveway. "I'm almost finished. But would you take a look at Kevin's tricycle. The chain seems frozen up or something." Then she returned to her grass cutting.

A few minutes later she cut off the mower and pushed it toward the garage. Larry stood over the tricycle, a screwdriver in one hand and a look of utter disgust on his face as he stared helplessly at the grease on the other hand. He made a motion as if to wipe the befouled hand on his clothes and then remembered, just in time, that he still wore his tennis whites.

"I'm a lawyer—not a damned mechanic!" he snapped irritably when she came up to him.

"Just leave it. I'll ask Dad to fix it," she said apologetically.

From this vantage point in time she could only feel impatience with that conciliatory person she had been, forced to acquiesce with his opinion that she had been unreasonable in the first place to bother him with repairing a broken tricycle. He commuted to the city all week, and weekends were his only time to relax and unwind. She hadn't blamed him then for not wanting to bother with irksome trivialities. It hadn't mattered that Kevin loved the tricycle and imagined it as all manner of other vehicles, a tractor, a fire engine.

The same afternoon, after she had prepared lunch and cleaned up afterward, she had driven the kids over to her parents, the tricycle in the trunk of the VW. It hadn't taken her dad five minutes to get the chain moving smoothly on the track again and, while he was about it, he checked all the bolts to make sure they were tight and lubricated the working parts.

The recollection, as vivid as it was, was pointless. She hadn't loved Larry any less because he wasn't a handy person to have around the house. From the first, he had been fastidious and disinclined toward any kind of physical work that required getting dirty. Daniel just was a different kind of man—that was all. There was no sense in comparing him and Larry.

Having finished cutting the grass, Daniel stopped the engine of the mower and pushed it toward the house. As he came closer Sydney could see rivulets of perspiration on his face, shoulders and arms and farther down on his taut middle where the thick growth of chest hair narrowed to a trail that disappeared inside the waistband of his trousers.

From inside the house Sydney could hear the voices of Jerry Simpson and the couple with him. They would soon be coming out onto the veranda to examine the view and, most likely, to walk over the property. She looked over her shoulder and then back at Daniel with raised eyebrows. He shook his head decisively, emphasizing what she already knew, that he did not want to be introduced as the owner and have to suffer the questions of strangers looking at his house and property.

She walked down the steps toward him and accompanied him around the side of the house to the garage. "I tried to call you a couple of times today and got no answer."

Nor did she get one now. His dark eyes skimmed over her, seeming to take special note of the light tan on her face, neck and arms. "I didn't peel," she blurted, reading the inquiry in his gaze and disconcerted by the memory of his ministrations to her reddened skin. That had been exactly a week ago, and she hadn't heard a word from him since.

As she walked beside him she recounted the week's activities in regard to his house, her mind busy with another subject entirely, the cocktail party next weekend. When they reached the garage she waited just outside it while he pushed the lawnmower into its storage place. He came back out almost immediately and stood a few feet away from her, eyeing the crisp white slacks and sleeveless buttoned vest she wore.

"I'm not exactly dressed for receiving ladies," he said wryly, looking down at his bare, perspiration-streaked torso.

Sydney had been working up her courage and took

the plunge. "Daniel, I'd like to ask a big favor of
you. Don't be afraid of hurting my feelings if you
don't want to do it. Would you go to a party with me
next weekend?" She had spoken the words in a rush,
anxious to get them out before she could change her
mind about asking him.

His raised eyebrows seemed to say *What's the big
deal?* but before he could reply, she hurried on and
told him the rest.

"The party's being given by Larry's senior partner
and his wife—they have one every year about this
time." She met the dark penetration of his gaze and
added quietly, "Larry will be there. With Connie, of
course."

He frowned. "How do I fit in? Bodyguard? Shill?"

Sydney flinched at his bluntness. "Neither. Just
my date. I don't have the nerve to show up by myself
or I wouldn't ask you." He hadn't refused, but his
expression did not bode well. "I don't know anybody
else I'd want to ask."

"What do you hope to gain by going?"

Her eyes were intensely blue as she considered the
question, never for a moment intending to tell him
anything other than the truth. Daniel would see
through a lie in an instant.

"To prove to myself I *can* see him . . . with
Connie. To show him I'm doing fine without him,
that I don't need him anymore." Her voice was
grave, shot through with uncertainty.

He started to speak and then didn't, looking
beyond her to the people coming around the other
side of the house. "Time for you to run interference
for the craven owner again. I'll go with you to your
party. Call when you get back to your office and give
me the particulars."

Sydney was elated. "Believe me, Daniel, I appreciate this," she said fervently and then, seeing his restive glance over her shoulder, hurried to intercept Jerry Simpson and his clients.

Driving back to the office, it occurred to her Daniel had been eager to get rid of her as well as the others, and the thought rankled a little. He might have invited her to stay and tell him the details of the party in person since she was in her own car.

But at least he *was* going to the party with her! That was the important thing right now, not her feelings.

"I hope you won't be too bored," she told him by way of warning when she called later. "It'll be mostly lawyers and judges, I'm afraid. A few prominent politicians, too, of course."

"I can stand anything for a few hours."

"I'll do something for you sometime, Daniel, I promise. I can't tell you how much I appreciate this." She considered inviting him over for dinner and then decided that might seem too much like payment in advance for the favor he was doing her.

"How are Stacy and Kevin?"

"Fine when I last saw them, which was this morning." On impulse, she reversed the decision of a moment ago. "Why don't you come over tonight and see for yourself. Cora's cooking spaghetti and meatballs and she always makes enough for an army."

There was a silence.

"I'd enjoy seeing them again. But don't feel you have to invite me."

Sydney heard some unspoken message in the reluctance underlying his words and tried hard to decipher it. He would enjoy seeing *them* again, he had said, not necessarily herself. Adding this to his earlier eagerness to get rid of her, she perceived his unwillingness to have her think he was interested in her personally. Good heavens! Did Daniel think she was chasing him?

Her cheeks burned as she recalled the last time she had invited him over. She had ended up naked on the sofa. Perhaps the prospect of a repetition of that evening's shedding of her inhibitions induced this hesitancy of Daniel's to accept her casual invitation to dinner. She would disabuse him of any such misconception immediately.

"I know I don't *have* to invite you. The kids will be thrilled to see you again. Stacy wants to show you her progress on the picture of your house. And Kevin has been saving up questions on you know what favorite American sport." There. She had made it plain the invitation was made on behalf of her children, not herself.

Apparently it was the assurance he required. "What time?"

"Why don't you just suit yourself. I'll probably be home at least by six. As far as I know, Cora and the kids will be home all afternoon."

His wariness irritated her far more than she would have expected. She could understand his not wanting to get involved sexually or emotionally with another woman until he felt he had recovered fully from his divorce, but was there any reason the two of them couldn't be friends? She liked him a lot and enjoyed his company. Why couldn't he accept her on that basis?

As it turned out, she got home earlier than she had told Daniel and had changed into old denim shorts and a tee-shirt by the time he arrived. She could have dressed more presentably, but she didn't want to alarm him by appearing to have dressed for a date, she told herself sarcastically.

Stacy and Kevin left no doubt of their welcome, and Daniel spent the two hours before dinner in their rooms, leaving Sydney to her own devices out in the living room. If she hadn't still been a little disgruntled at him she might have joined him and the children, but, instead, she turned on the television and watched the news with Cora.

Later, she unbent when she saw Stacy's and Kevin's obvious enjoyment of their guest. Dinner was a jovial and relaxed affair with even Cora displaying a level of entirely uncharacteristic animation.

In his unassuming way Daniel made himself at home, accepting generous seconds of spaghetti and meatballs and salad and, after dinner, getting up from his place and helping to carry dishes over to the dishwasher without even asking if he could help clear up. Sydney noticed the startled expression on Kevin's face and then smiled to herself when her son hurriedly reversed his exit from the dining area and began to pick up glasses and silver without grumbling, as he was prone to do when it was his turn to help Cora clear the table.

In a short time the work was done and the five of them were able to settle down in the living room to watch television. Since it was the weekend, Stacy and Kevin were permitted to stay up later than on a week night, and they pushed their liberty to its furthest limits.

When Sydney finally insisted it was time for them to go to bed Daniel seemed to take that as a signal for his own leave-taking, confirming her feeling that he was leery of being alone with her.

She told herself firmly that only her pride was hurt and sat up alone after he had left, thinking about the party next weekend. One day during the week she would take a day off and drive into the city to shop for a special dress. She had just the thing in mind. If only she could be lucky enough to find it . . .

The dress was perfect!

Sydney turned slowly in front of the mirrored doors of her closet, surveying herself with deep satisfaction. The dress was classic elegance and perfect for her, complementing her slender height. Strapless and daringly low-cut, the black taffeta sheath fit snugly in the bodice and waist and hugged the slim curves of her hips. The narrow skirt, which came down to her calves, would have imprisoned her legs, making walking all but impossible if it had not been slit to above the knee on either side. A transparent overdress made of a single layer of sheer black chiffon covered her neck and shoulders and arms, was gathered in at the waist by the narrow brilliance of a rhinestone belt and then billowed out in a soft, diaphanous cloud to her calves.

The dress had cost a small fortune, but it should be an eloquent statement to Larry Stanton that she had changed her life-style for the better. No more bargain counters and sales racks for her.

Her eyes were indigo blue in the creamy oval of her face and charged with a brilliance that she knew was a combination of anticipation and apprehension. So much seemed at stake this evening. She felt oddly as if she had been preparing for some big test for the past two years, and tonight was the night for it.

The peal of the doorbell roused her. Picking up her evening bag from the dresser, she went to answer it herself. Cora had taken Stacy and Kevin to a movie at Sydney's own request. It might be silly but she had wanted total privacy while she dressed— *armed* might be a better word—for this evening.

"Don't you look handsome!" she marveled with candid admiration when she saw Daniel. It was the first time she had seen him in anything more formal than slacks and a knit sports shirt. He wore an oyster white suit that was perfectly tailored to fit his broad shoulders and tall length. His silk shirt was a pale gray-blue, his tie a shade darker than the shirt. While she hadn't doubted he would be a presentable escort she hadn't expected him to look quite so magnificent.

He was looking her over, too, and whistled softly. "Not just a regular season game, is it?"

She met the challenge in his dark eyes and smiled in admiration of his perceptiveness. It wasn't the kind of terminology she would have used, but it was apt. No, this wasn't a regular season game tonight. At the very least, it was some kind of play-off, if not a bowl game. How did *he* know that?

They talked little on the drive across the Causeway. Sydney felt as though she were summoning all her energy for what lay ahead, and Daniel mulled over his own thoughts, whatever they were.

She sat up a little more erect as they neared the Parkers' residence. The party had begun an hour earlier and the street was already lined with expensive automobiles. Daniel parked behind a Rolls-Royce and came around to open Sydney's door.

She was grateful for his hand at the small of her back and for his quietly imperturbable presence beside her as they approached the entrance of the ultramodern house which was all white cubes and rectangles and great expanses of glass.

Once inside, it didn't take long to spot Larry and Connie among the clusters of people in the vast central room into which the foyer opened. He was in conversation with Judge Garrett of the state civil court, a man for whom he had always expressed private contempt but to whom he was now listening with exaggerated deference.

Having greeted her hostess and presented Daniel, Sydney maneuvered herself and him into a position where Larry had only to look up to catch sight of her. He did so in just seconds, and the expression on his face was worth every penny the dress had cost her, every second of thought and effort in preparing for this party. He was clearly stunned, presumably at her appearance, since he must have known from Gladys that Sydney had accepted the invitation.

Catching his eye, Sydney nodded and smiled and then moved off languidly toward the bar, Daniel at her side. Along the way she stopped several times to greet acquaintances and introduce them to Daniel.

"That was Larry back there, I take it."

The low words from Daniel took her by surprise. She glanced up and met his quizzical gaze. "That was my ex-husband," she confirmed with open satisfaction. "You don't miss much, do you?"

When they had gotten drinks from the bar they strolled over to a giant potted tree and stood looking around the starkly modern room with its white stucco walls and huge abstract paintings.

"How do you like it?" Sydney asked idly, making conversation. It was impossible for her to concentrate on anything except the inevitable confrontation with Larry that would take place before the evening had ended.

"An impressive entertainment center. A showplace. Not the kind of home that makes you want to put your feet up."

She followed the path of his eyes as they roved around the room and noticed he was getting more than his fair share of female attention. Why should that surprise her? Daniel was an impressive figure of a man, standing head and shoulders above the other men present. Something aloof and assured in his bearing made people take a second look at him.

His eyes had come to rest on Larry and Connie, who still stood talking to the judge, or rather, listening to him. "Why don't you introduce me to your ex-husband?" he suggested unexpectedly.

At first she was taken aback. Daniel couldn't really expect her to walk right up to Larry and his mistress and start talking as though they were just old school friends or something! But then, why not? What better way to prove how little she minded coming face to face with her former husband in a social situation when he was escorting her replacement.

With sudden decisiveness she slipped her hand inside Daniel's arm and gave him a smiling nod. "Introduction to one ex-husband coming up," she said flippantly. Her voice was the slightest bit husky from the constriction of her throat muscles and she didn't feel as casual as she strove to appear as she approached Larry across the expanse of black and white marble tiles.

"How are you, Larry? I'd like you to meet a very good friend of mine, Daniel Bates. My ex-husband, Larry Stanton, and his law associate, Connie Bell."

Sydney was spared introducing the judge because he slipped off at the moment of her arrival. She had never liked him anyway.

"Glad to meet you, Bates."

Larry had to tilt his head back a little in order to look into Daniel's face. Connie, looking ill at ease, managed a stiff smile to acknowledge the introduction.

"You're looking marvelous, Syd." Larry's eyes

assessed the expensive chic of her outfit and the sleek new hair style she'd acquired since their separation and then slid over to Daniel again.

Sydney could read his mind. He wondered just who the hell Daniel Bates was and whether she was having an affair with him.

"You're looking good yourself, Larry. As always. And so are you, Connie. How are things at Parker, Hoyle and Denton? Connie, I know you're doing some title work for some of Pontchartrain Realty's clients." While she spoke, Sydney moved a little closer against Daniel as if emphasizing their intimacy.

Larry groaned. "Oh, no, did you have to bring up the subject of real estate with Connie? That's a sore point with her these days."

"Damned right it is." Connie spoke for the first time, her normally cool blue eyes snapping with irritation. "I didn't make law review to sit in an office and do all the grunt work while some other people I know get to shine in court and make a name for themselves. Just because I'm a woman . . ."

"That has nothing to do with it and you know it," Larry scoffed. He had taken on a pleased expression at her mention of "some people" shining in court. "Every junior partner has to put in his—or *her*—time on the less exciting aspects of a firm's practice. Even law review people."

His voice held a trace of condescension on that last. Sydney knew for a fact that *he* hadn't made law review and had lamented his failure to do so.

"What kind of work do you do, Daniel? You have the untainted look of one who does not practice law." Connie's voice held an edge of bitterness.

"I'm a geologist."

Sydney rather thought his smile was warmer than

mere politeness required. What *was* there about Connie that made men fall at her feet? She was certainly attractive, her blonde hair falling to shoulder-length, her figure nicely proportioned and shown off to advantage in simple, expensive clothes —tonight a midnight-blue dress exposing the tops of her breasts.

Still, Sydney failed to find anything sensational about her appearance and felt a twinge of annoyance and betrayal when Daniel eyed Connie's empty glass and suggested, "Could I get you a refill?"

"Yes, thank you. I'll go with you."

Without a glance at Larry, Connie appropriated Daniel's free arm, smiling up into his face as though he were her rescuer in a storm. Sydney had little choice other than to free her own hold on his other arm. *Traitor!* her eyes flashed at him as he turned and left her standing with Larry.

"Where the hell did you come up with that guy? He looks like a bouncer." Larry transferred his frowning gaze from the back of the tall, broad-shouldered man moving away from them to Sydney's face. "Are you living with him?" The tawny eyes so like Kevin's bored into hers.

"Of all the brass!" she spat out between clenched jaws, taking care to keep her voice low. She had always abhorred making scenes in public. "It's none of your business one way or the other. I don't even have to *ask* if you're living with Connie. You've made no secret of the fact."

Larry didn't even have the grace to look sheepish. "I'm not the mother of two children who live with me and see me as an example, either." He was using the tone she had always despised, that of someone being very patient with a person of lesser intelligence.

Sydney's cheeks developed brilliant spots of color and her eyes were illuminated with her fury. "Don't you talk to me like that anymore, Larry Stanton. You no longer have any right to criticize me. Don't forget children need a male role model, too."

He seemed fascinated with the animation anger lent her features. He studied them closely and then let his eyes slide down her slender length before coming back up to note, once again, the new hair style. "I can't accept the idea of you and another man, Syd. I know that sounds strange to you, but you were *my* wife for nine years."

Sydney steeled herself against the caressing timbre of his voice. This was the Larry who always had been able to undermine her anger.

"Do you think I liked the idea of you and another woman, Larry? You were *my* husband for the same nine years, and I believed all that time you were faithful to me the way I was to you."

He did manage to look apologetic then. "I was faithful, Syd, I swear it, up until the last few months before I told you—" He glanced around restlessly. "I wish there was somewhere we could talk privately." His face was somber, the golden eyes eloquent as they plumbed the indigo depths of hers. "When Gladys said you were coming to the party I was surprised at how glad I was at the thought of seeing you. Do you know how long it's been? You're never around when I come over to pick up the kids." His eyes swung away to avoid the reproach in hers. "I *know* I should see them more often. It's difficult—"

"What's wrong? Doesn't Connie like children?" she asked crisply.

"Connie doesn't like a lot of things most women like," he replied tersely. "Frankly, Syd, I'm beginning to think I made a terrible mistake leaving you for her. I want to be man enough to tell you that. You deserve that much from me."

Countless times during the past two years Sydney had dreamed of hearing Larry say those words. She had imagined the satisfaction she would feel and debated in her mind what her reaction would be. And here he was telling her what she had yearned to hear: He was sorry he had left her. He wasn't happy with Connie after all.

"What's wrong, Larry? Doesn't she cook your meals and wash your laundry? Take your suits to the cleaners? All those things I did that you took totally for granted?"

"I don't blame you for being bitter, Syd. I can't deny I was ungrateful most of the time. But those aren't the main reasons I'm not satisfied with Connie. Hell, I can hire somebody to cook and clean and do the laundry. She's just not warm and understanding of me the way you were. Not *supportive*." He searched her face anxiously for a reaction.

The pensive expression on Larry's face failed to melt Sydney's heart with tenderness as it had always done before. Something had changed inside her. She found herself looking underneath the words for the unspoken message that lay there: *Connie didn't build up Larry's ego the way Sydney had done.*

"Maybe you just can't take the fact that Connie thinks her career is as important as yours. You want somebody to play second fiddle, Larry. Connie's too much competition for you."

He stiffened in annoyance. "You were never like this before, Sydney," he reproached. "Hard and— and *vicious*. Have I done this to you?"

"You're probably partly responsible, Larry, but it's a real cop-out to blame other people for what we are, isn't it? In a way I'm grateful to you for waking

me up when you did. You made me realize what a
vulnerable position I was in, depending on someone
the way I depended on you. Not just financially, but
emotionally as well. It makes me shudder to think
what would have happened if we'd stayed together
another ten years and you came home one day
and . . . told me what you did."

She literally shivered at the prospect she had
conjured. "I'd have been devastated. As it is, I have
a new confidence in myself, a self-esteem I lacked
before. The old Sydney doesn't even exist anymore,
Larry. There's no chance you could go back to her."

He stared at her intently, as though processing her
words carefully. "What if I told you I like the new
Sydney," he said softly. "You're a beautiful woman.
Would you go out with me some time, Syd? We
could get to know each other all over again. Maybe
we've still got something going for us."

She was saved from having to answer him because
they were joined by Daniel and Connie, who had
been gone long enough to get several drinks and
drink them, too, Sydney reflected with uncharacteristic bitterness.

"I thought you'd abandoned me for another
woman," Sydney chided, realizing too late how
tactless her impulsive words were, given the present
company.

"Not on your life," Daniel said and amazed her by
bending and kissing her possessively on the mouth.
She brought her expression under control when she
took note of Larry's face. He looked for all the
world like an outraged husband.

"Shall we circulate?" she suggested to Daniel.
"Would you two excuse us, please?"

"Syd, I'll call you soon so we can finish our
discussion," Larry said quickly before she could

leave. His eyes searched her face for some sign of softening toward him.

"I'll think about what you said, Larry," she promised, feeling completely noncommittal. "I can warn you, though. It's not easy to get in touch with me a good part of the time. I'm awfully busy these days."

She felt Larry's eyes boring into her back as she walked away from him. What a triumph this evening had been for her, successful in every way. To stay longer at the party would be anticlimactic. She had no interest in mingling with the other people present. They meant nothing to her; none of them had been more than casual acquaintances when she had attended these gatherings as Larry's wife.

"Had enough?" Daniel inquired when they were far enough away from Larry and Connie to be out of earshot.

"I've had enough," she agreed thoughtfully. "Let's find Gladys and then get out of here."

She didn't have to add that she had accomplished her goal in attending the party in the first place. He probably already knew that, the way he always seemed to know what was going on around him. She couldn't wait to find out his reactions to Larry and Connie.

They had barely pulled away from their parking place when she prompted, "Well, what did you think of my ex-husband? My next question is what did you think of his girlfriend?"

Daniel didn't appear to be in a great hurry to answer. "How about some coffee at Morning Call?" He looked over for her assent, which she gave with a nod, and then turned his attention back to the street in front of him.

"What do I think of Larry?" he said after a long

pause which had made her wonder if he intended to ignore her question altogether. "I think Larry jumped out of his cozy little nest to explore the big world outside and now he wonders if he did the best thing. He probably thinks he might want to climb back in again."

"The problem is—the straw has all been rearranged in the nest," Sydney observed cynically, neither affirming or denying his surmise. "What about Connie?"

"Attractive, likable, has a lot on the ball intellectually. Not really happy with her job, as you were no doubt able to gather."

His analysis was a little too complimentary for Sydney's liking, but she managed not to say as much, knowing she would sound jealous. In truth, she could only agree with everything he had said about Connie. Sydney, too, had liked Connie when she first met her, seeing the other woman as what she herself would like to have been.

The conversation was general after that, touching upon the house, its dramatic decor, the guests at the party. They found Morning Call brightly lit and crowded, as always, and had to sit on stools at the central counter since all the tables were occupied.

Half an hour later Daniel had driven up to the toll booth at the south end of the Causeway, paid and begun the long, quiet drive across the night waters of the lake. Sydney nestled down in her seat, lost in her own recollections of the evening, in particular that conversation with Larry.

"Well, did you accomplish what you wanted?"

The question startled her. She didn't reply immediately, not entirely sure of the answer now. She watched the funnel of light created by the headlights of the car surge into the darkness ahead of them.

The blackness jumped aside and then closed in behind them. She always felt so isolated, such a tiny speck in the universe, driving across the Causeway at night.

"I don't know. I *think* so," she said finally. "Have you ever wanted something really badly and then when you got it not been sure it was so great after all?" Daniel met her earnest gaze in the semidarkness of the car, but he didn't answer. "Well, that's the way I felt tonight. For two years I've been longing to hear Larry say he made an awful mistake when he gave me up. Tonight he more or less said that—and I don't feel the way I imagined I would. In fact, I don't feel much at all."

Sydney spoke slowly, as if discovering her own reactions as she answered. "I wanted Larry to take one look at the new me and eat his heart out at what he had let slip through his fingers. He reacted just the way I wanted him to, but . . ." She lapsed into silence, unable to fathom her own feelings. It would probably just take some time for her to sort things out and decide if she were interested in pursuing a relationship with Larry. The idea was strangely unappealing, considering that, until recently, she thought herself still in love with him. "I hope you weren't bored."

"Not at all," he assured her. "I found it very informative."

She might have known he wouldn't elaborate, leaving her to form her own conclusions as to his meaning. Little more was said between them after that. Daniel switched on the FM radio and strains of soft music filled the interior of the car. Rather than soothing her, though, it evoked a poignant uncertainty. The lights on the Mandeville shore became clearer as they neared the north end of the Causeway, and then she saw the toll booths up ahead on the left. In minutes she would be home.

"Daniel, I don't feel like going home yet." She spoke impulsively.

He took the first left coming off the bridge, crossing the two southbound lanes and entering a street that led back into the older Golden Shores subdivision and then into the section known as Louisburg, where his property was located. It seemed darker and quieter there than anywhere else in town, despite the occasional streetlamps.

When he emerged from the black tunnel of his own driveway and parked the car behind the house, near the rear porch, she reflected whimsically how familiar Daniel's house had come to be. Like some place she had visited for years, the home of a favorite aunt or uncle or grandmother, perhaps.

The house had an inherently welcoming air about it, quite lacking in the modern brick ranch-style house she rented, which was comfortable but blandly minus personality, its only invitation coming from the presence of those who lived in it and their possessions. She supposed the quality she sensed in Daniel's house was much of the reason some people preferred an older home in spite of its time-consuming upkeep and possible inconvenience.

"I'd buy your house if I could afford it," she announced impulsively, opening her own door and getting out before he could come around and open it for her.

"That surprises me," he said as he mounted the steps and fit the key into the door. "I wouldn't have thought an old-fashioned place like this would appeal to you."

"Oh, I'd have to make some changes," she admitted. "Notice I said 'if I could afford it,' and that means more than just your asking price. I'd have to be able to install central air and heat and put in some insulation to help cut down on utility bills. But there's something so peaceful about this place. I'm sure the location has a lot to do with it."

"Wouldn't you feel isolated with no neighbors in sight?"

She followed him into the kitchen, giving thought to his question. "Maybe I would," she conceded. "It's a moot point anyway, since I definitely *can't* afford it."

He took two wine glasses from a top cabinet and then a bottle of chablis from the refrigerator. After filling both glasses, he handed her one.

They went back out into the central hall again and into the living room with its old-fashioned brocade and mahogany furniture grouped around a fireplace. "Do you mind?" he asked, setting his glass down on a carved end table and proceeding to strip off jacket and tie. Unbuttoning the top two buttons of his shirt, he sat down next to her on the sofa.

Sydney sat with one leg bent under her so that she was turned toward him. "I hope you didn't get a case of the big head tonight with all those women eyeing you at the party," she teased, noting the way the silken fabric of his shirt molded his powerful shoulders and chest. Her hands itched to reach over and touch him.

He slid a little lower, his head resting against the back of the sofa and his long legs sprawled out in front of him. "I didn't see another woman there who compared with my date," he replied and rolled his head sideways to look at her.

The frank sensuality in his dark eyes awoke a sensation of languorous warmth that spread gradually from a point of concentration in her midriff throughout her body, traveling slowly until even her outer extremities tingled with the pleasurable transfer of heat from cell to cell. She brought her wine glass to her lips and sipped, her eyes meeting his and becoming lost in their expression. His maleness was a powerful, captivating force ensnaring her in its field without any struggle on her part to elude it.

His eyes dropped to her lips, which were moistened with wine, and watched intently as her tongue appeared and made a leisurely job of licking them. He didn't move at first, but there was a subtle change in his long reclining frame, a tautness which indicated she had destroyed his state of relaxation. He set his wine glass on the table at his end of the sofa and reached over and took hers. She neither resisted nor inclined toward him as he turned toward her and slid closer until his thigh pressed against her knee.

Curving one hand along her cheek, he lowered his head toward her, his eyes locked with hers and burning with an intensity of purpose that made her heart pound deafeningly. Finally he was so close it made her dizzy to look at him, and she dropped her eyelashes and waited breathlessly for his lips to meet hers. Instead she felt the warm roughness of his tongue as it traveled along the soft crevice where her lips met, as if tasting the residue of wine her own tongue had left behind. Sydney gasped with pleasure, leaving her mouth totally vulnerable to further invasion.

He didn't take advantage immediately, as he might have. His mouth brushed against hers in a tentative, exploring manner as if he were kissing her for the first time. Her lips instinctively softened and clung, enticing him to harvest the sweetness they offered. Her hands indulged themselves in the irresistible urge to slide up his chest, her palms savoring the titillation of crinkly hair under the silk and coming finally to his shoulders and neck with their muscular hardness. The cool silken texture of his shirt combined with the solid tautness of the flesh underneath gave rise to an exquisitely sensual pleasure that made her hands all the bolder.

She felt a quiver ripple through him, but he didn't crush her against him as he had out on the steps of the veranda that night he had come close to making love to her. Instead, he framed her face in both hands and deliberately deepened the kiss, intensifying her hunger for his lips until she was answering their demands with pressure and innovations of her own. When his tongue sought entry into her mouth hers welcomed it.

His hands dropped to stroke along the sensitive curves of her neck and then down over her back and around her waist, finally working their way up to capture her breasts in an intimacy that made her clutch his shoulders as a spasm of pleasure rocketed through her. When his thumbs found her hardened nipples and rubbed slowly against them the vague ache she had felt sharpened into strident need.

"Daniel," she murmured helplessly against his mouth, wrapping her arms around his neck and pulling him against her.

But his devastation of her senses continued. His hands had moved away from her breasts now, one of them slipping around her waist to her back while the other one trailed along the curve of her hip to her thigh. She groaned as it slipped under the hem of her skirt and began an upward ascent. To further the inflammation of her senses his lips lowered to her neck, tasting the soft, fragrant skin and then her earlobe, his tongue making a foray that melted what little brittle tissue was remaining in her bones.

"I want you, Sydney," he said softly, bringing both hands to her waist and pulling her a little apart from him.

"I want you, too, Daniel," she said huskily, tilting her head back to look at him, her face rapt and dazed with her passion. "I think I'll die if you don't make love to me."

He stood up and held his hand out to her. She took it and allowed him to lead her out into the hall and up the stairs. In his bedroom, he turned on the lamp beside his bed and then took her into his arms. For the first few seconds as he began to kiss her the judgmental faculty in her brain was in full operation. *I'm in the bedroom of a man who is not my husband. In a short time we will be making love. There is still time to stop,* a detached part of her spoke warningly.

But there wasn't time. Her arms had gone up around Daniel's neck and her hands were fondling the hard column of his neck and running rampant in his thick, unruly hair. His mouth was against hers, tender at first, imploring, asking for a response, and then pressing harder, hungry, demanding, his tongue plunging and searching for her own. Daniel's hands, those marvelous, incredible, all-knowing hands, were sliding down her back, shaping her hips, cupping her buttocks and lifting her up against him, leaving no doubt of his arousal and his great need of her.

Her breathing was rapid and shallow, her heart-beat resounding in her ears, when he unclasped the rhinestone belt at her waist and slid down the zipper of her dress. She stood without aiding him as he slipped the dress off her shoulders and then pulled it lower, past her breasts and waist and hips. She balanced one hand on top of his head while she stepped out of the dress, which he tossed aside across an enormous old rocking chair.

Still crouched low at her feet, he lifted first one foot and then the other and removed her high-heeled sandals. One by one the undergarments went, with Daniel stopping to kiss and caress each newly exposed portion of her body until at length she was naked. His eyes burned her with their passion as he stood a little apart, looking at her.

"You're lovely, Sydney."

She had a sudden image of him in the brief black nylon swimsuit. The way he was looking at her made her think he was feeling the same sense of awed admiration she had felt that day staring at him. A sudden urgency removed all reticence and she stepped closer to tug his shirt free of the band of his trousers. He made no effort to help her as she freed all the buttons down the front of the shirt and those at the cuffs as well and then slid the shirt off his shoulders and down his arms, taking her time as he had done and savoring her task, filling her eyes with his male beauty. Finally, he was naked, too.

His restraint broke and he pulled her against him, his arms crushing the breath out of her. "I want you," he said in a low voice that vibrated with his immense need. Picking her up without any effort he laid her on the bed. His breathing was audible and his hands trembling as he caressed her, fondling her breasts and stroking down the curve of waist and hip to her thighs, slipping along their soft insides until she made helpless gasping sounds of pleasure.

She grasped his head in both hands when he bent

and kissed her breasts, nuzzling their curves and taking the sensitive nipples between his teeth. Her hands were insatiable for the feel of his body; they stroked his shoulders, his powerful back, his taut, flat stomach, loving the vital firmness of his male flesh.

At length he rose up on one elbow and looked down at her, his eyes like live coals in a face tense with the effort of controlling his passion. "I can't wait much longer—" he began, but she didn't allow him to continue, reaching up and clasping his shoulders and drawing him down to her.

He was as patient in the ultimate union as he had been beforehand, bringing her with him from one plateau of passion to the next, higher, ever higher, until she wondered how one could feel such exquisite delight without exploding into millions of fragments. Still Daniel coaxed her with his voice, urged her with his body, to climb to the tip of the pinnacle. She knew the moment she had reached it there was no going any further. He was there with her and there was a moment of electrical oneness as they both surrendered to the convulsive wonder of release, their bodies melting together, two streams of volcanic lava merging into one and spilling down a mountainside, cooling only gradually as it came lower into the valley.

Sydney was grateful that Daniel didn't say anything afterward, just held her close against him so that his thudding heartbeat pounded against her breasts. Words would be hopelessly ineffectual in expressing what had just happened for them.

His breathing quieted, as did hers. For a moment she was bereft when his arms loosened around her and she thought he meant to get up. The room plunged into darkness and she knew then he had only been rising to turn off the lamp. He lifted her a little to free the covers and then pulled the sheet over them.

She relaxed against his long, masculine length, loving the intimacy of their satisfied naked bodies, the warmth of the cocoon he created with his chest and arms. She was drifting off to sleep when she felt his lips pressed against her hair, his hand fondling her cheek. Her mouth curved into a smile and she sighed contentedly.

"I can't stay here all night," she murmured drowsily.

"Don't worry. I'll wake you up a little later." Even in her somnolent state she noticed that he sounded wide awake.

Some time later she was annoyed by someone shaking her shoulder and complained irritably, "Stop that!"

"Sydney, it's almost three o'clock."

She tried to shut the voice out, snuggling closer against a wall of solid warmth. "Leave me alone," she muttered.

Gradually consciousness intruded and she realized that she had her arm around Daniel's waist and her face snuggled against the hairy contours of his chest. He was trying to awaken her so she could drive home before the hour grew so late that everyone, including Cora and any light-sleeping neighbors, would suspect she had spent the night somewhere else.

"'S not fair," she grumbled. "You get to stay in bed and I have to drive home." With a sigh she sat up, pushing her hair back from her face and blinking against the dim light from the lamp. He evidently had turned it back on. A chuckle drew her attention. She peered over her shoulder and saw Daniel grinning at her.

"Sweetheart, I have to drive you."

The endearment, as casual as he no doubt meant it to be, created a little rippling sensation inside her. She longed for him to pull her down beside him and say he wished she could stay the entire night and sleep beside him.

"I forgot," she said sheepishly and swung quickly out of bed, acutely conscious the whole time she was dressing that he was watching her. "Do you have a comb?" she asked, walking to the mirror over his bureau and grimacing at the tousled state of her hair.

"Top right-hand drawer."

She found it and began to use it on her hair, scarcely paying attention to what she was doing for watching him as he got out of bed and got dressed, too. How smoothly coordinated and fluid he was in his motions, not at all clumsy, as one might expect of a man his size.

On the drive to her house she sat slumped down in her seat, half asleep, her mind too fuzzy to cope with any kind of penetrating analysis of what had happened tonight. She'd think everything over tomorrow. All she wanted now was to go back to sleep.

When he turned into her driveway, she said, "Don't get out. I can let myself into the house."

He ignored her suggestion, turning off the ignition and getting out and coming around to open her door. When they got to the front door she couldn't seem to locate her key. After watching her fumble around in her evening bag he took it from her and found the key immediately.

He unlocked the door, pushed it open, dropped

the key into the purse and handed it to her. Eyelids drooping with sleep, she stood there searching for something to say and finding the words that came to mind far too inane. How could she say "Thank you for a wonderful evening" after what had happened between them tonight?

"Sleep well." Daniel bent and kissed her on the lips, took her firmly by the shoulders and gave her a little push through the door.

Chapter Seven

Sydney awoke with an inexplicable feeling of gladness. She stretched languorously, her mind like a featureless landscape bathed in sunshine. Then recollection came quickly. She and Daniel had made love last night and it had been past all belief. One of those once-in-a-lifetime sensual experiences she had read about in novels but suspected never happened to real people.

Never during her marriage to Larry, nor even afterward, when she was bitter and angry, had she harbored any dissatisfactions with their sexual relationship. Now she could only wonder if it had been all it should or might have been.

She had been innocent when she married, having enjoyed a few kisses and embraces but never more than that. Only after she had married Larry did she discover her sensuality, never having been aroused before by even the most urgent caresses of her dates.

Some inner control in her brain prevented her from responding because the culture in which she grew up insisted that a girl "save" herself for her husband and go to her wedding night a virgin.

Sydney had done that and felt glad that she had, vaguely complacent that her offering of innocence upon the altar of marriage was just one other strengthening factor insuring her starry-eyed hopes for the future. It would be easy now to look back with the penetrating vision of hindsight and scorn her former naïveté, but she had no regrets for having adhered to her parents' old-fashioned code of sexual conduct. The promiscuity one read and heard about among high school and college students of today did not seem right to her. She still regarded sex primarily as a part of married life, enjoyable for man and wife alike, but more than just pleasure. It was a kind of symbol of the marital bond, a physical welding of bodies representative of the oneness of the lives, purposes and dreams of two people.

And yet, clinging to her ideals as she had even after the devastating experience of divorce, she had willingly, urgently, *gloriously* made love with Daniel last night. And no matter what condemning charges her mind might bring against her actions she felt wonderful this morning in the aftermath of her passion.

Skirting for the moment any consideration of what significance last night might have for the continuance of her relationship with Daniel, she let her thoughts drift backward to the party and the encounter with Larry and Connie. Carefully and deliberately, like a projectionist running a film in slow motion, she recalled each word, each expression between the time she arrived at the Parkers' residence until she departed with Daniel.

Suddenly she sat bolt upright in bed, perceiving for the first time the enormity of her actions following the party. Larry had intimated that he was sorry he had broken up his marriage with her. He had made overtures leading her to believe he still had feelings for her and would like to explore the possibilities of their building a new relationship on the foundations of the old one.

And what had she done? She had left the party with her ex-husband's entreaties reverberating in her ears and gone almost directly to the bed of another man. And what was more, honesty made her admit that at no time during that passionate lovemaking with Daniel had she imagined him as anyone other than himself. She couldn't rationalize things by telling herself that the meeting with Larry had awakened sexual longings for him and she had merely used Daniel to assuage them, imagining he was Larry. That simply was not the truth.

Dear God, what have I done? she wondered in dismay as the full implications dawned. Would Larry even want her now that she had slept with another man? The absurdity of that thought hit her immediately, awakening the anger that had lain dormant more and more frequently the last few weeks. What kind of sniveling female mentality was she exhibiting by even thinking thoughts like that? Larry had been unfaithful to *her* originally, not she to him. *He* had broken up their marriage, not she. *He* had been living with another woman. Why should she feel guilty over one sexual interlude in two years?

Throwing back the bed covers with an angry gesture, she leaped out of bed, furious with herself. One tentative lapse into being a woman again, and look at the results. All manner of doubts of herself, not to mention lying in bed wasting valuable time on a Sunday morning when she had appointments with two clients today, both referrals who had asked specifically for *her* and both corporate executives who had only to *want* to buy in order to do so.

Chalk up last night to experience and let it go at that, she decided cynically, eying with distaste the black dress draped across a small velvet armchair near the window. The rhinestone belt caught a ray of sunlight and twinkled brilliantly, mocking her. Firmly, she told her mind not to wander capriciously to another room and another chair across which the dress had lain, an old wooden rocking chair built on generous lines to accommodate a large man's frame. With brisk, economical movements, she hung the dress on a satin-padded hanger and put it away in a garment bag at the far end of her closet. She wouldn't be needing it again soon.

"How was the movie last night?" she inquired of Cora and the children when she entered the living room half an hour later dressed in a turquoise linen suit with a cream silk blouse. The question was essentially rhetorical since she hardly listened to the replies, which ranged from "so-so" to "swell" to a shrug from Cora.

Both Stacy and Kevin were eying her business attire with a discernible air of disappointment which puzzled Sydney until the reason for it dawned. Their grandparents were out of town for the weekend on a rare visit to their son in north Louisiana. Fred Junior's wife had borne a child, long-awaited by Pauline Cullen, who couldn't understand the six-year delay. A child born to their only son was occasion enough to make Pauline and Fred Senior journey north to see their newest grandchild.

Consequently, Stacy and Kevin were denied their usual Sunday's itinerary: Sunday school and church with their grandparents, then lunch afterward and an entire afternoon's indulgence.

"Shouldn't you two be getting ready for Sunday school?" she prompted, bringing her cup of coffee over to the table.

"Yeah, I guess so," Kevin said gloomily, resting his head to one side on a small fist and eying her with woeful hazel eyes. "You don't reckon Daniel would want us to visit him today, do you?" he ventured hopefully.

Sydney felt a surge of empathy with her small son. To a child his age, Daniel's place must seem like paradise, especially at this time of year, when the outdoors beckoned. When she compared the meager yards in their subdivision with a long stretch of sand beach and acres of woods to play in she could hardly blame Kevin for his wistfulness. She *could* resent Larry, though, for not having more interest in his children. It wouldn't hurt him to entertain the children one day on the weekend while she was busy supporting them.

"If Daniel wanted you to visit him I think he would have asked you," she said crisply, dousing whatever thoughts he might harbor of wangling an invitation. The deep sighs and the glance exchanged between Stacy and Kevin told her that they had indeed discussed such a possibility.

Gloom hung so heavily in the air that she decided on impulse to divulge a plan that, up to now, had been only tentative. "I haven't mentioned this to you guys before because I don't know the exact date yet, but I thought we'd drive over to Florida and visit Disney World later in the summer."

The announcement brought a resurgence of hope, a chorus of exclamations and excited questions. She was suddenly glad she had told them because now she wouldn't be able to back out. They would hold her to the commitment and, in the meantime, it would give them something to look forward to on days like today.

Leaving the house a few minutes later, Sydney looked forward to the day ahead almost with a touch of desperation. Work was her haven. Today, more than usual, she wanted to bury herself in it, obliterate all other nagging concerns, even thoughts of the children. It was the one area of her life where emotion did not intervene to cloud the issues. She felt sure of herself when she was working and the rewards for her endeavors compensated for disappointments and filled the vacuum the failure of her marriage had created.

At least a dozen agents were already at the office when she arrived. The repartee, the ritual complaining, the bits of telephone conversations—Sydney found all of it familiar and soothing. She luxuriated in the sense of belonging to this world which, on the surface, had elements of a gambling casino. Every day held immense promise—a big sale, a million-dollar listing. The counter side of the coin was the expenditure of hours, days, even weeks or months of effort that might never pay off. For Sydney it was all worth the effort because it absorbed her and left her little time to think of anything else.

Her first client, a handsome man in his fifties, was in banking and had just accepted a position with one of the better-known banks in New Orleans. Sydney drove him around for an hour and a half to acquaint him with the area and point out locations of hospitals, schools, and shopping facilities. He offered to take her to lunch, and upon her refusal—she had only thirty minutes before her next appointment—asked if she would have dinner with him.

Something in Raymond Sandifer's manner warned her his interest exceeded that of client for real estate agent and she blandly invented another dinner engagement. Careful not to offend him with any indication of a personal rebuff, she made arrangements to show him and his wife houses the next time he would be in town, three weeks from today. With his wife present there would be no problem of unwanted attention.

Lunch was an apple which she ate at her desk while she filled in the details of her morning in a daily log. When the button with her own code number lighted on her telephone, she answered as distinctly as she could with a mouthful of apple.

"Sydney Cullen speaking."

"Hi. How are you feeling?" The deep, masculine voice was Daniel's.

A piece of the apple went down the wrong chute in her throat. She was caught up in a spasm of coughing which prevented her from speaking for several seconds.

"Sorry," she finally manged to choke out. "I was eating an apple—when you called—and forgot—not to talk and—swallow at the—same time. Other than that"—she took a deep breath—"I feel fine."

"I guess you've already answered my next question. I was hoping you might not be too busy to have lunch with me."

She listened carefully for some timbre or intonation that might indicate he was disappointed, but he sounded calmly matter-of-fact.

"'Fraid you guessed right. I have another client showing up in about ten minutes."

"I called your house before I tried the office. You didn't mention your parents were going out of town or I'd have invited Kevin and Stacy to come over here today. If you have no objections, I'll go over and pick them up now."

Not a trace of regret that she wasn't able to lunch with him. No mention that she might be able to join them during the afternoon when her work was finished. She could only wonder if the lunch invitation had not been a polite ploy to cover his real desire to spend time with Kevin and Stacy. The train of her thoughts appalled Sydney when she realized she was feeling jealous of her own children.

A sudden suspicion occurred to her. "You didn't happen to speak with either Kevin or Stacy when you called my house?"

"Why, yes, as a matter of fact, I did. Kevin answered the phone. Why do you ask?"

"He didn't *suggest* you invite them over to your place this afternoon, did he?" Her voice intimated she would deal later with the young man if he had been so bold.

"Indeed not. He may have mentioned that he and Stacy were at loose ends this afternoon when I inquired about their plans." An undertone of amusement rippled through the deep voice.

Sydney felt her lips quirking in spite of herself. It was easy for her to imagine the conversation that had taken place between Daniel and her son.

"I'll bet he did mention that fact—in his best poor-little-orphan-boy manner, guaranteed to wring the heart with pity," she said caustically.

"Have you forgotten how terrible it is to be young and bored?"

Sydney had to quell the self-pitying words which rose to her lips. No one was entertaining *her* on this gorgeous April day, and a well-dressed, middle-aged couple were approaching her desk at that very moment, her clients for the afternoon.

"By all means, take pity on my deprived urchins and think of their mother slaving away," she said with an abortive attempt at gaiety.

"Don't worry about them. See you later."

He hung up, leaving her quivering with a sense of injury. The least he might have done was suggest she join them during the afternoon if the opportunity presented itself. This was no time to nurse her pique, though, for the couple had arrived at her desk.

Perhaps she was less tolerant than usual, but within the first fifteen minutes in the company of Mr. and Mrs. Laden she knew they would never rank among her favorite clients. Every other phrase from Janet Laden was "In our neighborhood in New York . . ." Sydney could predict with relative certainty that the woman would be miserable during her two-year stay in Louisiana. Nothing about her new location would measure up to what she was leaving behind, and her attitude was guaranteed to alienate her new neighbors and acquaintances. Sydney could hear her several months from now after she had moved: "These Louisiana people are so stand-offish, not friendly like the people in my neighborhood in New York." Never once would she suspect that *she* was the one at fault.

Trying hard to ignore the woman's querulousness, Sydney showed them several houses that met with their restrictive conditions. Today she'd discovered they were looking for something almost exactly like their present home, right down to the floor plan and a private swimming pool in the backyard. Janet Laden disliked having to share a pool, even with other members of a country club.

By the time Sydney drove them back to the office, where they had left their rented car, her strongest desire was never to see them again, and seldom did she react so negatively to clients. Mr. Laden had said little, but his wife had found one fault after another with the houses they had examined, in one embarrassing instance voicing her criticisms within hearing of the present owners, who were still in residence.

"Good riddance," Sydney muttered ill-naturedly when they had departed. She hadn't invited them to come into the office to discuss their reactions to the houses she had shown them nor had she pressed for the date they would be returning to New Orleans. Let some other agent put up with them. He or she would be welcome to the commission.

Glancing at her wristwatch, she noted it was almost five o'clock. Maybe she should rush home and change clothes and drive out to Daniel's. That wistful conjecture was squashed by a disgruntled reminder that she hadn't been invited. In her present mood, though, she had no desire to go back into the office. She didn't care to discuss her afternoon with the Ladens, nor did she care to think real estate.

In an action unprecedented for her she climbed into her car and drove straight home without so much as popping briefly into the office to check her telephone messages. Whatever they were, they could wait until tomorrow.

Her mood didn't lighten when she arrived home and found an empty house. She hadn't expected the kids to have returned from Daniel's yet, but she had assumed Cora would be there. Instead she found a note on the dining table.

Daniel wouldn't hear of me staying home. Cora.

Sydney wandered down the hallway to her room, feeling ridiculously like a high school girl who hadn't been invited to the prom. She shed her suit and hung it neatly in the closet before slipping into shorts and a sleeveless cotton knit blouse.

Feeling empty, since she had eaten neither breakfast nor lunch, she opened the refrigerator and rummaged around for something to snack on. While she was slicing some Monterey Jack cheese and arranging it on a paper plate with crackers, the telephone rang. Thinking it might be Daniel, calling to invite her to join him and the others, she rushed to answer it.

"Hi, Syd."

It took a second or two to make the necessary adjustment from expectation to reality. Larry's voice, not Daniel's, came over the line. Her reaction was remarkably akin to disappointment.

"Hi, Larry."

"It was great seeing you last night, Syd. I can't get over how terrific you look."

Her mind was working rapidly, remembering Larry's insistence last night that he would call her and arrange a time when they could get together. Strange thought—dating your ex-husband, the man you'd lived with for nine years.

"Thanks, Larry. I feel good about myself these days." Today she hadn't felt good about anything, but that was beside the point.

"Are you busy tonight? I thought I'd drive over, see the kids, and then maybe the two of us could go somewhere for dinner and have a chance to talk. Get reacquainted, you might say." His voice had a surface note of cajolery but underneath that was smooth assurance. He was certain she would accept his overture.

Perhaps his smugness made it easier for her to refuse him. "Sorry, Larry, but that's not possible. The kids aren't even here, and I'm not sure when they'll be back."

"Where are they? At your folks?"

He thought she was just putting him off for pride's sake and would come around with a little persuading. Had he always been so cocksure where she was concerned?

"No. Mom and Dad are out of town. They went to Shreveport to visit Fred Junior. He and Janie finally—"

"Where are they, then?" he interrupted with a steely edge of suspicion in his voice. He made no pretext of being interested in the lives of the members of her family.

"They're with Daniel. He has an old house and ten acres on the lake." She would have been less than human had she not gotten a measure of satisfaction from telling him that and then from sensing his annoyance even before he spoke in reply.

"You *are* having an affair with that big hulk, aren't you, Sydney?" No soft-toned cajolery now, just righteous accusation.

"I'm involved with Daniel, Larry, professionally as well as personally. He's contracted with me to list his property." Her calmness was not pretense, but it seemed to infuriate him.

"To think I've been hoping you and I might get back together! You haven't heard the last from me about you and this man, Sydney. The courts take situations like yours into consideration when they decide on child custody, you know!" And with that vaguely menacing threat Larry hung up the phone with a sharp bang.

Sydney's lip curled with contempt. How like Larry to think he could intimidate her. As though he would seriously consider taking her children away from her when he didn't even have time for them on weekends. Not to mention the fact that he was hardly in a position to point the finger of moral outrage.

She walked back over to the counter and finished the interrupted task of preparing herself a snack and then took the plate and a glass of iced tea into the living room area. The draperies were pulled to either side of the sliding glass doors opening onto a small concrete patio. Outside she could see the big clay pots Cora had planted with petunias and begonias and geraniums. Beyond the patio was the lawn, green in the lushness of spring and bathed in afternoon sunshine.

Heaving a self-pitying sigh, Sydney sank into a deep armchair. Munching cheese and crackers and sipping iced tea, she gazed longingly out the glass doors. They were all over there at Daniel's, having a wonderful time and not even missing her.

When she had finished the snack she snapped on the television and tried without success to concentrate on the news, which was followed by a situation comedy. Her irritation and restlessness grew as the hour became later and still the others did not return. When the telephone rang, she dashed over to it and snapped into the receiver, "Yes."

There was a brief pause.

"What are you doing?" This time it *was* Daniel.

"I'm doing nothing but wondering where the hell everybody is!" she said waspishly.

"But surely you knew. You gave me your permission to pick up the kids. Cora said she left a note. Why didn't you come over and join us?"

The evenness of his voice only increased her irritation. "Because I wasn't *invited!*"

Another pause. "I see. Kevin and Stacy and Cora

are all over here and you don't come because you aren't invited."

She was beginning to feel both foolish and defensive. "Are you calling to say you're on your way here?"

"I was calling to find out if you were home yet and to tell you that by popular consent dinner is a wiener roast on the beach. Kevin and Stacy have been busy all afternoon gathering driftwood and building a fire."

A certain grim patience in his tone made Sydney wish fervently she had not acted and spoken so childishly. "That sounds like fun. Can I pick up something at the supermarket? One of the big ones is open on Sunday."

"Cora took my car this afternoon and bought everything we needed."

How frustrating it was to deal with someone so reasonable and controlled. If Daniel had only shown a little justifiable irritation she could have reacted against it with a spurt of temper. As it was, she promised meekly to be over there in a few minutes.

"Good. I suggest you wear long pants and bring a long-sleeved shirt. I have insect repellent but the mosquitoes can get pretty vicious right after sunset."

"What about Kevin and Stacy?"

"Cora brought along jeans and long-sleeved shirts for them."

Sydney felt tears clog her throat as she hung up the receiver. In her absence everything had been taken care of. All she had to do was show up, a kind of forced guest on everybody.

Admonishing herself not to be so hypersensitive, she changed into jeans, as instructed, and took a long-sleeved blouse from her closet before leaving the house. She could wear it over her knit blouse later. It was that hushed time of day, hovering delicately between afternoon and evening, when the light is mellow and golden, as if the sun is leaving with utmost reluctance. If Sydney had not been so stubborn earlier, refusing to go to Daniel's as she wanted to do, she would be enjoying this time on the beach.

Making an effort to push aside her glumness, she concentrated on appearing cheerful. It wouldn't do for her to put a damper on everyone else's fun just because she hadn't been included in the planning.

She had barely parked her car behind Daniel's and gotten out when Kevin and Stacy came tearing across the lawn from the beach yelling "Mom! Mom!" They almost knocked her over in their enthusiasm and she wrapped an arm around each of them, chagrined to realize how selfishly she had behaved this afternoon. What had been wrong with her?

"Come see our bonfire we built almost all by ourself!" Kevin urged.

She ran across the lawn arm in arm with her young son and daughter down to the edge of the beach. Cora was there, ensconced in a folding lawn chair and looking quite contented. Daniel sat cross-legged on the grass.

"Glory be," Cora said prosaically. "Thank goodness you're here. These two have been beside themselves worrying about you getting here and seeing the fire they built."

Sydney stood with her arms hugging the slim shoulders of her two children, their arms entwined around her waist. She felt the dark weight of Daniel's gaze but avoided meeting it, exclaiming instead over the fire and declaring, "So far today I've had one apple and a few crackers and slices of cheese. I can't wait for supper!"

"Hunger can make people aggressive." With those cryptic words, Daniel rose and came over toward them, forcing Sydney to look at him.

"Sometimes people take too much for granted," she countered quickly, fighting desperately against the weakness attacking her legs as he came close and towered over all three of them.

"We'll finish this discussion later," he said softly, his eyes saying that Stacy and Kevin were listening with puzzled curiosity, as was Cora, and that the matter between himself and her was private. Then, in an entirely different tone, he announced to everyone in general, "Ready to start cooking your supper? Every fellow for himself."

Sydney's response was as enthusiastic as anyone's, and her high spirits were not forced. The intimacy of that glance between Daniel and herself had warmed her through and through. Hadn't that been what she had been pining for all day, just some little indication that *she*, Sydney Cullen, was important to him? She didn't want beautiful words of adoration or passionate declarations of love, because she didn't put much stock in those anymore. All she wanted was something direct and honest like "You're not just anybody—you're somebody special." His eyes had told her that just now, and instantly all her fretfulness and paranoia had vanished like fog burned off by the sunshine.

She doubted she had ever been hungrier before or that food had ever tasted any better. A safe distance from the fire a makeshift table had been set up, a rectangular piece of plywood laid across two sawhorses and covered with a sheet to serve as a tablecloth. Metal folding chairs were placed around the table, which held all the fixings for hot dogs plus paper plates and napkins and plastic knives and forks. There were also bags of various kinds of chips and a huge heavy-gauge aluminum pot containing boiled whole potatoes and corn on the cob.

The last was one of Sydney's favorites and she ate two pieces of corn dripping with butter in addition to a well-dressed hot dog. Kevin and Stacy declared more than once throughout the meal that it was the best they'd ever had. While obviously not truly offended, Cora couldn't resist teasing them. "Wait and see when I cook another meal for you two since you're so good at cooking your own."

Everything about the occasion was perfect, Sydney reflected happily to herself when they were roasting marshmallows after supper. Cora had been included and was looking more relaxed and younger than Sydney had ever seen her look. Kevin and Stacy were model children, spontaneous and appreciative and not lapsing into the competitive squabbles that were unavoidable from time to time between siblings close in age. And, surprisingly, Sydney felt happy that for a short time *she* wasn't in charge of their behavior. Daniel wore the cloak of authority tonight, and wore it with genial ease.

Sydney was content to sit back and enjoy herself as a catered-to guest, allowing Daniel to officiate when the question arose as to who had collected the most firewood or was the most expert at roasting a marshmallow. The brief respite from her parental role made her realize just how constant the pressure was, even with Cora's invaluable assistance. Sydney was always the one responsible for her children, even when she was not physically in their presence, not just because the law had granted her legal custody, though that was part of it, but more so because she had felt each of them grow inside her body and she loved them in a special, protective way no one else could.

From experience, she knew the ultimate test of their good behavior would be the news that the evening was over. Like most children having a good time, they didn't want it to end. Why couldn't a party go on forever? they reasoned with childlike resistance to the inevitable ending.

An inner clock in Sydney's head told her when it was growing near the time Kevin and Stacy should be returning home and unwinding from the exhilaration of their day and evening. But she said nothing. Daniel spoke up not more than ten minutes later.

"Time for everybody to pitch in and clean up. Come on, Kevin and Stacy, you start carrying the chairs, one at a time, up to the house. You saw where they were stored in the hall closet. See if you can put them back exactly as they were. Cora, would you supervise, please?"

There were a few regretful sighs, but the two children set about following his instructions with alacrity. Sydney waited until they were out of earshot before teasing softly, "Why do nonparents always try to make us parents look bad. *Ouch!*"

He had come up behind her where she stood at the table and administered a stinging slap to her posterior, snugly encased in denim jeans.

"That hurt!" she accused, turning toward him while she rubbed the tingling area with one hand.

"I meant it to hurt," he said, bending forward and slipping his arms around her waist. Then he straightened, tightening his hold and bringing her up with him so they were on eye level, her feet dangling off the ground.

"That wasn't just for being a smart mouth just

now. It was for staying away all afternoon and sulking like a little kid."

His lips took hers in a hard, deep kiss she could have avoided with ease since his arms were wrapped around her waist, holding her against him. Instead she held his head in both her hands and kissed him back, opening her mouth to his questing tongue, welcoming it, not giving a fraction under the hungering pressure of his mouth.

When they finally tore their lips apart they were breathing audibly, their hearts pounding. Kevin and Stacy were returning across the lawn, their high-pitched children's voices floating ahead of them down to the beach. Sydney could feel the hard arousal in Daniel's body and her own throbbed and pulsed with an answering need. She shared his reluctance to pull away as he slowly lowered her to the ground and loosened his hold around her waist. Her hands trailed from their clasp on his head down the powerful convex curves of his chest to his stomach and waist, savoring the solid, warm feel of him.

She stood in the loose circle of his arms as Kevin and Stacy slid to a halt on the sand, giggling self-consciously. "We saw you two *kissing* out here!" Kevin announced.

"And so you did." Daniel's voice and the hand he held out to Kevin said he didn't mind their seeing him kiss their mother nor were they intruding now. "I hope you don't mind."

Kevin sidled closer and allowed Daniel's hand to tousle his hair and then fall to encase a slender shoulder. Not to be left out, Stacy came closer, too, declaring in an adult manner, "We don't mind, Daniel. You can kiss Mom."

Without seeming abrupt, Daniel eased the process

of cleaning up into motion once again. In a short time all the leftover food and other items on the table had been carried to the house along with the sheet and the remaining chairs. Daniel stated that he would take care of the plywood and sawhorses and douse the fire later himself. He also deftly handled a situation which had been worrying Sydney's mind.

"Cora, you drive the kids home in my car. It won't matter if it gets a little sand in it since I don't have to chauffeur people around. Sydney and I will come on a little later in her car. We have some real estate business to discuss."

The solution was so skillfully conceived she could have kissed him right there in front of everybody. She had been wondering how she could arrange to stay behind while everybody else left. And while she would have allowed Cora to drive her car, she liked this arrangement much better. She kept her car impeccably clean, not just for the sake of her clients but because she was so proud of it.

When the tail lights of the Buick had disappeared she turned to Daniel with a touch of diffidence now that they were alone. "How did you know I don't like anybody but me to drive my car?"

His smile held a hint of indulgence. "I remember how proud I was of my first car. I'd been driving my folks' cars through high school and college, but this one was different. It was *mine*."

Sydney regarded him in amazement. "I guess I do feel like this is my first car, the first really decent one, anyway. I always had something to drive while I was married, but they were just transportation. This one I picked out myself, brand new, and I love it."

"Wait here a minute."

Daniel was striding away in the darkness toward the garage, his movements fluid and effortless as they always were. He was back shortly with a large, dark bundle under one arm.

"A tarp," he explained. "It's a shame to waste that fire down there when it's getting to the nicest stage."

"That's a great idea!" She slipped her hand into the free one he offered and walked beside him.

He stopped suddenly. "Maybe you'd like a drink? Wine, beer, a cocktail?"

"Not unless you do. I seldom drink alcohol except at a party, and that's mostly just to be doing something."

"Same here." Satisfied with her answer, he resumed walking across the lawn.

The fire was a bed of glowing red-gold coals by now, having a vibrance and fascination all its own. Daniel unfolded the tarpaulin and spread it on the sand nearby.

Sydney lay on her stomach, elbows propped on the thick canvas and chin cupped in her hands so that she could gaze into the embers. Daniel followed suit.

She sighed. "At the risk of sounding like Kevin and Stacy, this was a wonderful idea. I'm so glad you included Cora. That was thoughtful."

"Cora's obviously a member of the family. Maybe I should confess to an ulterior motive, too." The teasing note in his voice made her turn her head to look at him and he leaned over to take a quick taste of her lips.

"You scoundrel!" she accused laughingly. "I do believe you had the whole thing planned so Cora would be here to drive the kids home and I would be left at your mercy!"

"When I suggested they leave without you, you put up quite a fight," he mocked.

"Why, *you*—" She pushed at him and he rolled

over on his back, pulling her down on his chest. She lay partly on top of him, feeling his heart beat against her breasts and looking down at his face, expecting him to claim her lips, wanting him to.

Instead, he reached and smoothed the wings of hair back from her cheeks. "I missed you today. I was disappointed when you were too busy to have lunch with me, and then when you could have joined us, you didn't. Why?"

Sydney was awkwardly at a loss to explain. Her feelings earlier today seemed silly now. She had to remind herself he hadn't made her feel in the least *necessary* when she spoke with him on the telephone at noon.

"You didn't *seem* disappointed when I couldn't have lunch with you—I *did* have clients, too. They walked in while you were on the line. And then you seemed more than happy to spend the afternoon with Kevin and Stacy instead of with me." The sound of her own voice gave her former grievances credibility. "Think back and you'll remember you didn't even suggest I might join you when I could. How was I to know I was welcome?"

His hands had fallen away from her face and weren't touching her. He was so still she waited breathlessly for him to speak.

"After last night you *didn't know if you were welcome?*" His deep, quiet tone held disbelief and something that might have been disappointment. Sydney felt as though she had slipped down a notch in his esteem and she wanted fiercely to regain the lost ground.

"Daniel, how was I to know what last night meant to you? For that matter, I still don't know."

She sat up, miserably aware of the gulf widening between them with every word she spoke. "I don't even know how *I* feel about last night, except that I'm not sorry it happened. This morning, when I first woke up, I felt just fantastic and then . . . well, I started thinking and trying to figure things out and got more and more confused." That's what she was right now. Confused.

He sat up, too, his powerful arms wrapped around his knees. "What were you confused about?" Judging from the remoteness of his voice his interest might be purely clinical.

She found it difficult to explain when he was on one planet and she was millions of miles away on another. "I just couldn't fathom *why* I had done what I had last night, especially considering the implications."

"Which are?"

"Well, that Larry might never want me back once he found out I'd been to bed with another man." She omitted telling him about Larry's telephone call that afternoon, which had done a fair job of confirming her conjecture about his reaction to her sexual involvement with another man.

"Do you *want* him to want you back?"

"I thought I did. That's why I was so confused this morning when I realized what I'd done—going to bed with you."

Daniel uttered a sound that was part anger and part exasperation. "Are you telling me *you* would be willing to have him back when, according to you, he's been living with another woman for more than two years, and yet suddenly you're a scarlet woman because you've been to bed with a man one time?"

It sounded even more ridiculous and inconsistent coming from him than when she had recognized the same contradiction herself. She reached over and laid her hand on his forearm, keeping it there even when his flesh twitched and solidified into steel.

"*That* made me mad, too, not just the double standard involved, but the fact that I was looking at everything the way Larry would and meekly going along with it the way I always had when we were married." She hesitated, getting now to the difficult part. "Another complicating factor that I didn't let myself think about this morning—I don't think I want *our* relationship to stop, Daniel."

His head turned sharply toward her face, his dark eyes raking her features in the golden glow from the embers. There was something vaguely despairing in the way he shook his head before he did what she longed to have him do—gathered her into his arms and held her close.

"I knew we shouldn't get involved with each other," he sighed.

Sydney melted against him, loving the gentle strength of his hands as they kneaded and stroked her shoulders and back. She would worry about the complications later. Right now she was immersed in the warmth and joy of being in his arms. Before long it wasn't enough and she wanted more from him.

"Daniel?" she murmured, raising her head from his chest and reaching up to caress the hard, rugged planes of his face before pushing into the vital thickness of his hair and drawing his lips down to meet hers. They kissed like two people starving for the taste of each other, insatiable for the clinging of tongue to tongue, careless of the pain of their lips grinding against each other.

Their hands reached and touched and then explored further, more and more urgent to get beneath the barrier of clothing to firm, resilient flesh underneath, flesh that trembled with the passion they ignited in each other. This time there was no patient, deliberate ritual of undressing each other. They ripped off their clothes, kicking and tossing them aside and then lying together naked on the coarse-textured canvas, shuddering with the ecstasy of flesh against bare flesh.

Sydney moaned her pleasure aloud. "Daniel, I've never known anything like this," she said in a voice that came to her ears rough with strange vibrations.

"Sydney, I want you. I want you," he groaned.

His great passion engulfed her as he covered her entire body with kisses that seared her flesh—her face, her neck, her breasts, her stomach, her thighs. She felt herself burning and dissolving into liquid flame wherever his mouth and hands touched, and they touched her everywhere.

Their bodies merged with a need too monumental for patience and gentleness. Sydney was like someone in a delirium, all her inhibitions cast aside along with her clothing. She and Daniel were primitive man and woman with raw, primitive appetites lying together on the sand under an immense open sky. He urged her upward with him the same way he had the previous night, but the ascent was faster and steeper and the ultimate elevation dizzying beyond anything she could ever have believed possible.

At the last she grasped him in desperation and held on with all her strength as they made the plunge together which took them out into space and beyond consciousness for a piercing, shattering moment as incapable of description as the events in a dream after one awakens.

Afterward they lay together, exhausted and only gradually returning to the present, where they became two people lying on a rough tarpaulin spread on the thick sand in the darkness, a dying fire nearby. Sydney was dazed, her voice hoarse when she spoke aloud the thoughts that awoke such awe.

"Daniel, that was even *more* . . ." She searched for a suitable word and found none powerful enough. "Than last night."

"I know." He sounded as off balance as she felt, not yet restored to normal.

At the risk of sounding unworldly, which no doubt she was, she had to say what was on her mind. "Daniel, sex was never like this for me before. Do you think it's because I've gone so long without it—or that I'm older or something?"

He rose up on one arm so that he could look down on her. By now the fire shed little light, and the night was a cloudy one, so his face was an unreadable landscape of shadows. With his free hand he smoothed her hair back and brushed his fingertips across the contours of her face as if flicking away imaginary grains of sand.

"I don't know. This morning I wondered the same thing about myself and decided maybe it's worthwhile in the long run to be celibate for a year. Or maybe we're just a dynamite combination."

He had answered the question she had not asked, out of timidity. She'd wondered if their lovemaking had been something beyond the ordinary for him as it had been for her. Having been reassured, she could not resist teasing him.

"For two people with virtually *no* appeal for each other . . ." she drawled lazily and then rejoiced in the rich spontaneity of his laughter.

"See what you missed all these years, thanks to your bias against us football jocks," he retaliated when he was able to speak.

Sydney was not to be outdone. "Just think what I

could do to you if I were well-endowed the way you like your women," she speculated with an ulterior motive.

His gaze slid down her long, slender form. "Sweetheart, if you did any more than you do now, I'd be in trouble."

The husky declaration wasn't exactly a revision of his earlier statement some weeks ago that she wasn't his physical type, but she was satisfied with it for the time being.

Chapter Eight

Sitting up, Sydney looked around for her clothes and saw them strewn helter-skelter on the sand. While she dressed, shaking each garment thoroughly before putting it back on, she remembered what Daniel had said when Cora was leaving with the children.

"Did you really want to talk to me about something related to real estate?" she asked curiously.

He had already finished dressing and was picking up handfuls of sand and pouring them on the remaining embers of the fire.

"Yes, but it can wait a few minutes until we walk back up to the house. A cup of coffee sounds good to me. What about you?"

"Sounds good to me, too."

She was more than mildly curious but didn't press him. Some sixth sense told her he was going to remove his house and property from the market and

probably wanted to break the news to her diplomati-
cally. Did he think she would be upset at losing the
listing? She wouldn't be. In her heart she felt he
should keep the property he loved so deeply. Maybe
that was the reason her efforts to sell the property
had been so perfunctory from the first.

Besides, she admitted to herself as she helped
Daniel fold the tarpaulin, wouldn't it be nice for
things to continue just as they were now? Daniel
living here and she and the children and Cora living
in their house, all of them enjoying wonderful times
together as they had today. If she sold Daniel's
house and land she would make a fat commission,
but Daniel would move away, probably abroad, and,
if true to his word, he wouldn't return to this area
again.

No, she'd rather forfeit the listing and have him
stay, and she'd tell him that when he introduced the
subject in his own time and way.

They walked together across the upward slanting
lawn, Daniel with the folded tarp under one arm and
the other one thrown loosely around her shoulders.
He seemed hardly conscious of her, having with-
drawn to some place inhabited only by his own
thoughts.

In the kitchen she sat at the table and watched him
as he made the coffee, having refused her offer of
help. At his prompting she told him about her day,
sketching in the details about the morning client who
had been too friendly for her liking and the couple in
the afternoon who had been impossible to please.

When the coffee was made and he had poured
each of them a cup she half expected him to suggest
they drink it in the living room or out on the
veranda, but he sat down at the table. Almost

abruptly, he introduced the subject on his mind and at first her premonition seemed correct.

"I'm having serious afterthoughts about my decision to sell this house and land. In fact, I've definitely decided to take it off the market." He paused, searching her face for a reaction.

She decided to find out more before letting him off the hook completely. "What are you going to do with it, then?"

He appeared slightly relieved at her level tone. "Believe me, I'm sorry I put you to so much trouble for nothing. All that measuring and typing up the contract and showing the place to people. Maybe I can make it up to you in the long run. And tell your manager I'll pay for the advertising Pontchartrain Realty's done so far."

Sydney made a dismissive gesture. "Don't worry about that part of it. Advertising is a big part of the operating budget." She sipped her coffee. He still hadn't answered her question about his plans now that he wasn't going to sell. Was he being deliberately evasive?

"Were you serious last night when you said you would like to buy this house if you could afford it?"

Sydney's heart began to race so fast she could feel the rapid pulsebeat in her wrists. Daniel wasn't about to propose to her, was he? And if he did, what on earth would she say?

"As serious as one can be when talking about something that's obviously out of the question," she hedged nervously.

Daniel's forearms rested on the table in front of him and one hand toyed restlessly with a spoon. Sydney noted the tremendous power in the size and musculature of those arms and then the sensitivity of the long, tapered fingers that could easily bend the delicate spoon double.

"You're not thinking of selling this house to me on special terms I can manage?" she asked when she couldn't tolerate the silence any longer.

He looked up. "No, I hadn't really considered that. I was thinking more of offering to let you live here as a kind of caretaker. Rent free, of course." Reading the expression on her face as instinctive resistance to his proposal rather than the intense disappointment it was, he quickly sought to remove whatever objections she might have.

"I'll install central air and heat and do whatever I can as far as insulating the place. You would have a free hand in decorating and making minor changes that wouldn't destroy the integrity of the house. If you're worried about me having a change of mind after you've gone to a lot of trouble, we can work out a contract agreeable to both of us."

What he suggested was advantageous for her in every way, but she couldn't muster the enthusiasm she should be feeling. Something inside her—she supposed it was nothing more serious than her pride—smarted at the discovery of how far afield she had been in second-guessing his intentions. Her spirits had collapsed like a punctured balloon when he proposed *not* that she marry him and live *with* him in this wonderful old house but that she take up residence after he was gone, a kind of custodian. She still didn't know what she would have said if he had asked her to marry him, so wasn't it ridiculous to feel as if she had been rejected?

"Why would you agree to an arrangement that seems to have so little benefit for you?" Her throat muscles suffered from the same tenseness as the rest of her and made her voice come out a little ragged.

He looked thoughtful but answered immediately, obviously having asked himself the same question beforehand. "The situation would have enormous benefit for me, not just in terms of personal satisfaction, but monetary benefit, too. The first because it would give me great pleasure to know Kevin and Stacy were growing up here, enjoying this place even more than I did as a kid since they'd have it year-round. And since I have every confidence you would take good care of the house, in time it—and certainly the property—will increase in value as the population in this parish increases."

Sydney felt like crying. She couldn't remember when she had felt more insignificant. It was Kevin and Stacy whose happiness and welfare he was considering, not hers. No doubt he wouldn't even be making this offer if she didn't have them. To him she was nothing more than the mother of two beautiful, healthy children he probably wished were his own.

For the first time she comprehended the meaning of the old saying, "Keep a stiff upper lip." Hers was bent on quivering and it took all the support of her hurt pride and resentment to conquer the weakness. Since she had to stiffen everything else, too, her voice came out stilted and excessively polite.

"It sounds too good to pass up. Why don't we both give it some further thought. I take it you're still planning to go abroad?"

He could tell something was wrong. His gaze was troubled as he studied her erect posture and controlled features. "Nothing is really definite yet, but I'll probably be leaving in August."

He got up abruptly from the table. "Like another cup of coffee?"

"No, thanks," she declined, still in the same polite voice. "I'd better be going."

"Are you terribly disappointed about losing the listing?" he asked hesitantly, his face a mask of concern.

She wasn't, but she would far prefer him to believe she was than have him know the truth. "Not *terribly,* but a little. I'll have to eat some crow from the other agents in the office, but it won't kill me."

"I can't tell you how relieved I am that you're taking the news so calmly." He moved around the table and tried to draw her into his arms, but she held herself stiffly aloof.

"I'd really better be going. Tomorrow's another busy day."

When they walked down the rear steps toward her car, Daniel went automatically to the passenger's side and climbed in, assuming she would drive. Sydney took note of the action and it warmed her, softening some of the rigidity she felt in all her bones and muscles. Daniel was a fine, sensitive man and she was making him feel guilty for a decision he had every right to make.

On the drive to her house she was able to talk more normally and the atmosphere between them relaxed. She stopped on the street in front of her house and waited for him to move his car so that she could pull under the carport. Lately it had become an annoyance to have a single car driveway.

When he pulled back into the driveway and got out, she assumed he intended to come inside and get the spare key he had given Cora, but when she mentioned it, he said, "I'll get it another time."

It occurred to her then that she had the keys to his gate and house and wouldn't be needing them unless she decided to accept his offer and live in his house when he was gone.

"Here," she said, pulling the keys out of her purse and offering them to him.

One hand caught her wrist and the other closed her fingers firmly around the keys. "Keep them."

"But I don't need them now!" she protested, puzzled.

He used his firm grip on her wrist to pull her up against him until she stood with the length of her body pressed against his. His gaze met her questioning eyes.

"I like to know you have the keys to my house," he said softly.

A chunk of something hard and cold dissolved inside her chest. To cover her emotion, she joked a little unsteadily, "You'd never know when I might steal in when you least expect me."

His grin was raffish and the dark gleam in his eyes suddenly made breathing a conscious labor. "If I'm asleep, don't hesitate to wake me."

The image he conjured up teased her mind with disturbing clarity: Daniel asleep, dark hair tousled and rugged features soft and vulnerable in repose, herself slipping quietly into his bedroom, sitting beside him, watching him, waking him . . .

"Can I come over tomorrow night?"

She blinked, a little dazed at the interruption. "Sure, if you want—"

"I want," he inserted firmly. "I'll come over after dinner."

"Why don't you come _for_ dinner?"

"I thought you'd never ask."

A brief, hard kiss and then he was gone.

"What happened to May!" Sydney wondered aloud as she tore a page off the calendar hanging over the desk in her bedroom. She had sat down a few minutes earlier to write out checks to pay the monthly bills and noticed the calendar. It set her off on a whirl of introspection.

More than a month had passed since the cookout on the beach when she and Daniel had made love under the vast bowl of the sky, and not a day had gone by since that she hadn't seen him. He had become a constant in her life, in her household, she might more accurately say, since Kevin and Stacy adored him. Every other statement out of their mouths contained a reference to him.

Cora liked him, too, but every now and then Sydney caught an expression or tone of voice that bespoke the older woman's underlying concern. She probably would have liked some reassurance as to where the relationship between Sydney and Daniel was headed.

Sydney didn't allow herself to dwell on that question. Insofar as she knew, nothing had happened to change Daniel's mind about going overseas to work. She had accepted his offer to live in the house after he had gone, and he was busy making the changes she considered essential for basic comfort, the main one being the installation of a modern heating and cooling system. The house had six fireplaces and numerous ceiling fans, but she did not care to live without a thermostat to control the temperature of her house, nor did Daniel expect her to.

Shaking her head ruefully at the direction of her thoughts, Sydney reflected that if she weren't careful she would find herself sounding like Kevin and Stacy with "Daniel says." Was it possible that in two months he would be gone and they'd all have to adjust themselves to *not* having him around?

She reached into the wire basket on her desk and

pulled the electrical bill out of the stack of mail there. A few minutes later her pen rested mid-word on the check she was writing. Daniel *not* sitting with them at the supper table at night, *not* having them all over to his place to share a big pot of red beans or jambalaya or boiled crawfish, shrimp, or crabs, *not* planning and supervising outings on his beach, *not* taking a genuine interest in every facet of Kevin's and Stacy's lives, in her own daily routine. *Not* making love to her . . .

By mutual, unspoken consent they always made love in his house, never hers. Whenever they did, the fiery intensity of their passion blazed up to consume them as it had from the first. The main difference now was that they had come to know each other's bodies more intimately and familiarity had replaced the initial shyness on Sydney's part. It felt utterly natural to be with Daniel in his bed. More and more she resented having to leave and drive home to lie alone in her own.

"You know," she had said whimsically one night recently when she lay in his arms after they had made love, "one of the few things I really miss about being married is having someone to sleep *with*. You know what I mean?"

He rubbed the hard line of his jaw against her forehead. "I think so. It's nice to turn over in the middle of the night and feel a warm, living body next to you. Even one that snores."

She had giggled at that. "Do *you* snore, Daniel?" She asked wistfully. With all her heart, she wished at that moment she could stay the entire night and find out for herself.

"Is that *all* you miss about being married, Sydney?"

The question startled her with its total unexpectedness and underlying seriousness. Neither of them spoke much now of their former marriages. That had been talked out those first weeks they had known each other, before they became lovers.

For her part, she rarely thought of Larry, not even to resent him as she had during the time when she had nourished herself on anger. She gave careful thought to Daniel's question and decided she liked her life better now than before. All she knew of marriage were the years with Larry.

"Well, maybe not *all*," she said slowly, "but the other things are just as minor. Like having an escort for parties. For the most part, I like my life now. It feels good to know I don't have to have a man to support me and that I can make my own decisions, come and go as I wish, within the limitations of my responsibilities to Kevin and Stacy, of course."

She thought she could read what he was thinking. "If you're wondering whether it ever occurs to me that they should have a father in residence, I can tell you it does. But they don't have one. It's as simple as that. Life can't always be perfect."

He was quiet for a long time, but she knew he wasn't asleep. His body was too taut for that. She wondered what he was thinking.

"What about you, Daniel? Do you miss being married?" Suddenly his answer was of the greatest importance. She awaited it with a disquieting sense of dread.

"Yes, I suppose I do. At least all the positive things, like having someone to share day-to-day living. You know, eating meals, talking about what happened at work, watching the evening news, making plans for tomorrow and next week and next year. Yes, I'd have to say I miss being married."

He sighed heavily. Sydney felt as if a band had tightened unbearably around her heart. His voice had echoed with such deep regret and loneliness that she was sure he was still in love with *her,* Deborah, and the knowledge was unendurable. She wished now she hadn't asked, for she no longer found it possible to remain where she was, lying next to him in bed, when his mind was full of his ex-wife.

She had gotten up, dressed, and driven home, miserable at the proof that Daniel, unlike herself, hadn't recovered from the breakup of his marriage.

Unlike herself! For Sydney, that evening had brought the revelation that she herself *had* "recovered" from the trauma of her own divorce. Now, as she sat at her desk and intermittently wrote checks, addressed envelopes and lapsed into long stretches of sitting immobile, captive to her thoughts, she made another discovery.

She loved Daniel! Maybe she wasn't *in love* with him as she had been with Larry at age nineteen, but he was important to her. He was a golden thread woven into the fabric of her existence, she thought rather fancifully, a little abashed at her bent toward poetry. It was going to be an intolerably dull piece of cloth, her life when Daniel left. Why couldn't he be content to stay and have everything continue as it was?

The inspiration, or brainstorm, came later that same afternoon. At the time she was lying back in a lounge chair on her patio, watching Daniel tutor Kevin and Stacy in the art of passing a football. Kevin hadn't mentioned a word about junior football since the day a month earlier when he had asked Daniel, "If I was *your* little boy, would *you* let me play?"

Awaiting the answer confidently, Kevin had slid a sly glance at his mother to make sure she was well aware of the trap he had set.

Daniel hadn't hesitated in answering. "If you were *my* little boy, Kevin, I wouldn't dream of spoiling your chances of playing sports in high school and possibly later, in college, which is what you'd be doing if you injured yourself permanently now."

Kevin's tawny eyes had widened with sheer disbelief and then darkened with pain at this betrayal from an unexpected quarter.

Daniel had continued. "I'd encourage you to do everything possible to build a healthy body and increase your strength and agility. Plus, if you were interested, I'd teach you a lot of the strategy involved in football. Then you'd see a lot more when you watch a game. You'd appreciate more of what's going on."

Here Daniel had flung Sydney a teasing glance which she had read plainly: If women understood the intricacy of football they would appreciate its mass appeal. She resisted the strong temptation to take up his challenge, choosing not to intrude in Kevin's conversation.

"*I'm* interested," her young son had announced earnestly, trying to salvage something worthwhile from Daniel's disappointing reaction to his question.

Since that conversation Kevin had taken an inordinate interest in his diet, wanting to know the specific body-building benefits of everything he ate. He viewed activities such as swimming and riding his bicycle as "training" now, and paid rapt attention during sessions with Daniel on football strategy and the roles of the various players. Sydney heard enough to question the popular cliché she had mouthed more than once herself: "dumb football player."

It occurred to her now, as she sat on the patio and watched Daniel arc the football gracefully through the air to Stacy, that her ten-year-old daughter would probably always view football and football players differently from the way her mother had. Because of the contact with Daniel, Stacy would more than likely associate the sport with manliness and intelligence allied with sensitivity and gentleness.

How many fathers spent as much time with their children as Daniel spent with hers? she marveled, watching him. And then the idea unfurled itself in her brain like a magician's flower popping miraculously out of a top hat. Her subconscious must have been working on the plan for hours or days or weeks, because it materialized full-blown, perfectly formed in every detail. It was so inevitable and reasonable, not exactly a solution to a problem so much as a design that worked beautifully for everyone involved.

She couldn't wait to present the idea to Daniel, but she wanted the time and place to be *right*, which meant when the two of them were alone at his house. To that end, she suggested after supper that she would like to go over to his house to make some decisions about what color paint she would choose for various rooms. She had picked up several color charts earlier in the week and had been looking them over.

Not surprisingly, they made love before the evening was over, but not immediately upon arriving at the house. Sydney wanted him to help her decide which rooms would be suitable for each child and for

Cora. They walked from room to room upstairs, inspecting each one and discussing what color it should be painted.

"What about you?" Daniel teased. "Which room will be yours?"

"I don't know . . ." She hid her smile, pretending to deliberate. "Don't you dare!" she yelled as Daniel grabbed her and began to administer stinging slaps to her posterior.

"Which room?" he asked threateningly, pausing.

"Yours!" she yelled, half angry at his manhandling and yet unable to keep from laughing.

"That's better."

He began taking quick, hungry little tastes of her lips, spacing his words between the kisses. "I'll . . . think . . . of you . . . sleeping . . . in my . . . bed . . ."

"I'll be sleeping in my own bed," she contradicted softly, wrapping her arms around his neck and returning the pressure of his lips so that the succession of brief kisses lengthened into one that went on and on until they were both breathing in shallow gasps and she no longer was standing on her own feet but was being held up against him so that she felt the burgeoning thrust of his arousal and his need for her.

Ah, Daniel, she whispered silently in her head, *How can you go away and leave me when we have this together?* But the time was not right to say it aloud.

He picked her up easily and carried her into his bedroom and stood her on the floor beside the bed. She remained standing, quiescent, while he pulled the skimpy cotton stretch top over her head and then bent and kissed her breasts with lingering attention.

While he savored the firm roundness of the curves his hands were busy unsnapping the waistband of her shorts and sliding down the zipper. He bent lower and pushed the shorts down past her slim hips, kissing her bared abdomen and exploring her belly button with his tongue.

Next he removed the wispy nylon of her bikini panties and stayed a moment longer on his knees, shaping the graceful curves of her hips and pressing his lips to her rounded thighs.

There were times, when they made love, that they tore off their clothes in a frenzy of urgency, as they had that night on the beach. Then other times, like tonight, they lingered over the process of disrobing, prolonging it like a connoisseur of art slowly pushing aside the curtain concealing a masterpiece.

Sydney took as much delight in Daniel's body as he did in hers, reveling in the masculine symmetry and the hard resilience of his flesh under her hands, the crisp, springy texture of the hair on his forearms and chest and legs.

"You're beautiful!" he exulted when she was completely naked.

"So are you," she murmured, high atop a wave of sensual pleasure. She could rely on him completely to attend to her physical needs as well as his own when they made love. Without fail he raised her to heights of exquisite pleasure and at times it was transcendent, taking them beyond time and space to a sensory plane excruciating and maddening in its intensity. Tonight was such a night.

Sydney clung to him desperately during the final, wild leap into nothing, her head exploding with colors of such brilliance that she felt like a human fireworks display.

"Daniel, Daniel," she murmured, going limp against him afterward, her heart a poor runaway beast slowly tiring after an arduous journey.

When they had lain together for some minutes and she felt her pulse and heartbeat return to normal, she pulled away from him, turned over on her stomach and rose up on her elbows so that she could look at his face. She wanted to see his reaction when she asked him.

"Daniel, would you marry me?"

Heavy eyelids snapped back to reveal startled dark eyes. He stared at her face, which was still a little dazed with passion.

"Are you serious?"

"Yes, I'm serious. Just think—if we were married, I wouldn't have to get dressed and go home in a little while. It would be perfectly acceptable for us to sleep together all the time."

The answer, not at all her only reason for suggesting marriage between them, came out sounding more whimsical than she had intended. He pushed himself upward against the headboard of the bed so that he was half lying and half sitting. His expression convinced her that he didn't think she was as earnest as she was, but he didn't seem amused, either.

"I really am serious, Daniel. I've been thinking about the idea and it has all sorts of advantages for all of us. We could all live in this wonderful house— you and me and Kevin and Stacy and Cora. You would have the kids you've always wanted—they're crazy about you—and they would have someone who was a father in fact, not just in name. You wouldn't have to go away and leave this place you're so fond of."

She searched his face anxiously for some sign of enthusiasm and disappointingly found none. He lay so that one leg was pressed against her side, but mentally he had retreated somewhere far away.

"We'd all live happily ever after."

The undertone of irony stung her. She sat up. "Why not? We certainly have enough going for us, don't we? You and I may not have stardust in our eyes, but look what that got us the first time around." A feeling of apprehension spread through Sydney. She had thought Daniel would like this whole idea as much as she did. How had she so misread him?

"What if Larry decides he wants you and the kids back? What happens to me then?"

She saw a ray of hope. If that was what was bothering Daniel she could reassure him without fail. "Larry all but told me the night of the party at the Parkers that he'd like us to get back together. He called the following afternoon to try to see me— remember the afternoon we all had the cookout here on the beach? I refused. I let him think I was having an affair with you, and I wasn't then. He hasn't bothered me since. That's all over, Daniel."

The eager rush of her words was doing nothing to soften the remoteness of his expression, she saw with despair.

"What if we get married and later I'm transferred? The East or West Coast, Scotland, Scandinavia, even an Arab country?" he asked quietly.

Sydney drew back, a small frown creasing her brow. Why was he needlessly complicating matters like this? Her tone was both beseeching and a bit accusing when she spoke.

"The kids' schools, my job, my parents . . ." Didn't he see all the reasons why they should remain here?

"That's what I thought. In other words, I can be

your husband and Kevin and Stacy's father as long as I can live here with all of you in this house. Under any other circumstances, I'm on my own again. No thanks, Sydney. That's not my idea of marriage."

The curt finality of his words slashed through her like a razor's edge, overwhelming her with pain and disappointment. He was being totally unreasonable, letting all of them down.

"I don't understand you, Daniel," she said, trying to hide her hurt.

"No, I don't think you do. Not if you think I'd be willing to marry you on those terms. Why, I'd be little more than a live-in lover. Flattering as the idea may be, it's not enough." He sounded weary, as though he was tired of the whole subject.

Sydney got up from the bed and silently began putting on her clothes. Nothing had prepared her for this reaction to the suggestion which, to her, had seemed so eminently practical and reasonable. How could she know a man so well and yet not know him at all? Suddenly she wanted *him* to bleed a little, too.

"I don't think it's fair for you to get us all so fond of you, so used to having you around, and then up and leave—just like *that!*" She snapped her fingers for emphasis.

He swung his legs over the side of the bed and stood up slowly, as if he was old and his joints and muscles were stiff. His voice sounded as if speaking were a monumental effort, too. "I suppose you're right. It isn't fair. Not to you and the kids—nor to me."

Immediately, Sydney regretted the impulsive outburst, but it was too late now to recall it. She had her pride to consider. During the following days and weeks, she would come to regret it even more and to recall time and again his reply.

He called and visited with far less frequency and then hardly at all. Eventually she saw him only when she took advantage of the fact that she would occupy his house after he had moved. She dropped by on one excuse or another, hoping to find him there.

When she first suspected he was gradually removing himself from her life and the children's she longed to confront him directly and beg him to disregard what she had said. She hadn't really meant it. She missed him already, and so did Kevin and Stacy. Surely he missed them, too, or he wouldn't have become so enmeshed in all their lives in the first place. He must have needed their companionship and affection as much as they needed his.

Only pride kept her from voicing these feelings to Daniel. It wasn't every day a woman proposed marriage to a man and was so bluntly refused. Her sense of rejection was severe, undermining her confidence where he was concerned. She always found herself arriving at the appalling conclusion that he was still in love with his first wife and the prospect of marrying another woman was unendurable to him.

By the end of June, when four weeks had passed, what she had suspected was happening was painfully evident. Daniel no longer telephoned or made overtures to indicate any interest in spending time in her company. In her heart she echoed the sentiments of Kevin and Stacy when they voiced their puzzlement and disappointment that Daniel never visited them or invited them to his house anymore.

Kevin, especially, was disconsolate at the absence of his mentor, and Sydney's heart ached for him when he lamented, "But, Mom, Daniel didn't finish telling me about the T-formation—and a lot of other stuff."

How could she tell her son that *she* was to blame for the cessation of Daniel's attentions to all of them?

With the advent of blistering July weather real estate activity quieted, as it usually did after the hectic pace of spring, and she had more time to think. Her emotions seemed to change from day to day. The deep, guilty awareness that she had deprived her children, as well as herself, of Daniel's presence during his last two months in this country gradually changed to resentment. Daniel was the one at fault. He was being cruel and unreasonable, cutting them out of his affections this way as though they had never really mattered to him. Then her resentment strengthened into anger, and she decided one day she had taken the silent treatment from him long enough.

Early one Saturday morning during the second week of July she drove to Daniel's house, her lips compressed and her shoulders squared with righteous purpose. There was only one way she could let him know the extent of her deep sense of having been wronged. It might appear to be a classic case of "cutting off her nose to spite her face," but she planned to do it anyway.

He was home. The doors of the garage stood partially ajar, revealing his car. But there was no answer when she stood just outside the screen door at the rear entrance, the pungence of some familiar scent assailing her nostrils, and called his name. Holding firmly to her sense of purpose, she marched around the side of the house and, still seeing no sign of him, proceeded briskly down to the beach. When she neared the point where the grass ended and the sand began she saw him off to the right, strolling slowly in her direction and obviously unaware as yet of her presence.

She stopped involuntarily and watched him, her heart pounding traitorously at the sight of him, wet and clothed only in the black nylon swimsuit. He had been out for an early morning swim before the sun warmed the lake and was returning to the house, his gaze directed somewhere in front of his feet, his whole demeanor one of somber introspection.

At least he didn't look any happier than she felt these days, but, surprisingly, the observation gave her little satisfaction. And then he glanced up and saw her. It might have been her imagination, but his feet seemed momentarily to falter.

Neither of them spoke until he had come closer and stopped about ten yards away from her, and he was the one to break the silence. She'd be damned if she intended to behave as though this was a pleasant social visit.

"This is a surprise. It's good to see you." The words appeared to cost him some effort in the speaking.

"Is it really?" Arched eyebrows emphasized her open skepticism. "Why do you deny yourself the pleasure, then?"

He neither flinched from the scathing sarcasm of her tone nor lowered his eyes from hers. "You know the answer to that."

"Oh, do I?"

Now that she was here facing him, Sydney was gripped with powerful emotions that played havoc with her determination. He looked so dear and familiar and so somber that she bitterly regretted the great gulf separating them and at the same time wished she had never met Daniel Bates. Hadn't she been perfectly happy with her life before he barged into it, all six and a half feet and two hundred plus pounds of him?

Taking a deep breath, she steeled her resolution. "I came here for one reason only, Daniel, and that's to inform you that I don't intend to live in your house. You can just find another caretaker!"

He was staring at her disbelievingly. "Sydney, you're not serious?"

"I'm telling you I *won't* live in your house!" she said shrilly, fighting against the threat of tears.

"It's damned considerate of you to change your mind after I've spent almost ten grand getting this place ready to meet your specifications."

Sydney stared at him, taken aback by the raised level of his voice and the barely restrained violence in his whole demeanor. She had never seen Daniel like this. His hands were clenched into fists at his side, as though he would like to smash something into pieces, and his face was twisted with rage.

"I can change my mind if I want to," she said defiantly, lifting her chin.

"You can, can you?" he shouted.

She wondered if he was going to hit her as he charged across the distance between them. Grasping one of her arms, he didn't even pause in his progress across the lawn toward the house. His fingers hurt, biting brutally into the flesh of her arm right to the bone. She had to take rapid, running steps to keep up with him or else resign herself to being dragged along behind him, for she sensed there would be no pity in him at this moment. He was too angry.

"You're *hurting* me, Daniel!" she protested breathlessly as he mounted the steps of the veranda and pushed her through the open screen door.

She stumbled into the hallway and managed to come to a halt without losing her balance completely. At first she was too overcome with the turmoil of her emotions to notice her surroundings. She stood rubbing the bruised flesh of her upper arm and wondering what Daniel intended to do to her. He had come inside, too, and was regarding her with an expression that promised further violence.

Meanwhile her brain dealt with the sensory message her nostrils automatically relayed. The faint odor she had smelled earlier was much stronger in here, and it was . . . paint. Looking around her, she saw that the walls and ceilings were freshly painted in the soft cream color she had chosen, and the beaded wainscoting had received a coat of varnish.

"But you weren't supposed—you didn't *have* to—" she stammered, turning toward Daniel, who had been regarding her in grim silence while she gazed around her at the evidence of his work.

He gestured peremptorily toward the open living room door behind her and she turned slowly, a rising sense of premonition warning her of what she would see in there. It, too, had been painted, and not just any color, but the dusky rose she had selected from the paint charts weeks ago.

Too overwhelmed to say anything, she followed him to the dining room and kitchen and to the other rooms on the ground floor, a large bedroom she planned to be Cora's and a huge old-fashioned bathroom as big as most bedrooms in a modern house. All the rooms had been painted according to her wishes and the bathroom renovated so that the major portion of it was a private bath adjoining Cora's room and the remainder a half bath accessible for general use from the hallway.

Cora had never complained of having to share a

bathroom with the children as she presently had to do, but Sydney had decided to provide a more private arrangement for her in Daniel's house. This bedroom had other attractive features, too, including large casement windows overlooking the lake and a door opening out onto the veranda.

It occurred to Sydney now just how selfish she had been in dashing over here today and telling Daniel she had changed her mind about living in his house. She had given no thought to what she would be denying the other members of her household. Her motive had been to exact revenge, and it had backfired in her face.

"When did you do all this?" she asked in a chastened voice as she followed him back into the hallway.

"I'm on vacation this whole month," he said briefly. The anger and threat of violence had dissipated, but the grimness was still there in his voice and countenance.

Sydney watched him mount the first few steps of the staircase, believing he was dismissing her without any further word. She stood rooted to the spot, overwhelmed by her despair and yet unwilling to have them part like this, with no friendly exchange, no expression of gratitude from her, no forgiveness from him, no admission from either of them that they missed what they had had together.

He stopped and looked back over his shoulder and she realized that he expected her to follow him. For one unreasoning second hope flared up in her heart and it pounded wildly, sending a gush of blood through her veins.

"I haven't finished all the upstairs rooms yet."

Her spirit collapsed like a pricked balloon. She

could feel her hopes oozing out of a hole inside her as she followed Daniel up the stairs into the bedrooms she had designated as Kevin's and Stacy's. These were repainted, but the upstairs bathroom she would share with them, Daniel's room, which would be hers, and the remaining bedroom were not yet painted.

"If you'll excuse me, I'll put on some clothes," he said in the same terse, controlled voice when she had inspected the rooms her children would occupy, Stacy's a cheerful yellow and Kevin's a vivid blue. They had been allowed to choose the colors themselves at Daniel's suggestion.

"The blue's too gaudy!" she had demurred when she pointed out Kevin's selection on the chart.

Daniel had only grinned and shrugged. "He's the one who has to live with it. And the great thing about paint is that it isn't permanent."

The final effect wasn't as bad as she had feared; the spacious size of the room and the height of the ceiling prevented the bright blue walls from closing in the way she had thought they would.

She waited for Daniel out on the landing at the head of the stairs, her mind a jumble of questions. Why had he gone to all this trouble and work and additional expense to get the house ready for her and the kids? Was it because he cared for them? Or was there some more practical reason, perhaps the desire to see that the house was lived in and protected as soon as possible after he had left.

Sydney had anticipated that it would take her at least a month, perhaps even two, to get all the painting and renovation done. Now she wouldn't have to wait at all, just have the movers come in and transfer her furniture and possessions.

It was obvious to her when Daniel emerged from his room that he was dressed for another day of work, having donned faded and paint-spattered denim jeans and a short-sleeved cotton shirt whose shirt-tails hung loose and whose top three buttons were unfastened, giving a glimpse of his chest. The sight of it aroused disturbing memories of her intimate explorations of those powerful, hair-matted contours and her hands clenched involuntarily, the palms tingling.

He looked so tall and big and cleanly male that something ached inside her at the thought of how soon he would be gone halfway across the world. It was really true that he was leaving, that she would have to face the business of living without him. Some recalcitrant part of her had been clinging to the hope that he would change his mind and decide to stay, if not here, at least in the New Orleans area, where he would be able to see her and the children. But he wasn't going to change his mind. *Dear God, he wasn't going to change his mind!*

The refrain echoing inside her brain made it impossible for her to speak until they had descended the stairs. "I insist on paying for all the paint and varnish and materials. It's the least I can do," she said finally, stopping in the middle of the hallway. She hoped he would give her some excuse to linger, offer her a cup of coffee, suggest they sit on the veranda and enjoy the morning coolness. She didn't want to get into her car and drive away and leave him.

But he walked around her, giving her a wide berth and leaving her little choice except to follow him reluctantly to the back door, which he held open. She passed through it and walked down the steps.

"I really insist on paying you back," she said, just

to have an excuse to stop and turn around and look at him.

He lifted his broad shoulders in an indifferent movement. "You can if you really insist, but it's not necessary. I don't want your money. I don't need it."

"But that wasn't in our agreement!" The fervor of her protest was entirely unrelated to the words. She didn't care one way or another about the money herself. What she was really crying out against was the inevitability of the future. She wanted to say, *Daniel, don't go away and leave me! Please, Daniel, don't!*

He didn't look at her directly as he elaborated or give any indication that he perceived the real reason for her agitation. "I did the work because I wanted to. I had the time and needed something to do with it. As for the money, it's of no consequence. My parents are dead. My wife makes more money than I do so I don't have to pay her alimony. If you make it a point of honor to pay me I'll be forced to take it, but I'd prefer you to buy something for Kevin and Stacy and consider it a gift from me."

His tone and manner were as distant as they had been that first day she saw him, the day she drove up in Cora's shabby blue Fairlane wearing a dowdy disguise. It seemed like years ago.

"Do you have anything in particular to suggest?" she asked out of sheer doggedness, prolonging the conversation, dissatisfying as it was, just so she could stand there gazing at his half-averted profile and noting its rugged strength.

"Something for their new rooms, perhaps, or fishing gear. Whatever."

He looked at her directly for the first time since they had come outside, his dark eyes flicking over her yellow polka-dotted halter top and solid yellow shorts and sliding quickly over bare slim legs to feet encased in flat sandals before returning to her face.

"Aren't you working today?"

She shrugged noncommittally, not having the nerve to admit the truth, that he would be the deciding factor one way or the other. She hadn't known that truth herself until just now.

"Things are slow this time of year."

He ignored the opening. Glancing at his wrist-watch, he shifted restlessly. "It gets hot during the day now. I don't mean to be rude, but I'd better get to work."

The dismissal was plain. Sydney made her departure hurriedly, fearful that the tears aching in the back of her throat and smarting painfully beneath her eyelids would break loose any second, and they did before she was out of the dim tunnel of his driveway. She stopped at the entrance and succumbed to the awful misery engulfing her body and soul. Never before in her life had she felt such raw pain as she felt now, such utter hopelessness for the future.

It wasn't until some minutes later when the deep, wrenching sobs had subsided and she was able to control herself enough to drive that she realized with a dull shock, *I feel worse at this moment than I did the day Larry told me he wanted a divorce,* and she'd wanted to die that day. Had her capacity for grief enlarged and deepened with maturity? Or was there something she hadn't faced up to before now?

Was she in love with Daniel even more deeply than she had ever been with Larry? If she were, it would explain the dreadful apathy that deadened her whole outlook on the future. It would explain why her work had lost all its charm for her so that only with the most rigorous discipline could she force herself to attend to its details. Not even a new listing or a sale had the power to lift her spirits.

By the time she reached her house Sydney had come to terms with the truth. If being in love with someone meant she couldn't bear to think of a future without him, well, she must be in love with Daniel. But he couldn't be in love with her because he wouldn't even consider changing his plan to work abroad in order to marry her, while *she* . . .

The train of her thoughts was suddenly clear to Sydney, and comprehension was like an electrical shock rippling through her nervous system. *Whereas she would uproot herself and her children and go anywhere with him!* Was it possible that she, who had sworn to remain self-supporting and independent for the rest of her life, was actually thinking like this? Would she really give up her work in real estate, even temporarily, if it became necessary? After all the hurt and anger and bitterness of divorce, would she again put herself in the care of a man?

Yes, she would.

The revelation was incredible, but irrefutable. Once she had accustomed herself to the notion that marriage to Daniel took precedence over everything else, even her all-important self-sufficiency, the question still remained—would Daniel want her if she came to him without any conditions whatever?

Slowly and painstakingly, she recreated in her mind the evening when she had so confidently and casually proposed marriage to him. He hadn't refused point-blank at first. He had asked questions, which now aroused a tiny flare of hope in her breast. She had brushed the questions aside or bristled at them, particularly the one that probed into the way she would react if he were transferred to work somewhere else.

Not once had she mentioned her affection for him, her belief at the time that she loved him but wasn't *in love* with him. Looking back now, she could understand his negative reaction much better than she had at the time. He thought she was offering him a temporary and highly conditional relationship that would end any time it did not suit her convenience. And indeed, hadn't she been offering him just that? It had taken his refusal and the subsequent loss of his companionship to awaken her to the depth of her feelings for him.

How, though, was she to determine his own feelings? Unless she made the effort herself, she wouldn't even see him again. If she went to him and told him she loved him, chances were he would only reject her again. He might very well still be in love with Deborah, whom he had referred to as his *wife*, not ex-wife, that very morning.

That was a chance Sydney would have to take.

She had been sitting in her car in the driveway for heaven knows how long thinking her way through the maze of her emotions, and without any further hesitation she backed out, intending to return to Daniel's house and confront him with all she had discovered about herself and her feelings. In her urgency to reach him she drove faster than she normally did, exceeding the speed limit. Why did everybody on the highway seem to be driving so *slow* today, she wondered irritably, zooming around a large car towing a motor home.

Normally she slowed down a little at this particular intersection where four lanes cut across Highway 190 and there was always the danger of cars darting across in front of her even though she had the right of way. She saw the van with its lurid blue and silver paint job, noted that it was approaching the intersection too fast, but she couldn't stop now. All she could do was press down on her horn and hope it didn't keep coming.

He's not going to stop! I'm going to hit him!

The sickening realization flashed in on her brain like a blinding light, and she hit the brake even though it would do no good. The collision was unavoidable.

"Daniel!" she screamed with all the power of her lungs as her car plunged into the broad silver and blue blur in front of her. There was the crunch of metal against metal, the explosion of breaking glass, pain, and then nothing more.

Chapter Nine

"Well, well. Look who's finally decided to wake up!" Dr. Powers chided from the foot of Sydney's hospital bed, his keen professional gaze touching her wan features and then dropping to study the chart in his hands.

Sydney's mind struggled to form questions which vaguely troubled her, but the effort was too arduous and she let her heavy lids sink down again. Maybe later . . .

By the following afternoon she was able to remain awake for longer periods and form coherent thoughts. She learned then, to her surprise and dismay, that she had been in the hospital over a week, most of that time in a coma. Dr. Powers and the hospital staff considered her "a very lucky young lady" and constantly assured her she was "doing great." She'd suffered a concussion, broken ribs and internal injuries, including a punctured lung.

"It'll take you a bit to get back on your feet," Dr. Powers warned several days after the first time he found her conscious when he made evening rounds.

"Why doesn't anyone come to see me?" she asked weakly.

He made some joking remark. Later she learned she had been in intensive care and hadn't been allowed visitors. In seeking to put her mind at rest, though, he said something that puzzled her greatly.

"Don't you worry about a thing except getting well. That fiancé of yours tells me everything is fine with your children, and some of the other agents are taking care of things for you with your real estate work. You just concentrate on getting well."

"My fiancé?"

Dr. Powers was busy jotting something down and giving the nurse accompanying him some instructions about a change in Sydney's medication. She had to ask again.

"Did you say my *fiancé?*"

He laughed his jovial laugh. "Don't tell me that crack on the head made you forget a man *that* big?"

She guessed then that he must be talking about Daniel. But how had Dr. Powers come to think Daniel was her fiancé? In the days to follow she learned the answer to that and other questions.

After she was moved to a semiprivate room she was finally permitted visitors. The first was her mother, who came by during the early-afternoon visiting period when her father was at work. Pauline fussed over Sydney in the way of a worried mother who feels helpless and wants to *do* something for her injured child. Sydney allowed her to comb her hair and dress her in the pretty lacy bedjacket she had brought.

Pauline, like everyone else, insisted Sydney must

not "worry about a thing" and made vague comments that greatly puzzled her. Pauline had been "a little hurt that Sydney hadn't confided in her, her own mother," but she and Fred were both "happy" for Sydney. They were sure Daniel would make "a wonderful husband and father." Pauline said her instincts had told her that from the first.

"Mom, what are you talking about?" Sydney finally managed to ask, growing impatient with the constant stream of chatter.

Pauline looked coy. "*You* know. It's not a secret anymore. Daniel's told everybody that you two are planning to get married. He's already—" She slapped a hand over her mouth. "But I'm not supposed to tell you that. I almost let the cat out of the bag."

A nurse whisked in at about that time and, after a discerning glance at Sydney's face, ushered Pauline away. Sydney slept most of the afternoon, but when she did awaken she puzzled over what her mother had said. Why had Daniel told everyone, including Dr. Powers, that he was marrying her when he wasn't?

She awoke in the early evening and found him there beside her bed, looking down at her. From the unguarded expression on his face, which mirrored deep concern, she realized she must look ghastly.

"Daniel," she murmured, her heart overflowing with gladness at the sight of him, so big and dear and dependable.

He took the frail hand she held out in both of his huge strong ones and bent to kiss her gently on the cheek. "You had us all worried there for a while," he said huskily, remaining outwardly bent over in order to maintain his hold on her hand.

"Here. Sit down by me," she urged, trying to move herself over further on the bed.

"No, don't do that." The firm command in his voice stopped her. "I'll just bring that chair over there up closer." He sat in the chair after he had moved it next to her bed and took her hand again, stroking it reassuringly.

"How are the kids and Cora?"

"They're great. Worried about you, of course. Anxious to have you back home."

"Not as anxious as I am."

At that particular moment, though, she wasn't anxious about anything. The warm contact of Daniel's flesh was like an injection of courage flowing into Sydney's body, giving her strength and hope. She intended to ask him more questions in a little while, but right now she was content to listen to the deep, resonant flow of his voice as he related a few incidents involving Kevin and Stacy. He didn't really have to tell her everything was all right with her household while she was lying helpless in the hospital. If he was looking out for her children and Cora she knew they were safe.

It must have been the medication she was taking, because in spite of her most determined efforts to stay awake she felt her lids drooping traitorously. The next time she awoke, Daniel was gone. *Oh, I meant to ask him*, she thought, and went back to sleep.

He came to see her every day after that first visit. She lived for the time when he would appear in the doorway, seeming to take up every inch of the large retangular opening.

"I was surprised to learn I had a fiancé," she said the second day, beginning to feel stronger and able to stay awake for hours at a time.

"I hope you don't mind. There were some practical reasons for me to assert myself as something more than just a friend."

He had obviously been expecting the question and was prepared for it. His explanation was not the one she would have liked to hear, but she trusted him implicitly and decided to wait until she was closer to being well and better able to cope with the thought of resuming her life before she probed any deeper into his reasons for the pretense.

At the end of her third week in the hospital she began to grow irritable and impatient with the slow business of convalescence. "I want to go home," she announced to everyone, including Dr. Powell. By the end of the fourth week he assented, giving her stern instructions to limit her activities and dire warnings of the consequences if she failed to heed his orders.

The day she left the hospital she learned one of the "practical reasons" why Daniel had posed as her fiancé. With the help of Cora, he had taken it upon himself to move all Sydney's furniture and possessions into his house.

The reasons he gave were so eminently practical she could find no fault with them. The house was ready for her occupancy. Why should her money be spent on rent when there was no need for it? And it would be months before she would feel up to the rigors of moving. Kevin and Stacy would be starting back to school in a couple of weeks, and it would be advantageous for them to be settled in their new home.

On the evening of her first day away from the hospital she mustered the courage to ask Daniel what had been bothering her with increasing urgency. Up until then she just hadn't had the nerve to ask because she didn't feel up to coping with what the answer might be.

At her cajoling he had carried her into the living room where she lay propped up on pillows on the sofa and watched television with the children for a while. Before long, though, he insisted it was time for her to go back to bed.

"Could we talk for just a minute," she wheedled when he had taken her back to her room, the capacious downstairs bedroom she had designated as Cora's.

"Just for a minute," he agreed reluctantly, smoothing the covers with all the competency of a professional nurse and then sitting on the edge of her bed.

She swallowed, trying to alleviate the lump of nervousness in her throat. "Daniel, when are you leaving for the North Sea?"

"Are you in such a big hurry to get rid of me?" he evaded teasingly.

"You know better than that. I never wanted you to leave at all. But you said you were leaving in August . . ."

He picked up a hand that had clenched into a fist on top of the covers and smoothed out the tense fingers. "I don't think you should worry about any of this now. It's too soon. But I don't intend to go anywhere until you're completely well, unless you want me to."

That news was enormously soothing, but she wasn't content to drop the subject. She had to know more.

"But what did you tell your company? I mean, how did you get out of going when you were supposed to? Weren't they depending on you?"

He hesitated, looking at her as if debating her

readiness to hear the truth. The fingers he had smoothed out clutched at his hand, and that pressure seemed to help him to decide.

"I told them I was going to get married. The job I was taking is strictly single status. Not even an oil company expects a man to stay away from his wife for two years."

Sydney was quiet, one part of her wondering why she wasn't more surprised at what he had revealed. Another one of those "practical reasons" for pretending to be engaged to her.

"Won't they be upset when you tell them you aren't getting married after all?"

He sighed. "Couldn't this wait until you're feeling stronger? There's plenty of time."

"Please," she begged. "I won't be able to sleep wondering about it. I wouldn't want you to get into trouble because of me."

His dark eyes noted the anxiety in hers, which were huge indigo orbs in her pale face. "I was hoping I wouldn't have to tell them that. Unless you're no longer agreeable to the idea of marrying me."

Sydney was too stunned at first to speak. Why had he changed his mind? Why was he now willing to marry her on terms that had not been acceptable to him before, since as far as he knew nothing had changed in her attitude toward him? She had been on the way to tell him she loved him and would go anywhere in the world with him when she had had the accident.

Now he apparently interpreted her silence as indecision. "Don't worry about it," he said gently, raising her hand briefly to his lips. "There'll be time enough to make up your mind when you're feeling better. My job is secure no matter what you decide."

"I don't have to make up my mind," she protested quickly. "I still want to marry you."

"Good. Then it's settled."

His tone was that of an adult soothing a child. It wasn't the way she wanted Daniel to talk to her, and it raised a host of doubts as to his motives for changing his mind about marrying her.

"No, it's not settled," she objected. "You're just feeling sorry for me, aren't you?" Tears welled up in her eyes and spilled over onto her cheeks. "I look like a skinny scarecrow and goodness knows when I'll be strong enough to go back to work."

She jerked her hand away from him and put it, along with the other one, over her face. The deep, choking sobs hurt her chest, but she couldn't seem to stop them.

Daniel muttered a savage curse. "Please don't do that, Sydney. You've got it all wrong. I don't feel sorry *for* you. Just sorry that it happened at all. That you've suffered so much pain. God, I could kick myself for giving in against my better judgment and talking about this tonight."

The self-condemnation in his voice helped her to control her emotions. "Don't blame yourself," she said huskily, wiping away the tears with the top of the sheet. "It's probably just an inevitable hysterical reaction. I'm feeling sorry for myself tonight. It would have happened if we'd been talking about the weather."

He wasn't convinced, not even when she managed to produce a watery smile.

"Are you going to be okay now?"

"I'm fine," she lied.

He leaned over and kissed her tenderly on a mouth that still quivered. Then he stood up, regarding her with somber eyes. She could tell he was still worried about her.

"I think I'll go to sleep now." Her tired, drowsy tone was genuine. She was only vaguely aware of him leaving the room.

Neither of them brought up the subject of marriage after that, but Sydney could think of little else during the following days. Why had he changed his mind? Time and again she arrived at the same conclusion: Daniel must be acting out of a kind, protective instinct. He was fond of her and the children, of Cora as well, and he must have decided that marrying Sydney would be best for all of them. They needed him.

At one time Sydney would have accepted him gladly on those terms, and she probably wouldn't be able to refuse him now when the time came. But she longed for more.

Inevitably, he asked the question she had been expecting. "Sydney, where were you going the day you had the accident?"

How could she tell him the truth without making him feel responsible for the accident? Aside from not wanting him to feel guilty, though, she had other reasons for not telling him. The day she had been hurrying to pour out the discovery that she loved him and would marry him on any terms he chose, she had been strong and healthy and self-sufficient. Now she was a frail, wretched creature who would arouse pity in the heart of any compassionate man. She didn't want Daniel's pity, so she told him a lie.

"Oh, just to the store to get a few things. Some shampoo, stuff like that."

Days and weeks passed and she grew stronger. Gradually she put on weight and began to feel less like a scarecrow. Daniel commuted to work in the city each day. The children went back to school. During the day Sydney had Cora for company plus visits from her mother and agents from the office.

Pauline Cullen brought up the subject Sydney and Daniel had tabled since the first evening Sydney got out of the hospital.

"When are you and Daniel getting married?"

Something restrained in her mother's manner warned Sydney that the question wasn't just a straightforward bid for information.

"We haven't really discussed it. Why?"

Pauline patted the tight curls of her new permanent in a nervous, characteristic gesture. "I just wondered, that's all. You'll be getting back to normal pretty soon, driving and going out where people will see you've recovered from that terrible accident . . ."

It came clear, then, what her mother was getting at. Pauline was worried about what people would say. Sydney was living in the house of a man who wasn't her husband, and he was still living there, too. Apparently Pauline didn't consider Cora chaperone enough to prevent gossip.

Sydney's first reaction was to get angry, but in all fairness she couldn't really blame her mother. The people in this area, people who were Pauline and Fred's neighbors and friends, settled, stable people, not the transient executive types, were conservative in their moral outlook and undoubtedly would look askance at Sydney's present situation, innocent as it was. Daniel slept upstairs in his old room, while Sydney had her room and bath downstairs.

Not for anything would Sydney cause her parents unpleasantness on her account. And there were the children to consider, too. Their classmates wouldn't hesitate to repeat any ugly gossip they heard at home.

Still Sydney did not bring up the subject with Daniel, finding the situation extremely awkward. And then there was no need because everything had changed.

Several days after the conversation with her mother Sydney got her new car, the Volvo having been completely totalled in the accident. In her excitement at being able to drive again and to go to the real estate office for short periods she didn't pay much attention to Daniel's increasing moodiness as she might otherwise have done.

One Saturday late in September Daniel had a visitor. At the time she arrived, he was walking down on the beach with Kevin and Stacy. Sydney, in the habit of sleeping late since her accident, had just gotten up and was sitting out on the veranda drinking a cup of coffee, basking in the sunshine. She still wore her nightgown and robe and upon rising had taken the time only to brush her hair and wash her face.

Hearing the sound of an automobile at the rear of the house Sydney didn't bother to move, thinking that whoever it was would come up to the back door and knock. Cora was back in the kitchen and would answer the door.

It came as an unexpected shock to see a small, blonde woman stroll past the veranda with the utmost confidence, headed for the beach, where Daniel was in full sight with Kevin and Stacy walking on either side of him.

Sydney stared at the stranger, who wore a crimson slacks suit that emphasized every curve of her tiny, perfect figure. Almost intuitively she knew she was looking at Deborah, Daniel's ex-wife.

The woman must have caught a peripheral glimpse of Sydney because she stopped abruptly and swung to face the veranda. "Who're you?" she demanded as though Sydney were a trespasser on her property.

Sydney wished desperately she had taken the time to dress and make up her face. Never in her life had she felt quite so dowdy as she did now in the presence of this exquisite woman, every detail of whose dress, makeup and coiffure was perfect. And to make Sydney's discomfort worse, she could see in the distance that Daniel was headed toward the veranda. He had seen the visitor.

"I'm Sydney Cullen. I live here," she told the woman with all the dignity she could summon. "Who're you?"

"Deborah Bates." The answer was delivered like a challenge, and then with a dismissive glance at Sydney, Daniel's ex-wife turned her attention to the three people approaching from the beach.

"I see Daniel has found himself a brood."

The sardonic remark came to Sydney's ears as she was escaping into the house, not bothering to excuse herself with normal courtesy since the situation was far from normal and Deborah Bates was ignoring her as though she didn't exist. There was simply no way Sydney could bear to remain there and have Daniel walk up and see her looking like some poor hag next to the chic woman he had married, the one who *had* been his type.

When she emerged from her room almost an hour later, her hair shampooed, her face carefully made up and her tall figure elegantly clad in dark blue slacks and a long-sleeved silk blouse of a paler blue, Sydney discovered that Deborah had already gone. The expression on Daniel's face took her sickeningly back to those times early in their relationship when they had shared with each other the disappointments of their broken marriages. Seeing Deborah again had evidently been a big shock for him, arousing painful memories of the past.

"I didn't know Deborah was coming here," he explained tersely. "She called and left a message at the office earlier in the week that she would be in New Orleans this weekend and would get in touch with me if she had time."

He hadn't bothered to mention any of that to Sydney, but now she could understand his moodiness the last few days. He had been thinking about Deborah.

"I hope she didn't think I was rude, but I had to get dressed and go down to the office this morning," Sydney lied, her pride forbidding that she tell him the real reason she had fled from the veranda so quickly.

Daniel frowned. "Aren't you already rushing things a little?"

"I can't wait to get back into the thick of things again," she declared. "I feel like I've been vegetating." She hadn't been feeling like that at all. On the contrary, she had been thinking she wouldn't let herself get as bogged down in real estate as she had been before the accident, but she felt a need now to let Daniel know he wasn't burdened with her any longer.

Sydney stayed longer at the office than she should have, arriving home in the afternoon so exhausted she went straight to bed and got up only long enough to eat supper. The next day she could feel the censure in Daniel's eyes when she got dressed and went off again, but he said nothing to reinforce what she knew herself—she *was* rushing things. But she had to. Some sense of foreboding warned her that the respite was over. For a brief time she had laid her heavy mantle of responsibility on Daniel's strong shoulders, but now she would have to take it back up again. If he had really intended to marry her, surely he would have mentioned the subject again by now.

Sunday night Daniel broke the news that he would be moving out of the house to an apartment in the city. She didn't argue with him or even question him as to his reasons. She knew already what they were, and she was so exhausted from her long day that she wanted nothing but to go to bed and sleep and forget everything, especially the fact that Daniel might be fond of her and the children, but he had never gotten over Deborah and probably never would.

"Will you still see us?" she asked him the next morning, her heart twisting unbearably at the thought of not seeing Daniel. Why couldn't he have learned to love her the way she loved him? *Why, why, why?* And yet, she reminded herself, he had been so good to her, to all of them, she mustn't do or say anything to make him feel worse than he probably already did. She mustn't make him think he was abandoning them. Whatever the cost to herself, she must try to act as if his leaving weren't tearing her apart.

"I don't know," he finally answered, his dark eyes full of pain as they met hers. "You'll have to give me some time."

That answer, when she thought of it later, seemed rather strange, but she tried not to dwell on it or on Daniel because her sense of loss was almost more than she could stand. As she had done once before when her life disintegrated, she immersed herself in work. And because her health was not fully recovered and she tired easily, the time she wasn't working was spent sleeping.

October and November passed and half of December. With the coming of the Christmas season, there was the usual lull in the real estate business, and Sydney had more time to herself, more time to try not to think about Daniel and the emptiness of her life.

And then, late one afternoon when she had gone over to the city to do Christmas shopping, she saw him. She was in Lakeside Shopping Center and had just emerged from a store into the congested mall when she heard her name and looked around to see Daniel striding toward her.

"Daniel!" she exclaimed softly. It was all she could do to prevent herself from throwing down the packages she held and reaching out her arms to him. Somehow she checked the crazy impulse and tried to restrain her joy, assuming the expression of someone who has accidentally run into an old friend.

"What a surprise," she said, smiling up into his face when he had stopped close to her.

"You look great, Sydney." His dark eyes took in the smart gray suit and high-heeled navy leather pumps, the color in her cheeks, the luster of her auburn hair.

"I'm back to normal," she declared, noticing that he was thinner than he had been before, his face gaunt and pale. "What about you, Daniel? Have you been ill?"

He shrugged. "I had a touch of flu. Mainly I've been working hard."

"Maybe you need some good advice about keeping a reasonable balance in your life," she chided, reminding him of the time he had lectured her on the same subject. "Do you have time for a cup of coffee?"

"Sure." He looked around them at the throngs of people. "How about the Crêperie? It should be about the quietest place."

She let him carry some of her parcels as they walked to the small restaurant at one end of the shopping center. It was crowded, too, but they managed to get a corner table.

Sydney would have been content just to sit there and look at him without carrying on a conversation, but he wanted to know about Stacy and Kevin and Cora, her mother and father, as well as about her. She answered all his questions, all the while thinking to herself how wonderful it was to see him again, to be in his company. Separation hadn't done anything to lessen the way she loved him.

"What about you, Daniel? Are you happy?" she asked anxiously. He didn't look happy. She wondered if he had seen Deborah again, or heard from her.

"Holiday seasons are lonely for people without families," he said abruptly and then looked as if he regretted having said it.

"Why don't you come over and have Christmas with us?" she invited impulsively. "I could use some help with the tree and decorating and all that. You could stay several days if you wanted. We have lots of room."

She was afraid at first that he was going to refuse. If he did, she might break down and cry in front of everybody. The images she had created in her own mind, all involving Daniel sharing Christmas with them, were so alluring that she couldn't bear to relinquish them. Her pride had abandoned her.

"Are you sure?"

"I can't think of anything I'd like better," she said simply, meeting his eyes without any attempt to hide what might be shining in hers.

"I accept, then."

He was the one to drop his glance and break the eye contact that had her heartbeat racing. She wasn't in any way prepared for what he said next.

"I'm being transferred out to the East Coast in June."

"Oh, no!" The words were out before she could stop them. "I mean, that's a long way away. Did you ask to go there?"

"No, but it's not really a bad assignment. I like New England." He hesitated. "Have you ever been up there?"

"No," she said ruefully. "I haven't really been anywhere. I meet so many people who've traveled and lived all over the country, sometimes I feel like a real provincial."

"Maybe you could come up and visit me. Bring the kids, too."

The suggestion was casual, but Sydney was desperate for any faint ray of hope. "They'd love it, poor darlings. I promised them a trip to Disney World in Florida this summer, and then I had the accident and they lost out."

Sydney mustered all her nerve and posed the question she had been wanting to ask. "Did you get into any trouble with your company for not getting married when you told them you were?"

His lips twisted in an ironic little smile. "As far as they know, I *am* married."

Sydney's eyes widened in amazement. "But wouldn't they *know*—I mean, you live over here—in an apartment—"

He shrugged. "It's a big city. Nobody has to know where I live. I was pretty much of a recluse before, and my colleagues just assume I drive back and forth across the Causeway every day. It's normal for a man to be attentive to a new wife."

Sydney's mind worked rapidly. "This new assignment, then, is family status?"

He nodded.

"But what if you get caught? Won't you be in trouble? They'll expect you to show up on the east coast with a wife, won't they?"

"It's a little touchy. I'll just have to get an imaginary divorce, I guess."

The whole story didn't make much sense to Sydney. She shook her head confusedly. "I just don't know why you didn't tell them the truth. That you were going to get married last summer and then it fell through. That's what happened, isn't it? You did intend to marry me and then you changed your mind."

"Something like that."

He obviously didn't want to discuss it any further, but Sydney wasn't willing to drop the subject. Back in the fall she should have pressed him for the reasons why he kept changing his mind about marrying her, but she hadn't had the courage at the time. First he wasn't and then he was and then he wasn't again. It wasn't like Daniel to be that capricious.

"Why *did* you change your mind, Daniel? Was it because Deborah showed up that day? Did you hope you might get back together with her some time in the future?"

He didn't answer, seeming to be distracted by a group of matronly women sitting down at the next table and all talking volubly at once. Then the waitress, having left the check on the table some minutes before, appeared to ask if there was something else they wanted. Sydney followed Daniel's glance and saw that there were people standing in the foyer of the restaurant waiting to be seated.

"Shall we go somewhere else?" he suggested with an impatient little frown cutting between his eyebrows at all the interruptions.

Sydney glanced at her watch and gave a horrified gasp. "Oh, my goodness, I had no idea it was this late. Kevin will never forgive me if I miss the Christmas program at school tonight. He's so proud that he has the main part."

There was no opportunity to continue the conversation as Daniel accompanied her through the crowds of shoppers to her car outside. He helped her stow her packages and admonished her to drive carefully in spite of her hurry.

"Can I tell the kids you're coming for Christmas?" she urged, wanting to commit him to the visit in some irrevocable way.

A smile touched his lips briefly. He wasn't fooled. "You can tell them. I'll telephone tomorrow night and make definite plans."

Sydney thought about the encounter with Daniel all the way across the Causeway. She played their conversation over and over in her mind. Part of her regretted that he had not answered her last question, while the coward in her gratefully accepted the reprieve. At least he had promised to have Christmas with them. It was something to look forward to with all her heart and soul, knowing that she must think in terms of grasping the moment and not depend on anything in the future.

"Guess who's coming to spend Christmas with us?" she told the two children that night after they had returned home from the Christmas program at Kevin's school.

Their enthusiasm was tempered with caution, as she had expected it to be, for Stacy especially had felt a sense of rejection when Daniel moved out of the house to the city two and a half months ago.

"But why isn't he marrying you like he said he was?" she had wanted to know.

"We *both* changed our minds," Sydney had explained, trying to take some of the responsibility upon herself so that Stacy wouldn't resent Daniel.

Kevin had been listening with troubled features. "Is it *our* fault, Mom, that Daniel didn't marry you? He said he wouldn't be my real dad."

"What?" Sydney had heard nothing of this before. "When did Daniel tell you that, Kevin?"

"Oh, Kevin, that's not what Daniel meant, and you know it," Stacy broke in with a big-sister tone guaranteed to irk her brother. "Mom, Kevin asked Daniel if he was going to be his father after you were married, and Daniel tried to explain to him that nobody except our dad could ever *really* be our father and we mustn't forget that."

Sydney had had to fight back tears of emotion. She could see the scene so clearly in her mind and hear Daniel, not willing to give a pat, dishonest explanation, even to a child. But Kevin apparently had not been wholly satisfied with the answer, and when Daniel left the boy had built up a private sense of guilt. Sydney did her best to alleviate his burden, assuring both of the children that Daniel did love them and her but had to go away for reasons she would explain when they were older.

For her children's sake she had also been forced to try to act as though she were not as devastated as she actually was by Daniel's departure. She didn't want them to have burned into their young minds the image of her as an abandoned, wretched woman. They had seen her grief after the separation with Larry and no doubt been aware of her unhappiness during the summer when Daniel had stopped seeing her before the accident.

"Why is Daniel spending Christmas with *us*?" Stacy wanted to know now.

"Yeah, why?" Kevin chimed in quickly.

It was a delicate situation for Sydney to handle. She wanted them both to welcome Daniel and enjoy his company, but she didn't want to leave them vulnerable to further hurt by allowing them to think Daniel was resuming his old relationship with all of them.

"Because I asked him to and he has no family of his own," she answered quietly.

Stacy hesitated. "He could have had *us* for a family," she said stiffly.

"Yeah, he could've," Kevin seconded.

Sydney didn't try to deny what was obviously irrefutable in their young minds. "Daniel is very fond of both of you," she assured them. "He wanted to know all about you when I saw him today. He's been sick lately and very busy with work. That's probably the main reason he hasn't been over to see us."

"He could have telephoned," Stacy put in stubbornly.

Sydney left the subject, confident that Daniel would be able to deal with it in person far better than she was doing now. He called the following evening to say he would arrive in the early afternoon on Christmas Eve and stay overnight, if that was agreeable to her. Before he hung up he asked if he could speak with Stacy and Kevin.

The conversation with each child wasn't long, but it effectively thawed their reserve about seeing him again.

"He has my picture of this house hung in his apartment," Stacy announced proudly afterward. "He said he wants to see what I've painted lately." With that, Stacy headed straight for the staircase on the way to her room and Sydney had a strong hunch about the reason for her hurry.

"Daniel asked about you, too," she told Cora, from whom she expected the greatest opposition to Daniel's visit. She didn't add that he had been delighted to hear that the older woman had a "friend," because Cora didn't welcome discussion of her courtship.

Basil Dunnings was the caretaker of the Humphries place farther down the beach. The owners lived in New Jersey and came down only for vacations during the year. A retired widower with married children, Basil lived rent-free in the garage apartment in exchange for keeping an eye on the place and maintaining the grounds. He also did gardening for several people in the Louisburg area, including Sydney, since Daniel had moved. Basil and Cora had met and apparently found much in common.

"What are you going to do if Cora ups and marries him?" Pauline, ever mindful of practical considerations, had wanted to know.

Sydney could only admit that it would inconvenience her, but she refused not to hope for whatever was best for Cora's happiness. The first strong hint that the friendship might be heading in a serious direction was Cora's rather terse announcement of her plans for celebrating Christmas. She and Basil would be spending Christmas Eve with his children and grandchildren on this side of the lake and Christmas day over in Metairie with her children and grandchildren.

Christmas Eve was cold and cloudy with a sharp wind blowing from the north. Daniel arrived and set to work putting up the tree Sydney had bought and had delivered from a tree farm in Folsum. In a surprisingly short time Daniel had Stacy and Kevin organized into work details. He might never have been gone at all, Sydney reflected with painful poignancy as she listened and watched and joined in the flurry of preparations.

They all traipsed through the woods gathering pine boughs and holly to decorate the mantel in the living room. When they returned Daniel built a fire in the fireplace while Sydney made hot chocolate. Before supper, they decorated the tree.

Sydney and Cora had gotten all the cardboard boxes of lights and ornaments down from the attic ahead of time. There were cries of recognition from Stacy and Kevin. "Hey, this is the rocking horse I painted in the first grade!" and "Mom, remember this gold angel! Miss Ethel brought it back to me from Germany!" For Sydney, a Christmas tree was a family chronicle, not an artistic creation to impress those who viewed it. From year to year, the collection of ornaments grew, some of them homemade by her and the children and some of them gifts. Decorating the tree was a poignant experience for her, bringing back other Christmases and reminding her of the growth of her children from one stage to another.

She was glad to be able to share the time with

Daniel. He strung the lights first and then obliged them by hanging ornaments according to their various instructions on the higher branches.

"Gosh! You don't even have to have a ladder!" Kevin marvelled.

"Isn't it beautiful!" Sydney exclaimed when the last piece of tinsel had been draped across the branches. She had never lost her childhood enchantment with Christmas trees and always felt this same sense of delight. She could never understand why some people considered Christmas trees too much trouble.

They ate supper in the dining room rather than in the kitchen. Afterward everyone pitched in to clear the table and carry the leftover food and dishes to the kitchen. Then they disappeared in different directions and presents began appearing as if by magic under the tree.

"Have you always opened your gifts on Christmas Eve?" Daniel asked, encountering Sydney at the bottom of the stairs and taking several wrapped packages off the top of the tall stack she carried.

"Yes. When the kids were younger Larry and I saved some toys for Santa Claus to deliver on Christmas morning. But since we went over to my parents' house on Christmas day, our special family time at home was Christmas Eve. What about you?"

He followed her into the living room where they spread the packages under the tree. "As you know, I was an only child and my parents were older. They always regarded holidays with forebearance more than anything else. Oh, I got presents, of course."

Sydney felt a pang of sympathy for the small boy whose picture he conjured up for her, but the conversation was interrupted by the entrance of Stacy and Kevin. With a great deal of giggling they made a production of adding their own packages to those under the tree.

"You two want to take turns handing out the presents?" Sydney inquired needlessly and immediately received enthusiastic replies. "I get as excited as they do about opening presents," she admitted to Daniel, standing beside him in front of the fire.

His dark eyes slid admiringly over her. She had changed for the evening into a hostess-style pyjama outfit of dull gold velvet. Her cheeks were pink with excitement and her blue eyes sparkled with animation.

"Here, Mom. This is for you from dad."

Kevin handed her a small square package which turned out to be perfume. She opened it without any self-consciousness or emotion other than pleasure.

"How is Larry these days?" Daniel asked in an undertone while Stacy and Kevin were absorbed in deciding which present to select next from under the tree.

"Oh, he's fine. He broke up with Connie and is dating a young widow with three children. Isn't that ironic?" Sydney shook her head.

"Here's a present for *you*, Daniel," Stacy announced with a self-conscious air.

It was her own present to him, a miniature painting of the lake with an oak tree in the foreground and a brilliant sunset on the horizon.

After that there was no opportunity for private conversation between Daniel and Sydney. All the presents were opened and admired to the strains of Christmas carols playing on the stereo. Daniel put more wood on the fire and Sydney made more hot chocolate for the children and poured glasses of sherry for herself and Daniel.

It was late when the two of them were finally

alone. Sydney knelt in front of the fireplace, feeding in the last few pieces of torn wrapping paper, thinking of the moment just past when Stacy had been almost through the door on her way upstairs and, stopping abruptly, had turned around to look directly at Daniel.

"You're not leaving tonight? You'll be here tomorrow when we wake up?" she had said uncertainly.

He had flinched a little under the relentlessness of her child's candor. "I'm not leaving tonight, Stacy. I'll be here when you wake up," he promised gravely.

Sydney could feel the heaviness of his mood now as she straightened and turned around to face him. He sat at one end of the sofa staring into the flames.

"They're so fond of you," she explained with a touch of apology. "They missed you terribly when you left."

He sighed, looking at her. "I missed them, too." His eyes touched the mantel with its greenery and lighted candles, flicked over to the shimmering Christmas tree and then swung back to her.

"This was perfect tonight. Exactly what I always dreamed Christmas could be like in this house."

She longed to go over and sit down beside him on the sofa, to touch him with tender fingers and smooth away the unhappiness in his dark eyes. But there were too many barriers between them.

"I'm glad you came," she said simply. "It was incredible luck running into you like that in the shopping center."

Sydney thought of the encounter in the crowded mall and the conversation between them in the restaurant. That conversation had to be completed. She had to know once and for all the reasons why he had left without marrying her as he had said he wanted to do. The thought of hearing those reasons from his lips filled her with dread, but she couldn't continue to live with the groundless hope that someday he might change his mind again.

But first, if everything was to be open between them, she had to correct the lie she had told him. "Daniel, after the accident you asked me where I had been going, and I lied to you." The only sign of agitation as she stood facing him was the slight twisting of her linked fingers.

"You *lied?*"

"Yes. I said I was just going on an errand. Actually, I was on the way here to see you. I was going to tell you what I'd just discovered about myself. That I was in love with you and—"

"My God—no!"

She flinched at the exclamation, dropping her head and shutting her eyes tight against the pain that shafted through her at his horrified tone.

"That's why I didn't tell you when you asked. I knew you'd feel terrible about the accident, as though it was your fault," she whispered miserably.

Daniel got up from the sofa and came over to her. She couldn't bear to look up and see what she knew would be on his face: pity for her and regret that he didn't return her love. Then she felt his fingers lifting her chin.

"Look at me, Sydney."

She opened her eyes, but a glaze of tears blinded her.

"I haven't been honest with you, either. I found out about my transfer to the East Coast in September, a week before I moved out," he said gravely.

Sydney blinked hard, trying to clear her vision so

that she could see his expression. "But why didn't you tell me?"

"Because I didn't want to take advantage of you in your weakened condition. I was afraid you would go ahead and marry me anyway and agree to go with me when the time came just because you were grateful—and I knew, God help me, that if you offered, I wouldn't have the strength to refuse."

"But I thought—Deborah came here that day— and then right after that—" Sydney was afraid to believe what she thought he might be telling her.

"I know what you thought. That seeing Deborah again aroused all my old feelings for her. I let you think that, even though it wasn't true."

"It wasn't? Oh, Daniel!" There were more tears flooding into her eyes now, but these were tears of hope.

His fingers left her chin and wiped away two big wet teardrops coursing down her cheeks. "No, my darling, it wasn't true at all. Oh, I suppose I'll never be totally indifferent to Deborah. She's someone who once meant a lot to me. But seeing her again was just another proof of what I already knew—that I was in love with you and wanted to spend the rest of my life with you."

Sydney blinked hard, got a clear glimpse of Daniel's face and the love for her written there, and then succumbed to all the emotions besieging her. She was sobbing and laughing with joy all at the same time, and Daniel was holding her close against his broad chest, his hands stroking her hair and shoulders and back and his voice crooning entreaties for her not to cry.

"I'm so happy," she whispered, tightening her arms around his waist.

"Reckon we ain't the only ones with something to announce," came a dry male voice from the door.

Daniel and Sydney looked up to find Basil and Cora regarding them, the latter looking highly self-conscious.

"Cora and me's decided to tie the knot," Basil announced without any further preliminaries.

"Congratulations!" Daniel exclaimed, not loosening his hold on Sydney even a fraction as the other couple advanced into the room. "I think this news deserves a toast, don't you, darling?"

The last was spoken in a voice of such tender possession that Sydney thought she might burst from pure happiness. "It definitely deserves a toast," she agreed unsteadily. "Why don't you two sit down while we get some more glasses."

"That was a clever ruse," Daniel teased in a low tone when they were in the kitchen. He caught her up in his arms and claimed her lips in a deep, hungry kiss that awoke all the old urgent need for his lovemaking. It took all their self-discipline to tear their lips apart and stay their roving, exploring hands and carry out the task of finding the glasses.

Sydney concentrated only with the greatest effort upon Basil's explanation of his and Cora's plans. They would be married in a few weeks and live in Basil's apartment until they found something a little bigger. He would continue looking after the Humphries place and doing his gardening work, and Cora was hoping she could work for Sydney the same as before, the only difference being she wouldn't live in the house.

"We might be able to work out something advantageous for all of us," Daniel said thoughtfully, but he didn't elaborate. Sydney wondered if he had been thinking the same thing she was.

Basil stayed less than an hour, and after he left, Cora retired to her own room. It had seemed like a lifetime to Sydney, who found it difficult to think about anything except the astounding discovery that Daniel loved her the way she loved him.

"I thought you might offer to let them live in this house when we move," she said, settling into the circle of his arms on the sofa when they were alone again.

"I wanted to discuss it with you first." There was a slight note of uncertainty in his voice. "Are you sure you're willing to move away from this area? There's your work to consider and your parents . . ."

"Daniel, I'll move anywhere in the world with you," she said dreamily, "as long as we can take the kids with us."

His arms tightened until she was hardly able to breathe. "I wouldn't think of *not* taking them. Next to you, they mean more to me than anything else."

There followed an interlude when they held each other close, not speaking because words were insufficient to express the depth and magnitude of their feelings. Sydney was the one to break the silence.

"When did you fall in love with me, Daniel?" she wanted to know with incurable feminine curiosity.

"I don't know. I think it just happened gradually. It probably started the day I drove you to your parents' house and Kevin came around the house and fell. The mother in you took over and you jumped out of the car and ran over to him, not in the least worried about that expensive suit you were wearing."

She remembered the scene vividly, along with her uncomfortable awareness that he was watching her. "Did you know there have been times when I was actually jealous of my own children where you were concerned. Sometimes I've suspected you were just putting up with me because you liked them."

"I did like them from the first; I think you can take quite a bit of credit for making them likable people. But I never 'put up' with you. You intrigued me because you were such a mass of contradictions. Miss Professional Real Estate Lady one moment and down on your knees on the concrete the next. Telling me very coolly to keep hands off and then giving me hell because I managed to stop myself before I ravished you on the veranda." His voice held a trace of laughter at that latter memory.

"Don't you want to know when I started loving you?" she prompted.

"When?" he asked agreeably.

"When I saw you standing in front of my mother's sink up to your elbows in dishwater," she teased.

"For that you get kissed," he said with mock severity and carried out the threat with her full cooperation. There were thousands of other questions to ask, insights to share and plans to make, but for the moment they were thralls to the miracle of their newly discovered love.

A log shifted in the fireplace and the flames flared up briefly. The wind gusted outside, and the old house creaked as if bestowing its benign approval.

If you enjoyed this book...

...you will enjoy a Special Edition Book Club membership even more.

It will bring you each new title, as soon as it is published every month, delivered right to your door.

15-Day Free Trial Offer

We will send you 6 new Silhouette Special Editions to keep for 15 days absolutely free! If you decide not to keep them, send them back to us, you pay nothing. But if you enjoy them as much as we think you will, keep them and pay the invoice enclosed with your trial shipment. You will then automatically become a member of the Special Edition Book Club and receive 6 more romances every month. There is no minimum number of books to buy and you can cancel at any time.

Silhouette Special Edition

Coming Next Month

Bitter Victory by Patti Beckman

She had left him years ago, but when Slade
appeared in her office, Veronica still felt the
burning desire and hatred that had driven her to
leave her husband. Could their love
mend their differences?

Eye Of The Hurricane by Sarah Keene

There were two sides to Miranda: the practical
miss, and the daring, wild dreamer. And in Jake
she found a searing passion that would weld the
two together.

Dangerous Magic by Stephanie James

Elissa fought her way up the corporate ladder and
into Wade's arms. Her sultry innocence intrigued
him, and his desire for her was overwhelming.

Silhouette Special Edition

Coming Next Month

Mayan Moon by Eleni Carr

Beneath the Mexican moon, beside the Sacred Well of Souls, Antonio Ferrara, a man of fierce Mayan pride, took Rhea on a journey that encompassed the ages.

So Many Tomorrows by Nancy John

Having been mistaken in her first marriage, Shelley wasn't thinking of love—until Jason found her and taught her the meaning of life, and of a love that would last forever.

A Woman's Place by Lucy Hamilton

Anna's residency under Dr. Lew Coleman was difficult—especially when she saw the answer to all her hidden desires and dreams in his compelling gaze.

Look for More Special Editions from
Janet Dailey and Brooke Hastings,
and a New Novel from
Linda Shaw in Future Months.

Silhouette Special Edition

MORE ROMANCE FOR
A SPECIAL WAY TO RELAX

Silhouette Special Edition

March Special Editions
Available Now

Silver Mist by Sondra Stanford

To free her mind from a disastrous affair, Laurel concentrated on the business she was organizing. Then a charming local rancher entered her world —and her heart.

Keys to Daniel's House by Carole Halston

All of Sydney's energies went into her family and her career in real estate, until Daniel lured her away and made his house their home.

All Our Tomorrows by Mary Lynn Baxter

Brooke lost a successful past in a tragic accident, but in the tropical splendor of Hawaii, Ashley Graham challenged her to love again.

Texas Rose by Kathryn Thiels

Returning to her old Texas stomping grounds to interview a ranch owner, reporter Alexis Kellogg was stunned to learn that he was actually a man she once loved.

Love Is Surrender by Carolyn Thornton

Amid the lush splendor of New Orleans, a blue-eyed, sensitive man taught Jennifer about passion, jealousy—and love.

Never Give Your Heart by Tracy Sinclair

Gillian was thrilled to land a new account, but all too soon her client, Roman Barclay, aroused more than professional interest.

Dear reader:

Please take a few moments to fill out this questionnaire. It will help us give you more of the Special Editions you'd like best.

Mail to: Karen Solem
Silhouette Books
1230 Ave. of the Americas, New York, N.Y. 10020

1) How did you obtain **KEYS TO DANIEL'S HOUSE**

( ) **Bookstore**   10-1   ( ) **Newsstand**   -6
( ) **Supermarket**   -2   ( ) **Airport**   -7
( ) **Variety/discount store** -3   ( ) **Book Club**   -8
( ) **Department store** -4   ( ) **From a friend**   -9
( ) **Drug store**   -5   ( ) **Other:** _____
                                        (write in)   -0

2) How many Silhouette Special Editions have you read including this one? (circle one number)   11- 1 2 3 4 5 6 7 8 9 10 11 12

3) Overall how would you rate this book?
( ) **Excellent** 12-1 ( ) **Very good** -2
( ) **Good** -3 ( ) **Fair** -4 ( ) **Poor** -5

4) Which elements did you like best about this book?
( ) **Heroine** 13-1 ( ) **Hero** -2 ( ) **Setting** -3 ( ) **Story line** -4
( ) **Love scenes** -5 ( ) **Ending** -6 ( ) **Other Characters** -7

5) Do you prefer love scenes that are
( ) **Less explicit than**   ( ) **More explicit than**
in this book 14-1   in this book -2
        ( ) **About as explicit as in this book** -3

6) What influenced you most in deciding to buy this book?
( ) **Cover** 15-1 ( ) **Title** -2 ( ) **Back cover copy** -3
( ) **Recommendations** -4 ( ) **You buy all Silhouette Books** -5

7) How likely would you be to purchase other Silhouette Special Editions in the future?
( ) **Extremely likely**   16-1 ( ) **Not very likely**   -3
( ) **Somewhat likely**   -2 ( ) **Not at all likely**   -4

8) Have you been reading . . .
( ) **Only Silhouette Romances**   17-1
( ) **Mostly Silhouette Romances**   -2
( ) **Mostly one other romance** _____ -3
                    (write one in)
( ) **No one series of romance in particular** -4

9) Please check the box next to your age group.
( ) **Under 18** 18-1 ( ) **25-34** -3 ( ) **50-54** -5
( ) **18-24** -2 ( ) **35-49** -4 ( ) **55+** -6

10) Would you be interested in receiving a romance newsletter? If so please fill in your name and address.

Name _____

Address _____

City _____ State _____ Zip _____

19 ___ 20 ___ 21 ___ 22 ___ 23 ___